Praise for *The Fire Thief*

"Bokur's welcome debut nimbly contrasts the Hawaii of sun and golden beaches with its less well-known underbelly of poverty, discrimination, and crime. Fans of strong female cops will look forward to Kali's further adventures."
—*Publishers Weekly*

"Debra Bokur's *The Fire Thief* has all the elements of a great mystery—crackling tension, brisk pacing, a vibrant setting, and a flicker of paranormal . . . or is it?"
—**Wendy Corsi Staub, *New York Times* bestselling author**

"*The Fire Thief* will make you an instant fan of its rock-solid protagonist, Kali Māhoe."
—**Lisa Black, *New York Times* bestselling author of the Gardiner and Renner novels**

"An exciting blend of Hawaiian folklore and mystery. From page one to a stirring finish, Debra Bokur delivers a real page turner here. And Kali Māhoe, wonderfully rich, complicated and compelling, is the real deal. I can't wait for her next adventure."
—**Tracy Clark, author of the Cass Raines Chicago Mystery series**

"With her series debut, *The Fire Thief*, Debra Bokur explores the hidden back roads of Hawaii and grabs you from page one with an island procedural full of twists and turns while introducing a phenomenal and unique protagonist in Detective Kali Māhoe—tough, flawed, and perceptive. This clever and addictive novel surprises at every turn, so grab your sunglasses and enjoy the ride."
—**Edwin Hill, author of *Little Comfort* and *The Missing Ones***

**The Dark Paradise Mysteries
by Debra Bokur**

The Fire Thief

The Bone Field

THE FIRE THIEF

DEBRA BOKUR

KENSINGTON
PUBLISHING CORP.

www.kensingtonbooks.com

KENSINGTON BOOKS are published by

Kensington Publishing Corp.
119 West 40th Street
New York, NY 10018

All Kensington titles, imprints, and distributed lines are available at special quantity discounts for bulk purchases for sales promotion, premiums, fund-raising, educational, or institutional use. Special book excerpts or customized printings can also be created to fit specific needs. For details, write or phone the office of the Kensington Special Sales Manager: Attn. Special Sales Department. Kensington Publishing Corp, 119 West 40th Street, New York, NY 10018. Phone: 1-800-221-2647.

The K logo is a trademark of Kensington Publishing Corp.

ISBN-13: 978-1-4967-2773-2
ISBN-10: 1-4967-2773-8
First Kensington Hardcover Edition: June 2020
First Kensington Mass Market Edition: April 2021

ISBN-13: 978-1-4967-2774-9 (ebook)
ISBN-10: 1-4967-2774-6 (ebook)

10 9 8 7 6 5 4 3 2 1

Printed in the United States of America

This book is dedicated to my husband, best friend, and world's best travel companion, James Rawsthorne; and to my mother, Jean Costa Smith, who taught me to never, ever go anywhere without a book.

Acknowledgments

My thanks to the wise and wonderful Shannon Hassan at Marsal Lyon Literary Agency, and to my family at Kensington Books: rock star editor James Abbate, copyeditor Rosemary Silva, production editor Robin Cook, and publicist Crystal McCoy. To Hawaiian kahu and cultural historian Danny Akaka, and to the people of Hawaii who have so generously shared their culture, traditions, and stories with me throughout the years, I extend my deep and abiding gratitude: *mahalo nui loa.*

CHAPTER 1

Police captain Walter Alaka'i struggled for footing in the warm, waist-deep water. In front of him, revealed by the morning light, the body of seventeen-year-old Kekipi Smith bobbed back and forth with the current, no longer encumbered by the constraints of will or desire. The deep gash in his skull had long since ceased to bleed, washed clean by lonely hours spent drifting along the ragged beach beneath the last shard of February moon. The boy's eyes were half open, as though he were struggling, out of politeness, to stay awake.

Walter braced himself as a wave crashed in, then drew away, tugged by the invisible force of the tide. The naupaka blossoms in the dense coastal bushes caught his eye—fresh, gentle, wrenchingly out of place this morning. He backed carefully toward the dense mangrove roots behind him in the shallow cove of water that had pooled between the scissory lava rocks along Maui's southeastern shore. With his right hand, he grasped one of Kekipi's ankles, and did his best to keep the body from jolting against the rocks and gnarled labyrinth of twisted tree roots as each incoming wave lifted it and pushed it forward.

There was a thud, thud, thud of running footsteps beating against the heavy sand along the shore, followed by a soft splash as Officer David Hara slid into the water behind him. Hara averted his eyes from the face staring up from the sea to the cloudless sky, and Walter noted how he kept just out of reach of the floating arm that stirred with the moving current.

"Reinforcements here?"

Hara nodded. "Coming down the hill now, sir, with the stretcher. Photographer's with them, but the coroner says she's about a half hour out if she gets on the road before the tourists. She said to go ahead and pull him out when we're through, since it's an accident." He hesitated. "And that old fisherman who called it in is waiting for you at the top of the hill path."

"Okay. Tell him to stay put until I've had a chance to talk to him. Surfboard's just past the entrance to the cove, washed up in some kiawe roots," said Walter. "I'll stay here with the body. Be sure they get photos of the board."

The tip of an orange surfboard jutted from a clump of thick brush about fifty feet away. Walter's eyes locked on the board, and he calculated the facts at hand. The entire scene clearly implied the savage results of a wave gone wrong—an innocent surfing expedition turned fatal. Walter shook his head. It was not the first surfing death he'd seen over the years, and he was fully aware that it was unlikely to be the last.

He braced for the next wave as Hara scrambled past him, using the snarl of roots and branches to pull himself onto higher ground. The current from the receding wave tugged at the body. From the shore, there was the sound of movement, then voices. The branches were pushed aside, and hands reached out. Walter kept his hold on one ankle as the police photographer recorded the morning's unfortunate discovery, not letting go until the medics had taken over and had hauled both the sodden body and Walter from the sea.

The sky above was regrettably blue, given the events occurring below. The boy was wearing swim trunks, and his brown, tanned torso and feet were bare. Walter watched, dejected, as the slender remains were maneuvered onto a stretcher waiting on a patch of thick grass, then covered over with a thin sheet.

Along the water's edge, the police photographer moved away from the spot where the surfboard had been jammed. He paused briefly as he passed Walter. "All yours, brah."

Walter grumbled. He looked back to where Hara was waiting next to the stretcher, then to the spot where the medics stood. They had walked away, down the beach, and Walter was aware that they were deliberately avoiding making eye contact with him. "You expect me to pull that damn thing out of the water?"

The photographer shrugged. "Not like you're going to get any wetter, you know? Give the rest of us a break."

Walter sighed. It was true. There wasn't a dry inch of him to be found. He edged himself back into the sea, then took a deep breath and ducked beneath the surface and came up with the board resting on one shoulder. He struggled over the sharp rocks, scraping his arms and legs, his bulky frame not designed for this much physical activity, especially not this early in the day.

He carried the board to where Hara stood, shifting nervously from one foot to the other. Walter ignored him, doing his best not to be bothered by Hara's persistent discomfort in his presence. Every junior officer who had ever worked for him had exhibited the same nervous response, and though Hara had been under Walter's supervision for nearly four months, he was clearly not going to be an exception.

No practical experience, but clearly eager to learn, thought Walter. Maybe too eager. At twenty-three, Hara was an absolute pain in the ass. And, in Walter's estimation, he was far too good-looking to be a cop. Wherever he went, it seemed that a small parade of women magically appeared in his wake. Walter had just enough sense of self to admit that he found this to be more exasperating than anything else.

"Captain, there's something . . . well, something you should take a look at in here. What I mean is, sir, I think you might want to—"

Walter held up an impatient hand. "What is it, Hara?"

"The body, sir."

Walter sighed. "Just spit it out, please."

"Well," Hara began, confused. "The head wound . . ."

Walter walked past him without saying anything more.

The body lay silent, the legs slightly splayed out, permanently stilled. Hara moved to the top of the stretcher, then pulled the sheet aside and pointed to the wound. "Looks like the bone around the cut is crushed, sir."

Walter frowned. He stared in silence, considering the inference. "And? He hit those lava rocks and split his skull open with the impact of coming off the board, most likely."

"Except for this, sir." Hara stepped to the side, pointed at the gash. Walter bent closer and peered at the wound. There was something there, embedded in the edge—something shiny and white caught in the flesh.

Walter glanced at the medics, now standing at the edge of the water engaged in conversation, their sensitivity dulled through necessity and long years of recovering drowning victims. He pulled a pair of wet gloves from deep in his back pocket and slipped them on.

"Flashlight," he said, his voice terse.

Hara fumbled at his belt and removed a small, powerful penlight.

"Angle it right here . . . no, more to the left."

Walter studied the uneven opening in the skin, probing gently at the edges, speaking to himself. Hara stood beside him, still fidgeting.

Walter shook his head in confusion. "Well, I'll be damned. If I'm not mistaken, that's a *manō* tooth."

"That's what I thought, too, sir. But what's a shark's tooth doing in his head? That wound isn't a bite. If he cracked his head open on the lava rocks while he was surfing, why would there be a tooth in the flesh? And wouldn't a shark have, well, eaten some of him? Wasn't—"

Walter held up his hand again, muting a vexed Hara. "Calm down, Hara." Walter peered off toward the distant haze of horizon. "That's all true, but it makes no sense."

Hara took a deep breath, then gestured to the surfboard lying nearby. "And the surf leash is still connected to the board but not fastened to his ankle."

Frowning, Walter squinted more closely at the wound.
Were his powers of observation slipping? Hara had made
a good point about the surf leash, not that Walter saw any
good reason to acknowledge it immediately. The fact that
the leash's Velcro collar hadn't been secured around the
boy's ankle was odd, as the cost of surfboards made
leashes a practical necessity for recovering one after a
fall. If he was correct about his unofficial identification
of the body as local surfer Kekipi Smith, he knew that the
family included five children and that a good surfboard
had likely been a luxury.

Something stirred in Walter, and his voice lost its edge
of sternness. "Right, then," he said. "Something here isn't
adding up." He turned to Hara and nodded. "Good observation, Hara. Time for Detective Māhoe to get her
tattooed-warrior ass over here. Let me have your cell
phone. Mine's over there on the beach somewhere. You
can look for it while I'm talking."

Hara handed over his phone and stepped toward the
edge of land that fell away to the cove where the body
had been found. Walter punched in his niece's familiar
number, beginning the climb up the steep path leading
from the sea to the parking area above. She needed to see
the body in the full context of its surroundings, before it
was taken away, while the boy's *'uhane*, or spirit, was
still lingering in the place where he had died.

"And tape off this area," Walter yelled after Hara's re-
treating back. "We might have a crime scene on our
hands."

CHAPTER 2

Detective Kali Māhoe stretched her fingers down as far as possible, her lean, muscled legs wrapped around the thick lower branch of the old mango tree in her yard in the small village of Nu'u, near Hana. She could almost touch the ground with the tips of her middle fingers, where the ends of her long ebony hair mingled with the thick grass at the tree's base. From her upside-down position, the horizon was reversed, and she watched as a bug labored through the green blades toward the edge of ocean-sky.

Kali had spent a lot of time in this tree when she was a child, dreaming of the day when she'd be tall enough to reach the ground, and being warned by her grandmother from the front porch that not only was tree climbing unlady-like, but it was also a guarantee of broken bones. She smiled to herself. Her thirty-fifth birthday had just passed, and she'd yet to break anything.

Being outside, hanging from the tree, was far preferable to being indoors, sitting at the wooden kitchen table, which doubled as her desk. She'd been up for hours, and things were not progressing well with the presentation she'd been working on, which was to be given in conjunction with an adult night course the following spring at the University of Hawaii's Maui College. Besides her detective status with the Maui Police Department, she held a degree in cultural anthropology and was a recognized specialist in the cultural and spiritual traditions of Hawaii—a unique insight and perspective that often proved useful in her role as a detective.

Her grandmother, the renowned author and historian Pualani Pali, had left her this house and, by extension, the mango tree. It was also Pualani who had identified Kali as her community's next *kahu*, a spiritual leadership role traditionally handed down from grandparent to grandchild, which had been revealed to the older *kahu* by subtle signs that included Kali's natural interest in plants, her rapport with animals, and her dreams and visions, which were often layered. Pualani had confirmed Kali as her family's next *kahu* when she was five years old, after Kali had insisted that a sea turtle had warned her of a coming tsunami, which had indeed arrived soon after, with deadly flooding.

She pulled herself upright, grasping an upper branch, and dropped gracefully to the ground. The movement caused her dog, Hilo—the enormous offspring of a Weimaraner and a Great Dane—to raise his head briefly from his stretched-out position in a patch of sunshine.

The water beyond the lawn was tinged with grayish

green. Bobbing gently on its surface was an old fishing boat badly in need of a new coat of paint. The name *Gingerfish* could just be made out along the length of the stern, and Kali felt a familiar sense of relief to see the boat still at anchor where she'd left it. Walter had purchased it from a friend moving to the mainland, and Kali had offered to let him keep it at the rickety dock at the edge of her property. Walter spent a great deal of his free time aboard in a comfortable deck chair, plucking away at a vintage ukulele, while she continued to point out the need to replace the aging anchor chain. So far, the only measurable progress was the amount of rust that had accumulated along its length.

The dog trotted beside her as she walked across the lawn to the cluster of papaya trees that separated her three-acre property from the neighbor's yard. She reached for a ripe fruit, then twisted it slightly until it came loose in her hand. There was a *hālau* partially obscured by the papaya trees' branches. The small shelter, with its roof of dried palm fronds, offered minimal protection to the unfinished canoe resting on sawhorses beneath it, caught forever in its half-carved form, unlikely ever to be completed.

Kali looked away from it, afraid of stirring up the memories it carried of her late fiancé, Mike Shirai. She took the papaya inside, placed it on the kitchen counter, then opened the refrigerator door and gazed idly inside. There was some rice and shrimp from yesterday's dinner and a bowl of limp sliced pineapple that should have already been eaten.

The papaya, she decided, would have to do for breakfast. While coffee brewed, she cut open the fruit. The soft orange-hued interior was filled with dark seeds that ran the length of its center, and she scraped these from their nest. The juice trickled onto the counter as she placed the halves on a plate.

Plate in one hand and coffee mug in the other, she passsed the kitchen table where her computer hummed and pushed open the screen door. She made her way out onto the lanai, which ran along the front and one side of the small house. The sky was growing lighter as the morning progressed. She walked softly along the wide porch and settled into the threadbare cushions on a wooden deck chair, her legs tucked beneath her, then scooped up the sweet flesh of the papaya fruit with a spoon.

The sea spread out before her. The calls of gulls and the wash of waves against the shore were usually sooth-ing, but this morning the sounds failed to relieve the sense of restlessness that troubled her. She hadn't slept well, having woken during the dark early hours that had yet to give birth to the dawn. Something was out of bal-ance, and she knew it as surely as she knew the cloudless morning sky would be filled with rain clouds before evening arrived. Just as she had felt the approaching tsunami when she was five years old.

Kali sighed, adjusting her legs beneath her on the cushion. She had just eaten the last of the papaya when her phone rang, harsh and intrusive. Still holding the plate, she went inside and located the phone on the small table next to her sofa. As she lifted the phone, it slipped between her fingers, skittered across the wooden floor, and landed between a ceremonial drum and a spear gifted to her years before by a visiting New Zealand elder. She bent over, careful to avoid knocking over the spear, and retrieved the phone. As she pressed the button to accept the call, the plate fell from her other hand and broke into pieces as it struck the floor. She looked around the small room uneasily.

The voice on the other end of the phone was familiar—the deep, resonant tones of her uncle, Walter. "Aloha, Kali. You okay? Sounds like you're throwing things around."

Kali took a deep breath. Walter sounded oddly strained. "Not yet, but it's still early in the day. What's up?"

There was a tense pause on the line. "Well, I hate to drag you away from whatever it is you're not doing, but we've got a body down here on the beach. No positive ID yet, but I'm pretty certain it's Kekipi Smith, Anna Smith's eldest son. She made a call last night to say he hadn't come home, and it looks like he drowned down there off the cliffs near Haleakalā National Park, probably sometime late yesterday. Surfboard washed up nearby, so it appeared to be an accident."

Kali frowned, tightening her grip on the phone. "Appeared?"

Walter's voice was carefully noncommittal. "Well, seemed that way to begin with. But now something's turned up that doesn't make any sense." His voice wavered, but just for a second. "Can you get over here and have a look before we send him off?"

Kali's eyes darted back to the sea, just visible through the window. A dull malaise fluttered behind the bones of her chest.

Walter spoke into her silence. "I'm not feeling good about this. I'll explain when you get here, but we're treating it as a suspicious death. There are elements that put it right in your wheelhouse."

She closed her eyes and felt a shadow leaping into the darkness.

"Okay. I'm on my way."

She picked up her keys and headed out into the sunlight. Hilo followed, pushing the screen door open with his nose. He jogged close beside her, his long body bumping against her legs. She reached down with one hand, patted his head briefly, already lost in the story she was about to hear.

CHAPTER 3

There was a rough clearing at the top of the hill over-looking the beach. Watched by a disappointed Hilo from his spot on the front passenger seat, Kali left her battered, doorless Willy's Jeep on the sandy ground beneath the trees. She made her way through the damp, heavy grass toward Walter, where he stood next to an elderly fisherman. She recognized the older man instantly: Sam Hekekia, who'd lived on this stretch of coastline for as long as she could remember. She glanced at his face. He looked deeply forlorn, his fishing nets resting in tangled piles on the ground beside his feet.

It had been Sam's phone call earlier that morning that had alerted the police to the body, setting in motion the dark events now playing out on the sunlit beach below. Sam stood quietly, holding a dented aluminum travel mug. He lifted it and took a sip of cold coffee as Kali exchanged glances with Walter.

"Not my idea of the best way to start the day," Sam said, frowning. He raised a hand to his eyes, shielding them from the sun's glare, and looked out over the water. "Doubt the fish will come back here for a long while. They'll see the boy's spirit and swim away."

Walter nodded slowly. Kali could see that he was nearly as dejected as Sam.

"You're probably right," Walter agreed.

"We'll do a ceremony, Sam," said Kali, smiling at him with what she hoped was reassurance. "You'll see. We'll make an offering to Kuula. You know that he takes good care of fishermen. He'll make sure your fish will come back."

"Maybe," said Sam, still looking doubtful. "Maybe when you do the ceremony, you can ask Kuula to tell the fish to bring their friends. My nets are never full these days."

He waited quietly on the hill, looking at them expectantly. Kali and Walter said nothing.

"I watched that young policeman down there putting up tape," Sam said, gesturing toward the beach, his voice flat. "I know what that means. I watch those television shows, you know." He cleared his throat, turning toward Kali and Walter with a questioning glance. Still receiving no response, he reached down and gathered his nets, then turned toward the road.

"Okay. I'm going now. You call me if you need anything." He stopped, his lined face clearly disappointed. "Not that there's anything else to say. I walked down to the water, and there he was. Heard nothing, saw nothing, smelled nothing. Just the boy, caught up in the rocks."

"Thank you, Sam," said Walter, his voice solemn. "But if you do think of anything . . ."

"We'll talk later, okay?" Kali smiled again.

Sam nodded, then trudged away, his nets thrown over his shoulder.

Kali looked pointedly at Walter. He cleared his throat and walked to the head of the steep path. She followed him as he made his way carefully toward the spot below where Hara still waited beside the body.

"This the only way down?"

"Yes, for a considerable distance. This is the main path the surfers use."

The sound of the waves washing ashore against the rocks was rhythmic, steady as a metronome. Regardless of how peaceful the surroundings seemed, Kali thought to herself, surfing accidents were far more common than the local rental shops ever let on to the tourists. She stepped carefully onto the path. To her mind, it was simply more proof that the water gods didn't care how young or old you were, or whether you'd lived here your whole life: when they were provoked, whatever the reason, nothing could protect you.

She surveyed the sea's deceptive shimmering face. No native Hawaiian took the sea or any part of the environment for granted. The weather patterns in this isolated island chain were unpredictable. Despite the fact that the dim coast of the Big Island could be seen across the channel this morning, the weather and the ocean's profile for the past several days had been erratic. A storm system had moved through, bringing huge waves and churning the water into wild eddies. Today the far gentler ripples meeting the beach rolled out from a blue-green sea that was uncharacteristically still, offering an uneventful passage for the boats making their way through the wide channel between the islands.

Walter seemed to sense the direction Kali's thoughts had taken.

"The storm brought some big waves, but it didn't cause as much coastal damage as we all thought it would," he noted. He grunted, grasping at the shrubs lining the path, as his foot slipped on the sandy surface.

"I guess that's something good," she acknowledged. "Though it certainly brought the surfers out."

He nodded. "Of course, that's the thing about storms. They pass, but you can count on there always being another one." He looked up at the blue, deceivingly calm sky. "Heavy rain moving in later today, possibly with strong winds. We'll have tourists driving off the edge of the road or getting caught in riptides."

"That's right," said Kali, shaking her head. "Go ahead and look at the dark side of everything, Walter. You're always such a gloomy bastard."

They reached the bottom, where the path gave way to a level stretch of sand and patchy grass. Walter turned away from her. Kali knew he'd never waste his time denying the truth. She considered, in his defense, that his original plans for the morning probably had had absolutely nothing to do with fishing a teenage boy from a tidal pool. Instead, they'd likely been focused on making it to the Ranch Restaurant before the last batch of macadamia nut pancakes disappeared down the throats of the tourists who had stayed overnight, choosing to delay the navigational challenges presented by the twisting road that covered the long miles between here and the resorts clustered near the narrow central part of the island.

A low grumble sounded. Kali raised an eyebrow, and stared questioningly at Walter, her suspicions confirmed. "Was that your stomach?"

Walter glared, one hand moving involuntarily toward his generous waistline. "Call came before the sun was up. No time to stop for toast and jam," he said defensively.

But Kali was already wandering away. Instead of approaching the body, she walked along the waterline, listening to the space. It felt to her as though it had been disrupted, fragmented. An image of the broken plate on her wooden floor flashed through her mind, and she turned abruptly and walked rapidly toward the stretcher. From the beach, the two medics watched her, well aware of her *kahu* status, offering her the respect of not interfering.

She moved to the head of the stretcher. Hara stepped away as she stood next to the body. Her heart cramped, squeezed by a rush of sudden misery. This was no good. Like Walter, she knew who this boy's family was, and had lived all her life in the same remote community on the island's edge.

She turned and scanned the shore in the direction of the current, then looked down at the outline beneath the sheet. She frowned. There was something else lingering in the air, like the faint shadow of residual fear. She closed her eyes. It hovered, still dissipating, never measurable to begin with.

"There appears to be a *manō* tooth lodged in the flesh around the head injury," Walter said, walking up beside her. "Inconsistent with the idea of a surfing accident." He glanced toward Hara. His voice barely registering a grudging pride, he added, "Hara noticed it."

Kali lifted enough of the sheet to expose the boy's face, then walked from one side to the other to study his expression. The hair was pushed away from the jagged cut, and she leaned over, discerning the bright white edge of the shark's tooth.

"It was just a couple of weeks ago his picture was in the paper," she said.

"Yeah. He won a full scholarship to the University of Hawaii to study marine biology," said Walter.

Kali recalled the photograph. He'd looked buoyant, the future stretching out before him. She shook her head, letting go of the thought. She only hoped that wherever Kekipi was now, he'd found a new surfboard and all the big waves he could handle. She considered the possibility that the boy had perhaps become a wave himself, joined for eternity with the vast ocean.

"Clearly, that's no bite," said Walter, interrupting her thoughts. "A shark would have left tear marks. Taken a lot more flesh than that. Remember that girl, surfer from California, got half eaten couple of summers ago?"

She grimaced. "Yeah. Kind of hard to forget."

"Had that silver ankle bracelet, and when old Manny Peebles caught the shark and cut it open, he found the bracelet still there, still on a chunk of ankle. Parents didn't want it. I think Manny still wears it."

Kali glanced sideways at Walter, appalled. "He wears it?"

"Yeah. Says it brings him luck fishing."

"Sounds like he's not thinking too clearly about what might be on the end of the line."

Walter made a face. "I hear that."

The rumble of a car came to a stop on the hill above. They turned together and looked up.

"Sounds like the medical examiner is here," she said.

They watched as the stocky figure of a woman appeared at the top of the path and began to head carefully down the slope.

Neither spoke as she approached. The coroner, Mona "Stitches" Stitchard, was a fifty-eight-year-old ex–family practitioner who managed to not get along with anyone, regardless of whether they happened to be dead or alive. The sarcasm behind the nickname—never used directly to her face—alluded nicely to both her absent sense of humor and her precise sewing of tissue. The fact that she was also a woman working with a predominantly male police force had given weight to the already large chip on her shoulder, and her generally gruff personality made her someone that both Kali and Walter preferred to avoid whenever possible.

"Doctor," Walter said by way of greeting, carefully avoiding her nickname.

"Walter," she said, her voice lacking all warmth. She turned to Kali. "Good morning, Detective. I suppose the fact that you're here means you think there's more to this than a drowning, despite the information I was initially given this morning by the good captain Alaka'i."

Kali nodded. "Possibly, but I suppose that's for you to determine."

"Didn't seem like anything more than a surfing accident initially," said Walter defensively. "Except for a shark's tooth lodged in his head at the site of the wound."

"Interesting." Stitches lifted the sheet and studied the wound closely. "The impact, whether from rocks or something else, was heavy enough to break the skull bone. Any sign of a weapon?"

"Not so far," said Walter.

She set her medical bag on the sand and turned back to them as though surprised to see they were still there. "You can go," she said impatiently. "Do what you do. I'll let you know what my initial findings are."

They walked to the trees in front of the area where the body had washed up. Walter made a phone call, arranging for a crime-scene officer to join them, then gave some instructions to Hara.

Kali knew he was simply delaying the inevitable.

He came to stand beside her and sighed. "I guess I need to go and see Kekipi's mother. Unless you . . ."

"No." She looked at him. "I'll see her separately, when she's had a moment to process what's happened."

"Okay. Probably better. I'll take Hara."

They lingered, watching as the coroner conducted her preliminary assessment. Finally, Stitches gestured to the medics, who walked over, looking relieved. They lifted the stretcher and adjusted their grip, then made their way carefully past Walter and Kali, with Kekipi lying silently between them. Stitches glanced down the beach and gave a brief wave in Kali and Walter's general direction. She disappeared from view, and the sound of the ambulance and the coroner's car could be heard as they edged out of the clearing, following the uneven coil of the grassy track leading to the main road.

From the corner of her eye, Kali saw Walter glance at his watch, and she noted that he seemed to grow more discouraged with each sweep of the second hand. She knew that by the time he'd visited the victim's family, gotten a firm identification, and dealt with the crime-scene officer's initial assessment, it would be noon. Or later.

Walter's stomach grumbled again, and he sighed.

Kali tried not to be judgmental. She knew her uncle was a wonderful person—looking at his watch didn't mean he was heartless or without compassion. It simply meant that he was hungry.

CHAPTER 4

The morning was growing old. Kali had been joined by the CSI, who was searching the beach and the path leading down to where the body had washed into the rocks. Hara had returned with a message from Walter, relaying that the trip to see Anna Smith had been emotional, but that Kekipi's mother had had little to offer in the way of information other than names of friends, including a girlfriend. The staff at the local surf shop Kekipi favored had confirmed that he had been by, and had mentioned to them that he planned to head out later in the day into the waves the storm surge had left behind, but that he had been alone.

The most useful information so far was a map provided by the manager at the surf shop, marked up with the favored surf haunts on this section of coast. The pathway and the area around it—where the search was taking place—had been confirmed as the most popular access point. Based on tides and currents, the section of beach most likely to have been Kekipi's intended destination was only a few hundred yards from where his body had been discovered.

Unfortunately, most of that area was covered in lush grasses, which were about to see heavy rain. The sky had gradually relinquished its azure blue, filling first with swiftly moving clouds and now growing ominously dark. As predicted, the wind had picked up in force. Already, loose branches were being tossed about, and the waves on the beach nearby could be heard crashing against the rocky shoreline.

By early afternoon, Walter had rejoined her. The crime-scene officer had departed after making it clear that as there was no defined crime scene, the chances were astronomically small that there would be any useful information to contribute.

Kali was working her way along the steep side of the path. She met Walter and Hara at the top, where the flat ground of the clearing dissolved into thick trees. They walked side by side, rechecking the ground.

"This seems pretty pointless," grumbled Walter, ducking as a branch from a coconut palm swept by, narrowly missing his head. Beside him, Hara wasn't so lucky: the edge of the branch caught his shoulder, and he winced as it struck.

"You never know, sir," he said, rubbing the spot. "It's like you always say. Most killers are usually not paying attention to details. He might have dropped something, which we've all missed."

"What makes you so sure it's a he and not a she?" Kali asked.

Hara glanced at her but made no reply. They had already been at their search for about an hour and had nothing to show for it. In novels and movies, Kali thought, there was always a squadron of fifty eager trained assistants on hand to help out with this kind of search. Instead, they had sundry members of the island's small police force, who had been assembled on short notice, and none of them had any idea what might have been used as a murder weapon or what it was they should be looking for.

Her back was starting to hurt when she turned a corner and came out ahead of the others into another clearing. The protected ground beneath a group of palms had plainly been used on multiple occasions as a parking area. She called out to Walter and Hara, and together they studied the crisscross of tire marks, many of which appeared to be from the same set of mismatched truck tires. One tire clearly had a large patch on it a couple of inches from the outer edge. Walter took a series of photos, while Kali and Hara made careful measurements.

Weary from the search, Walter sat down, his back pressed against the trunk of one of the palms, and sighed. Hara, damp and clearly uncomfortable, waited silently for further direction.

"Take the cruiser and head back to the station, Hara. I'll catch a ride with Detective Māhoe."

Kali watched as Hara's figure faded into the shadows cast by the trees. She knelt on the ground next to Walter.

"Okay, one clearing, obviously being used as a parking lot, but no indication why," said Walter. "Probably just the surfers, or maybe the local lovers' lane. The spot where forlorn housewives sneak out and meet their sweethearts."

"Or," said Kali, "someone dealing. This is a nice, secluded spot. Close to the road, but invisible until you turn the corner in the path. Plenty of shade, in case the driver has to wait."

"More likely, someone living out of their van."

It was Kali's turn to sigh. "Okay. Probably. But what if the boy stumbled through here while some big meth deal was going down? That would be motive. And we know those guys from Kahului have been up here near Hana, operating in this area."

The rain began to fall in earnest, its big drops spattering the ground. For a minute, neither Kali nor Walter moved, enjoying the cooler air that followed the arrival of the rain. A soft breeze carried the scent of rich, damp earth and the hypnotic fragrance of a thousand tropical flowers.

"We've still got to talk to his friends," said Walter, half to himself.

"I'm going to go from here to the girlfriend's house. Maybe one of these kids can share something useful," Kali responded, her voice far from hopeful.

"Happens," agreed Walter. "Get in touch with the high school principal and see if you can set something up for the morning. We'll go there and talk to the kids. It's a familiar place, and will be a less intimidating setting for them."

He stood up, then brushed off the seat and legs of his trousers. The spot beneath the trees was protected to a degree by the thick weave of branches, but he and Kali would be drenched by the time they made it back to the car.

They hurried along the path, and climbed into the waiting Jeep. The rain drummed against the canvas roof.

"Any initial thoughts?" Walter asked.

Kali shook her head. A loose surfboard. A nice local boy with a shark's tooth buried in his head. She didn't have a clue.

CHAPTER 5

Kekipi's girlfriend was watching from the front window of her home. Kali could see her waiting, her young shoulders slumped. She opened the door before Kali had a chance to knock.

"Aloha," said Kali. She waited politely. "You're Alyssa, aren't you?"

The girl looked at her. Her face was puffy; her eyes were red and slightly swollen.

"Lys," she said. "That's what Kekipi called me. Lys."

She turned away and stepped aside so that Kali could walk into the small kitchen. An older woman was standing by the sink. She smiled at Kali.

"Aloha. You're the policewoman who called?"

"Yes. Detective Kali Māhoe." Kali held out her badge for the woman to see. "Are you Lys's mother?"

The woman nodded, then moved closer to Lys.

"Ronda," she said.

"Would you like to sit with us while I ask your daughter a few questions?"

"I'll be right here. You can sit at the table. I've just made some pineapple tea. I'll get some ice and bring you a glass." She put her arm around her daughter's shoulders and pulled her close, then kissed her lightly on her cheek.

Lys said nothing but went to the kitchen table and pulled out a chair. Her back was to the light coming in through the windows behind the table. Kali sat across from her, overcome with the sense that the girl had become transparent. She shifted her chair, bringing the girl's face into focus.

She leaned forward slightly, her gesture meant to be reassuring. "I know this is very difficult for you," she said. "But if I could ask you a few questions, it might help us figure out what happened on the beach."

"What do you mean, what happened? He drowned." She looked questioningly at Kali. "Didn't he?"

"We're simply trying to piece together the way things played out," Kali said, her voice gentle. From the other side of the kitchen, Lys's mother listened. "One of the things I've been wondering about was why he set out to go surfing so late in the day."

Lys shrugged. "He went all the time. In the morning before school, after school, in the moonlight. Everyone does."

"So whether or not the waves were good was the only factor?"

"Pretty much." The girl looked around the room. "Except, you know, if the weather was really bad. Kekipi wasn't stupid. He knew how dangerous that could be."

Kali waited. Ronda brought the iced tea to the table and set glasses in front of Lys and Kali.

"Mahalo for the tea," said Kali. She sipped slowly, aware that the other woman wanted to say something.

"None of these kids are . . . were . . . are reckless." Ronda stumbled over her words. "All of them are responsible. They grew up here, next to the water. They know to respect it."

Kali nodded. She knew that it was true, but that even the most responsible person was subject to accidents, and even more so to the deliberate mayhem planned by other human beings. "Was he careful in the water with his board? Did he use a surf leash?"

Lys shook her head. "Always. He had a new surfboard. Well, not brand new, but new to him. It was his birthday present last year, but he helped pay for it himself. He was really worried about losing it." She hesitated. "I gave him a new surf leash to go with it. I earned the money myself. Did it . . . come loose? Is that why this happened?"

Kali watched the girl's face. It was important that Lys understand that none of this was her fault. She felt the weight of her own private collection of guilt pull and stir.

"No, that's not why this happened. The leash is in perfect condition. It was something else, Lys. That's why I'm here. Can you tell me if Kekipi ever mentioned that he was worried about anything? Anything at all? Do you know if he'd met anyone new in the area?"

Lys frowned. "No. He always hung out with the same people. Mostly me. A couple of people we go to school with. He knew how much I was going to miss him when he went away to college on O'ahu. He told me . . ." Her voice broke. She looked down at the table, and Kali knew from the small movements of her shoulders that she was crying. She reached out and placed her hand gently on the girl's shoulder.

"It's okay, Lys," she said. "It's okay. I lost my boyfriend, too, a few years ago. I understand how it feels."

Lys looked up, her eyes wide and still innocent. "Does it ever stop hurting?"

"Not for a long time," she said, knowing it would be unfair to say anything but the truth. "But it changes."

The girl waited.

"What was it that Kekipi told you?"

Lys's voice was no more than a whisper. "He told me that he loved me."

Kali felt her heart wrench. The light grew brighter behind the girl, the sun streaking in between the flowered curtains that framed the windows. The girl sat sobbing quietly, and Kali thought of all the love that had been stopped in its tracks, and wondered if it was still out there somewhere, in a different shape or form, moving through the universe, simply waiting to burst forth again.

CHAPTER 6

The phone rang, the harsh jangle startling Walter, disrupting his nap. He raised his head from the surface of the desk and rubbed at the now-sore muscle at the spot where his neck and shoulder met. He pushed the speaker button on the phone.

The brusque, no-nonsense voice of the coroner filled the room.

"Wake you up, Walter?"

"Don't be ridiculous." He tried to hide the sound of his yawn. Outside his office window, Hara was diligently applying wax to the patrol car, the shirtsleeves of his uniform rolled up to the elbows.

"I've got a preliminary report here on Kekipi Smith, which, incidentally, does not contain details of how you failed to wait until I arrived at the scene and instead dug around in his head with a penknife."

"It wasn't a penknife," he said, his voice unconvincing, even to his own ears. "And we didn't realize that it was anything more than a surfing accident."

"You mean a suspicious death, which is handled here, not at your rebel outpost in Hana."

Walter bit his lip, determined not to engage in an argument he would never, in a million lifetimes, stand a chance of winning. Stitches continued speaking, equally aware of this truth.

"Still. It looks as though we have much more than an accident to deal with."

Walter sat up straight, his drowsiness immediately evaporating.

"Death was caused by a blow to the back of the head, which shattered the skull and created the significant cavity you noted. The body was placed in the water after death, and there is absolutely no possibility that death resulted from drowning. Not a drop of water in the lungs. There's some discoloration and swelling around one knee, which means he probably twisted it sometime shortly before he was struck."

Walter scowled as he considered this bit of information. The knee injury must have occurred fairly soon before he was hit, or he would never have made the steep hike or even planned on going surfing.

"What about the chance he hit his head on a rock, died, then rolled into the ocean?" he asked.

"You mean, hit his head on a rock that had a shark's tooth protruding from it?"

"Okay. Had to ask, though."

"Of course you did. The force of the blow and resultant

bone damage to the skull more or less rules out a fall, unless he fell from a considerable height. Perhaps you're suggesting he was sitting at the top of a coconut tree with his surfboard, waiting for the right set of waves, and accidentally toppled onto an upright tooth embedded in the ground below?"

Walter used all his willpower to refrain from commenting. "Looks like we got ourselves a homicide, then," he finally said.

"No, it looks like *you've* got a homicide. I'm on my way to a dinner party. I have a few more tests to run, and we'll keep the body here until you come up with something. Call the family, will you?"

"Yes, ma'am," he answered, dreading the prospect of telling Anna Smith that there would be no service, no closure for her grief—at least not right away. Far, far worse would be explaining that it appeared that her son's life had been taken deliberately—and that he didn't have the faintest idea why.

He picked up his hat and walked out to the car. Hara looked up from the far side, where he was bent over, inspecting the cleanliness of the running board. His forehead was damp with perspiration.

"That's enough, Hara. We've got work to do. We just got confirmation that the Smith death was no surfing accident."

Hara tossed the polishing cloth he'd been using into a bucket beside the car and began to roll down his sleeves. "But did he drown?"

"Appears not. Coroner just called. I'll fill you in on the ride. Get through to Kali and let her know we'll meet her over at the school. She's there doing the interviews."

As Hara prepared to open the car door, Walter shook his head, frowning. He ran his eyes meaningfully over the car's now-gleaming surface.

"Always use circular motions with wax, Hara. Especially the final coat. Always. Otherwise, you get streaks."

CHAPTER 7

Across the scratched Formica surface of the long cafeteria table, Jamie Tagert shifted in his seat. His eyes flicked across Kali's face, then looked away. She was used to that reaction and knew there could be a thousand reasons why a face-to-face with a police officer might cause someone being interviewed to be uncomfortable. She tried not to communicate her discouragement. This boy was the last interview of the day, and so far not a single useful bit of information had been gleaned.

Stiffly, Jamie acknowledged that he almost always surfed in Kekipi's company, and that the spot they usually frequented was the beach at the base of the cliff path where Kekipi had been found.

She did her best to put the boy at ease, but he fidgeted and continued to look away when she addressed him.

"You and Kekipi were pretty tight, from what I've

heard today," she said, watching as he twisted his hands together and shoved them beneath the table, out of sight.

"Yeah, sure. We been at school together, like, our whole lives, you know?"

"And you surfed together a lot? Down at the foot of the park path?"

He nodded, still not looking directly at her. "I already said. Best spot, right?"

"Can't say that I really know. I don't do much surfing myself, but I enjoy watching it."

He glanced at her briefly. "Aren't you a kahuna or something?"

She nodded. "Or something."

"And you're a cop?" he said, shaking his head. "Weird, you know?"

"Is it? I mean, aren't most people more than one thing? You, for instance. You're a surfer, a son, a friend, a student."

"Yeah, but that's different."

She waited, giving him time. She could see he was trying to reconcile what he'd so far told her with what he hadn't.

He leaned forward. "Kekipi, he was a good guy. Straight-up brah. He—" Jamie stopped.

"He what?"

Jamie leaned back and looked toward the door of the cafeteria where several students were waiting and watching. A cluster of mingled parents and teachers stood with them.

"Nothing." Jamie pushed the chair away from the table. "Nothing. I can go now, yeah?"

"Sure." She took a card from a stack on the table and pushed it toward him, doing her best to end the brief conversation on a friendly note, urging him to get in touch if he recalled anything that might be useful. "I'd really be grateful for your help, Jamie. You know, if you remember anything. Anything at all."

"Yeah. Sure."

She watched as he made his way to the cafeteria door. As he passed the group of students clustered in the opening, a tall boy with sandy hair reached out and shoved him lightly; the gesture was one of familiarity, and not unfriendly. There was a slightly older man standing next to him, peering curiously into the room. Kali recognized him and scowled. It was Chad Caesar, a local B-list actor who'd become a thorn in the side of the Maui police with his sensationalist podcasts and blog.

Kali saw him hold up his phone and speak to Jamie. She watched as Jamie shook his head and said something, but she couldn't make out his response. She rose from the table and made her way to the door.

"Didn't realize you were old enough to have kids in high school, Chad," she said.

He grinned, his lopsided mouth showing a few teeth that were too even and too white. "Miss Detective. I must say, you're looking particularly well today."

"What are you doing here? This is an official investigation, and unless you give me a good reason not to, I'm going to have you dragged out of here."

"In front of my fans? Cold, Detective. Very cold." He waved his phone briefly. "Just a quick note that I'm recording. And for your information, I'm here in an official capacity as a journalist."

She reached forward and took his phone, then shut it off. He spluttered and grasped for it, and she dropped it into her bag.

"You played a journalist on a really awful television show. That doesn't actually make you a journalist, you know."

"Doesn't it?" He grinned again. "For your information, I'm the most popular blogcaster in the islands. People depend on me to get the real scoop on things."

Kali snorted. "Mind telling me what you're doing here? From where I stand, it looks like a thirtysomething male is hanging out in a high school cafeteria, leering at the girls. Possibly leering at the boys, as well."

Chad threw back his head and laughed. "I hear you found a body. And as a citizen and taxpayer, I have a right to know what you're doing about it. And a responsibility to share what's up with my listeners and readers. Why don't you come on the show and fill us in on the details?"

"Tracking us with your police scanner, Chad?"

He shrugged. "Someone has to do the difficult work of keeping the public informed of the truth." He leered. "In case you haven't heard, I'm Chad Caesar, and I rule the news."

She pushed past him. She could feel his eyes following her but refrained from further comment. There was no telling how he would twist anything she said. And he was right: his podcast and blog were wildly popular, regardless of whether or not he traded in the truth. She pulled his phone out and dropped it into a pile of lunch debris that had been left behind on a table.

She was glad to get home. The day had been difficult, and the interviews with Kekipi's friends and teachers had been emotional. She had learned that his surfing friends were planning a tribute for him, and had listened with compassion as one of them explained how they planned to paddle out just before sunrise and form a circle with their surfboards past the point where the waves were visible. They would drag an empty board behind them, symbolizing that one of their own was missing, then would turn and ride back in together as the sun peeked above the edge of the horizon.

The image of the empty surfboard stuck with her as she stood beneath a stream of hot water, then stepped carefully from the shower onto the worn wooden-plank flooring of the small bathroom. The room had been built without a window, and the long hot shower had filled the tiny space with clouds of swirling steam. Her reflection gazed back at her from the full-length mirror on the wall, the edges of her body slipping in and out of view with the movement of the thick mist. She stood perfectly still, watching as the tattoo on her hip appeared, then disappeared.

She and Mike had spent months deciding on designs and had finally settled on the symbol of a turtle sketched from an ancient petroglyph along the Kona coast for Mike, as a tribute to Kali's Hawaiian heritage, and the Japanese characters for eternity for her, her gesture to Mike's Japanese blood. She reached down now, and her finger gently traced the outline of the black ink. She stopped suddenly, startled at a small movement in the mirror, just behind her. For the smallest fraction of a heartbeat, she thought she glimpsed a tall, familiar figure standing just over her shoulder, but it was gone as quickly as it had appeared. She closed her eyes, reaching for the edge of the sink, then grasping the cold porcelain.

In the next room, there was a whimper, then a persistent rattling as Hilo did his best to open the door. A thick enough mist could trick anyone into seeing anything, she told herself reproachfully.

That night was humid. She slept fitfully, not falling into a deep slumber until it was nearly morning. At first, the pounding on the front porch door seemed no more than part of the dream she was having, in which huge bones were spewing from the mouth of a fiery volcano. In the dream, she stood at a safe distance, watching as the bones hit the ground and broke apart. Each time a chunk hit the ground, it made a crashing noise. She sat up, fully awake, realizing with a great deal of regret that it was morning, and that this was not a strange dream, but the very real banging of a fist on her front door.

"Kali! I know you're home, because Hilo's out here. Open the door!"

She recognized the voice, but without pleasure. It was Birta Elinsdottir, who lived in the house on the next piece of land. As usual, she sounded thoroughly aggravated about something. It was Saturday, and Kali wasn't in the mood to deal with excitement. She was in the mood to sleep for another hour.

"Yes, hold on. I'm coming," she mumbled, and to her annoyance, she heard the door swing open in response. Hilo bounded inside and jumped onto the sofa, then stared down at Kali.

"Isn't it time you were up?" Birta asked, clearly rhetorically.

She plunked herself down into one of the two large easy chairs in the room and regarded Kali with a calculating look. In her lap, she held a covered plate.

"You don't even have any coffee made. For crying out loud, Kali, it's almost eight-thirty. Elvar's already been working on the forge for a couple of hours, and I made muffins. I brought some with me, but I'm not sure you've earned anything delicious. And why are you sleeping on the sofa again?"

Muffins. This sounded mildly interesting and would relieve her of the task of preparing her own breakfast. And there was always the remote possibility that Birta was actually crisis free today and just wanted to have breakfast with someone other than herself. Or that she simply hoped to escape the sound of clanging hammers coming from the covered terrace where her brother, Elvar, had set up the forge he used in his custom knife-making business.

Her mind flickered over an image of the tall, muscled Elvar, with his shy blue eyes, swinging his hammer, shirtless beneath his leather forging apron. Something in her stirred softly at the image, and she pushed it away. She rose from the sofa and wandered toward the kitchen counter to start a pot of coffee, yawning as she pulled two mugs from the dish rack, where they'd been left to dry.

"Coffee on the way. What kind of muffins?"

"Banana and macadamia nut, and I didn't just come for a chat. I need help with a theft."

Her heart sank. Work, after all. The muffins were nothing but a warm, fragrant bribe.

"One of Elvar's knives or swords?"

"No. Someone's been stealing our solar panels."

Kali paused with the coffeepot suspended over the mugs. "You sure?"

"Of course I'm sure." Birta scowled, watching as Kali filled the mugs. "Looks like someone's pried two out of the array up on the roof. One a few weeks ago, and one more last night. We found out this morning."

"That someone took one a few weeks ago?"

"Don't be ridiculous. Of course not. I noticed that *then*, and I noticed this *now*." Birta snatched one of the mugs off the counter, spilling coffee in the process. She seemed oblivious to the trickle running toward the edge of the counter, and was already pushing open the screen door to the front porch.

Hiding a smile, Kali wiped up the puddle of coffee and walked toward the porch with her own mug in hand, reflecting that her Icelandic neighbors couldn't possibly be more unlike one another. In his late thirties, Elvar was calm and friendly. Birta was the elder of the two. Bossy, sensible, and demanding, she'd moved to Hawaii to teach sixth and seventh grade at the local middle school—a task she approached with a zeal and intensity that kept most of the local kids in a state of perpetual terror. Kali wondered idly if her overpowering need for order and control was some deep psychological response to the crowds of tourists and the largely unstructured life she'd found in Hawaii, which was no doubt a huge contrast to the smaller population and stark orderliness of Iceland.

Followed by Hilo, she joined Birta on the lanai, settling into her seat next to the other woman. A small wooden table separated them, and Birta had placed the plate of muffins on its surface. Hilo found a space on the wooden boards, curling himself up as close as possible to the legs of the table. Kali reached for a muffin, waiting for Birta to elaborate. Looking out across the yard, she realized with some surprise that it had rained heavily during the night. She was just thinking that she must have slept pretty soundly when Birta's voice interrupted.

"So what are you going to do about it?" she demanded.

"I'm not clear why you're telling me about the theft.

You need to file a report and then contact your insurance agency. What exactly is it that you'd like me to do?"

Birta's eyes narrowed. She didn't smile. "Aren't you a detective? Do you know that each one of those damned panels cost us more than a thousand bucks?"

"Yes, I know. My grandmother paid the same for hers."

"And it wasn't an ordinary thief. It was some kind of spirit. That's why I came to you, as a neighbor. The police will just laugh."

Kali said nothing. She looked at Birta's no-nonsense face, at the unblinking gaze challenging her to say she had imagined it. Then she spoke slowly. "A spirit?"

"Yes." Birta crossed her arms over her chest, defiant.

Kali kept her voice neutral as she responded. "What exactly did you see? Can you give me any kind of description?"

For a long moment, Birta said nothing. Finally, she nodded, a sharp downward movement of her head. "It was some*thing*, not some*one*." She lingered again before continuing. "What I mean is that whatever it was, it didn't have a face."

The air grew still. Against the window screens, flies buzzed, their movements slowed by the heat already gathering. The brilliant sunshine belied the image of a faceless intruder making its way across Birta's sturdy roof. Kali studied the other woman carefully.

"Are you saying you saw a *noppera-bō* or a mujina?" Kali asked, then watched for Birta's reaction.

The older woman's pale eyes remained steady, and the only indication that she'd heard Kali's question was an added layer of defiance appearing in her tightly drawn lips.

Kali waited, patient.

When Birta spoke, her voice was matter-of-fact. "I am saying no such thing. We have plenty of folklore in Iceland, too much for me to be dismissive, but Hawaii's spiritual nonsense is your department. I'm reporting a factual observation. Whatever it was that was climbing on my roof did not have a face."

Kali frowned. Legends of supernatural events in the islands were not uncommon, but encounters with the faceless *noppera-bō*, which Hawaiians of Japanese heritage at times referred to and which they occasionally called mujina, were the subject of rare, frightening stories whispered in the dark. She spoke thoughtfully. "You have to admit that it's a highly unusual statement."

Birta waved a dismissive hand in the air. "You should be taking this a little more seriously, shouldn't you?"

Kali split the last muffin in half and offered a section to Hilo.

"Well, I don't completely understand. Why didn't you file a report when the first panel went missing? Did you see something then, too?"

Birta shrugged, then glared at Hilo and the muffin crumbs gathering around the dog's front feet. "Stop feeding that wretched animal. He's already enormous." She looked up. "When the first panel was stolen, Elvar and I were on the Big Island for a knife show. When we got back, the power didn't seem up to snuff. I called the maintenance people, and they found that a panel was missing. I couldn't be sure if it had happened the week we were away, or if maybe it had been longer ago than that. I felt silly calling the police when I couldn't even be sure of when the actual theft occurred. Reporting it to the insurance company would have simply raised the rates."

Kali nodded. "And the second panel?"

"As I said, it was last night."

"And you still didn't report it?"

"Why do you think? I'm reporting it now, to you, because I know you. The last thing I need is to have the local police force regarding me as a crazy old woman who makes things up. But it absolutely must have happened sometime last night."

"How can you be sure?"

"We drove down to Hana for dinner, and when we came home, Elvar went straight to bed." She paused. "I was in the kitchen, getting a glass of water, and that's when I saw the ghost. I hadn't bothered to turn on the lights, and there was moonlight coming through the window over the sink. There was something like a shadow moving in front of the window outside, blocking out the moon. It separated itself from the darkness and turned toward me. Instead of eyes and a mouth, there was nothing. Just a blank space. As though it wanted me to see."

She shuddered. "Then it was gone. It wasn't until this morning that we realized the power wouldn't come up all the way. We got out the ladder, and Elvar climbed up to the roof, and sure enough, there's another panel missing."

Kali shook her head. "Well, there's very little I can do until you make an official report."

Kali stood up and went inside, returning with her phone. She called Walter, and explained about the theft. Her brow wrinkled as she listened to Walter's reply. The conversation was brief. She turned back to Birta, her face serious.

"Walter's just a few minutes away. He said we should meet him over at your place." She saw the impatience in Birta's eyes. She spoke slowly, choosing her words carefully. "It seems we've had reports of similar thefts from other areas of the island."

Birta nodded. "All right, then."

Kali headed down the porch steps. Birta picked up her now-empty muffin plate and followed Kali slowly down the porch steps and across the wide lawn in silence. Hilo trotted along contentedly behind them, the three of them reaching a path that led through thick shrubs and palms to Birta's property.

In less than three minutes, they were next door. Elvar was standing under the overhang of his makeshift workshop in a small building in the garden, attaching a carved-bone handle to a newly finished knife. He turned when he heard them approach, then smiled warmly at Kali.

He was bare-chested and sweaty from the heat of the forge, a heavy leather forging apron protecting his skin and his long golden hair tied back to keep it from interfering with his work. Kali's heart gave a small, involuntary lurch as the muscles across his back rippled beneath his skin.

"Aloha," he said politely, then turned to his sister. "The solar company people are sending someone over with a couple of replacement panels, and I know you're not going to be thrilled, but I also phoned the insurance company." He grinned. "I'll warn you that no one seems to be in much of a hurry, though. I'm guessing they're on island time."

"Naturally," said Birta, her disapproval evident. "Anyway, it turns out we're not the only ones to have had panels stolen."

Elvar looked at her inquisitively. "What do you mean?"

Birta glanced at Kali, who hesitated.

"It seems there's been a sudden rash of thefts," said Kali. "It's anyone's guess where they're all disappearing to, but it seems unlikely that someone's driving them across the state border."

Elvar's laughter was interrupted by the sound of a car slowing on the main road. Walter's cruiser pulled into the driveway and rolled to a stop. They watched as he climbed out of the car. He greeted Birta and Elvar and listened as Birta relayed her tale of the faceless intruder, his expression neutral. He frowned and looked inquiringly at Kali, gesturing for her to step away from the others. He spoke quietly, just out of earshot of Birta and Elvar.

"*Noppera-bō* stealing solar panels?"

She shrugged. "Who's to say? Give me the details about what was going on when I called you."

"Theft with violent assault during the night on an elderly woman living near the airport at center island, in the Kīhei area. Grace Sawyer. She'd been on Kaua'i for several weeks, visiting her daughter, and came home a few days early. Her daughter phoned nine-one-one after getting an incoherent call from her mother that there was some kind of noise on the roof. Apparently, she went outside to see what was going on, and was attacked. We know part of the story because we got it from the daughter. The responding officer found the woman unconscious. Eighty-one years old, and someone smashed her over the head. But . . ." he said, then took a breath, "according to the emergency room staff, she drifted to for a few moments, mumbling something about monsters. Hasn't woken back up since."

Kali looked back to where Birta waited. "Could have been social commentary. Comparing thieves to monsters isn't necessarily a stretch."

"Could be. Or it could be something far more literal."

"And I'm guessing the theft involved solar panels?"

"Yup. Two. He, she, or they left the woman on the ground, unconscious and bleeding heavily from a head wound, and carried on with the theft."

Unaware, Birta crossed the lawn and took up a position at the foot of the ladder that had been left leaning against the roof of the house. She glared at Walter, her arms crossed tightly, and called out to him. "I saw what I saw. Now do your job and take a look at my roof. I left the ladder waiting."

Walter suppressed a smile and gestured to Kali to help him. Together, they walked to where Birta waited. Walter stood for a moment at the foot of the ladder, looking up, then directed his gaze at the thick lawn as he walked around slowly.

Kali walked with him, peering at the carefully mown lawn. They examined the area along the side of the house for some indication that another ladder had been set up the night before, but there was nothing.

Walter moved to the side of the house where the kitchen window faced out toward the sea. The shade was deeper here, and the roofline was slightly lower. Kali followed, her eyes raking the ground. Here, the lawn was broken up with patches of bare earth that edged a garden. She knelt, and peered into the dirt where the broad, waxy leaves of a bush had protected the ground from the rain. She stopped and pointed, and Walter came to stand beside her.

"There's a huge jumble of prints everywhere there's dirt," she said. "Mostly the same shoes, by the look of it. I know Birta spends a lot of time out here puttering around and gardening, so they may mean nothing."

They followed what seemed to be a logical line between the prints and the driveway. The grass was short
and dense, and there were no bare patches that might
have revealed more markings. Birta's Volkswagen was
parked at the far end of the drive where she usually left it.
Walter knelt and studied the ground beneath it, but there
were no signs of anything useful. After rising, he walked
the length of the driveway, but if there had ever been any
tire marks, they had been washed clear by the rain.

"Ask the scary woman and the knife guy for their shoe
sizes and find out if either one of them was walking
around that kitchen window in a pair of rubber-soled
shoes since the last rain," Walter said, eyeing Birta with
some trepidation.

Kali frowned uncomfortably. "I'd rather you did. This
isn't my case."

Kali could feel Walter's eyes boring into her.

"What's the deal?" he asked.

She shifted, looking back toward the house. "They're
my neighbors, and I'd prefer to let you handle it. I'm just
a little hesitant to get involved with them on any kind of a
personal level."

Walter smothered a laugh. "What?" He looked at her
knowingly. "Wait a minute. Let me make a wild guess—
you're hoping the guy with the ponytail might ask you to
the prom someday, and you think asking him questions
about his shoe size is too personal?"

"Asshole. And not true. They're my friends. Kind of."

"Yeah, well, you're lucky I'm not going to send you
up the ladder for being disrespectful. I'm the officer in
charge. Plus, I'm your uncle. So I'm doubly offended."

"Noted. Not that I particularly care."

Walter was still grinning when they returned to where

Birta waited. Kali gripped the sides of the ladder as Walter made his way up the rungs. He climbed carefully to the roof and even more carefully swung one leg up over the edge. The roof was empty, washed clean in the rain. The solar array wasn't far away. He climbed the sloping distance until he was standing before it. He dusted the panels closest to the empty spaces for prints.

"Nothing especially odd or out of place," he said to Kali as he climbed back down. "Doesn't look as though the panels were removed in a hurry. There's no scraping or broken attachments."

"They were probably taken out very carefully," said Kali. She and Walter walked to the edge of the lawn, looking back at the house. "Whether someone's stealing them to use or to resell, they'd have to be in pristine condition." She looked up at the edge of the roof. "The whole thing seems deliberate, right down to the thief knowing exactly when Birta and Elvar would be away from the house." And, she thought to herself, *knowing when the old woman would be off-island, on Kauaʻi, visiting her daughter*.

"Agreed. But the ghost part of the story is pretty weird." He looked at her sideways. "And it means you're officially on the job, regardless of the neighbor angle. Outside of the attack last night, none of the other theft victims mentioned anything unusual like that in connection with their panels going missing, but people are more likely to tell you that kind of thing, anyway. Like you understand or something."

"Or something. Send me the list of burglary victims," Kali said, her voice resigned and low enough not to be overheard, "and I'll see what I can find out. And let me know when—or if—the attack victim is able to talk."

They turned to walk back to Birta. Elvar had joined her, and Hilo leaned against him. Elvar reached down, scratching the big dog's ears.

As Kali drew near, Hilo wriggled out from beneath Elvar's hand and ran to her, his tail wagging madly.

"We might get some prints," Walter told Birta and Elvar. "But I doubt it. The whole job looks pretty professional." He grinned broadly and patted Kali on the shoulder. "But here's the good news. Kali's officially on neighborhood watch for you. Meanwhile, if you think of anything else, give me a call."

Birta made no comment. She simply turned and trudged toward the house, the sunlight glinting on the edge of the muffin plate, which she still held in her hand.

The others watched her go. Elvar turned to Walter.

"Thanks for coming over and having a look. Birta gets so excited about everything."

Walter smiled. "No problem. It sucks to come home and find out you've been robbed." He turned and looked across the lawn toward Elvar's workshop. The red glow of the hot forge could clearly be seen. "I saw something about you on the news, didn't I? About your knives? I think the reporter said you'd made some swords for a movie that's going to be filmed on Kaua'i."

Kali looked at Elvar in surprise. "Really? Birta never said anything."

Elvar shrugged modestly. "Yes, I was asked by the set designer to make a replica sword and a battle hammer. I've made a few before for films, but they were small budget movies shot back in Iceland. I don't think anyone ever saw them."

Walter looked impressed. He winked at Kali. "Sounds like a pretty cool job. You must be excited."

Elvar nodded. "Honored. They've given me some direction as to the size and length of the blade, but the design and inscriptions are up to me, provided they conform to the time period of the film. It should be a fun project." He gestured toward the workshop. "I've already made a few models to run by the film people before I start on the full-scale pieces."

Walter glanced at his wristwatch. "Well, good luck with it." He turned toward the police car. "I'll let you know if anything turns up. Kali, see you at the station."

As Walter drove away, Kali stood awkwardly in the yard. There was a slight breeze, and her hair lifted across her cheek. She pushed a strand away, trying to think of something clever to say, but Elvar had already turned back in the direction of his shop.

"Back to work, I guess," he said over his shoulder as he walked away.

Kali smiled briefly. She stepped into the shadows of the trees where the path between the houses twisted away, whistling for Hilo. Elvar, stoking the fire in his forge, didn't seem to notice.

CHAPTER 8

Kali and Walter tried to make themselves comfortable on the hard, narrow bench that served as a visitors' seat in the austere exterior office of the medical examiner, placed there deliberately by Stitches to discourage lingering. It wasn't easy, especially for Walter, whose bulk required considerably more space than that offered by the bench.

Even Kali was ill at ease. There was a faint chemical smell clinging to the air, and she was hyperaware that just a short corridor away, the boy's body lay stretched out on a cold autopsy table.

"You checked in with Kekipi's mother this morning?" she asked, overcome by the image.

Walter looked off into the distance. "When I got there, she was in his room, gathering his belongings."

"Getting ready to give them away, of course," said

Kali. "The traditional way. Holding on to the belongings of the deceased keeps their spirit trapped."

"Yeah. Said she was going to donate them." He faltered. "She's anxious to get him home."

Of course she would be, thought Kali. There were important rituals to perform. The body needed to be washed with salt water before burial; the family's mourning would not be complete until he had been sanctified and his spirit freed to begin its journey to *lani*, into the Hawaiian heaven.

They sat, waiting. Somewhere in one of the offices leading from the reception area, a clock ticked, measuring out the morning.

"I wonder," she said to Walter, "if the boy knows where he is now. Maybe he thinks he's dreaming."

His face filled with sadness.

She knew he was likely thinking of his own kids. She didn't need to have any of her own to wonder how anyone could survive such a loss—to marvel at how those who were faced with the task of burying their children were able to carry on.

"There were boxes stacked on the floor, all of them already labeled—books, posters, music. There was part of a sweatshirt poking out of one of them. She pulled it out to show me. It was new, one of those logo shirts from the University of Hawaii. She said the guy from the university who came out to tell him he'd won the scholarship had brought it as a gift."

Kali waited.

"She folded it up. Real careful, like. And then I told her what we'd found, that maybe it wasn't an accident."

Kali closed her eyes for a moment, imagining the mother's distress.

"But she had nothing to add to what we already know?" she asked.

"Just what I told you. He'd been frequenting the same beach access point for as long as he'd been able to carry his own board, and had surfed with pretty much the same group of friends for years."

Kali considered this.

"Not much from his friends, either," said Kali. "No quarrels or fallings-out with anybody, no change in his behavior, no indication of drug or alcohol use, no pregnant girlfriends. Everything we hear just reinforces the picture of a well-liked, intelligent, hardworking kid who loved to spend his free time riding waves."

Yet two days had passed since the body had washed ashore, and the trail—such as it was—wasn't only cold but invisible, too. No one had seen anything, heard anything, or offered anything in the way of even the most tenuous lead. And there was no sign of a murder weapon.

"You know," Walter said, "we have to consider this could be some kind of freak accident. Maybe he did just crash into the lava. Maybe the tooth was caught up in the stone, and there was some perfect storm of events that led to this."

Kali looked at him sideways, knowing he didn't believe a single word of his own speech. "Sure, Walter."

He looked affronted. "You saying crazy things never happen?"

"Of course not. I'm saying—"

The hallway door near the reception area opened, and Stitches stepped out, cutting short the conversation.

"You're both here. Good." She turned without another word and walked back into the her office. Kali and Walter exchanged glances, then got up and followed her. She was already seated behind her desk by the time they entered. She pointed to two chairs drawn up across from her, indicating that they should sit.

Stitches regarded them over the rim of her narrow, silver-framed glasses. Only a few traces of gray could be detected in her wavy, thick brown hair. The hair framed a pleasantly proportioned face, and her intelligent deep blue eyes were a rare shade, nearly purple in the right light.

She leaned across her desk, pushing a small glass vial toward them.

"Here you are," she said as if the vial was completely self-explanatory.

Kali picked it up, turned it slowly in her fingers, then looked up questioningly. "What's this?"

"A glass vial," Stitches said, her voice weary.

Kali hid her own annoyance. "Yes, I got that part. What's this little chip of a thing inside it?"

"Wood. To be more precise, a splinter of wood that came from something quite old."

Kali held the vial up to the light, and studied it more carefully. "Where'd you find it?"

"His head, in the main wound. There were abrasions, of course, from the lava, but those followed death. This splinter was buried a bit deeper than a surface examination revealed, and I've only just recovered it."

Walter raised an eyebrow. "If he didn't drown and was carried to the water after he was killed, is it possible it's something unrelated, like a splinter that worked its way out of an older wound?"

Stitches shook her head. "Not even remotely possible. If this had been there for a while, the area leading to it would have completely healed over, and there would still be scar tissue—perhaps just a miniscule amount—around it, indicating where the injury had been. If it had been more recent, then the area immediately surrounding it would have shown signs of trauma, such as pus and irritation where the body was rejecting the presence of a foreign object. No, this splinter was lodged at the same time the tooth found its way into the tissue."

Walter took the vial from Kali and stared at the small, narrow shard inside.

"The lab ran a few tests to determine the type of wood," said Stitches. "It's definitely tropical, but we're waiting on an exact species match." She watched them carefully as she answered. "More important it's quite old. At least a hundred years old, probably more. So, the object with which he was struck was an old, heavy piece of wood. I still don't understand the shark's tooth, but I guess that's your department."

She waited.

Walter shifted uncomfortably.

"How about one of those old fishing plaques? You know, with the fish mounted on them." He looked at the two women, both of whom were regarding him skeptically. "Someone could have used an old piece of wood they had lying around to mount a prize, like a shark."

Kali leaned back against her chair, shaking her head. Before she could say anything, Stitches spoke.

"The tooth is from an adult shark. It seems highly unlikely that a fully grown and extremely heavy shark, mounted, as you suggest, on a large piece of wood, and perhaps hanging randomly on a tree close to the beach as decoration, would be the first thing a killer would reach for to smack a young man over the back of the head."

Walter flushed. He raised his empty hands, palms up,

admitting defeat. "Some adult sharks aren't that big," he answered, his voice defensive.

"No . . . ," said Kali slowly. "But there may have been something ritualistic about this death. At least we should consider the possibility. The tooth may have come later, after he'd already been struck down with a wooden object. Placed as a talisman. Or as a signature."

"Well," said Stitches, turning to Kali, "I suppose you're the person to figure that out."

Kali's face showed no expression. "I guess it's possible. Though nothing comes to mind, really, as far as a legend or myth."

Stitches stood up, having offered both her latest findings and her opinion. "Well, we've all dealt with killers before. Narcissists at the core. Their reasons and behavior are rarely rational in nature. Though they are quite frequently selfish."

Walter stood, as well, clearly grateful that the meeting was drawing to a close.

"That's true," he said in agreement. "The real rationalization comes later, while they're trying to come up with an acceptable excuse for their actions."

"There's never an acceptable excuse for cold-blooded murder," Stitches said, her voice firm.

Kali gave a grim smile. "Couldn't agree more," she said.

Walter and Stitches looked away, knowing she was thinking of someone else. Kali rose, as well. Walter followed her to the office door and out into the reception area. They left the building, letting the doors close behind them, shutting out the scent of chemicals and sadness.

CHAPTER 9

Kali drove to the station later that morning, overwhelmed by a combined sense of urgency and frustration. The attack victim had still not regained consciousness, and the doctor in charge of her care had already pointed out several times that the combination of the victim's advanced age and the severity of the injuries left no guarantee that she would recover to a point that made questioning her a possibility.

Yet someone certainly knew what had happened—just as someone had also been there with Kekipi Smith and had likely watched as the last breath left his lungs and dissipated in the warm island air. Most likely, that person was the very one who had taken his mana—the spark of his life fire—from him.

She parked the Jeep and went inside. Walter was

seated at his desk, and looked up as she pulled a chair close and sat down, her legs crossed.

"I don't know where to turn on this," she said, weariness evident in her tone. "It seems so random. All we've got is a splinter of old wood and an island full of trees."

"Maybe we just can't see the forest yet," offered Walter, half serious. He held up a single sheet of paper. "Meanwhile, here's something to keep you occupied. I checked with the main station in Wailuku to see if there have been any updates since last night regarding panel thefts or anything weird on other parts of the island. There's been nothing new for a week, except for the nighttime attack and what your neighbor reported."

Kali glanced around the small, cluttered satellite police office. There was still an old fax machine in one corner. Kali recalled the former humming of the printer as pages made their way through before falling unceremoniously to the floor, the machine's basket having long ago been removed to serve the purpose of dish rack for the multitude of coffee cups continuously cycling across the counter near the small sink.

She took the sheet of paper from Walter and studied it. On it were the most up-to-date addresses and phone numbers for everyone reporting missing panels, and the contact information and Web sites for four companies supplying solar panels and related equipment to homeowners throughout Hawaii. For a moment she was surprised there were so few suppliers—this was followed almost immediately by a sense of profound relief that she wouldn't have to chase down fifty separate businesses spread across the entire chain of islands.

Only one of the supplier addresses was on Maui. Two of the businesses were located on Oʻahu, near Honolulu, and the fourth was on the Big Island, up the coast from Kona, in the quiet town of Waimea. Kali frowned, calculating. The off-Maui addresses would have to be dealt with later. The Big Island meant a flight or crossing the dividing water in the *Gingerfish*. Oʻahu would also require a flight and negotiating heavy traffic and, most likely, an overnight stay.

"All the theft victims have been interviewed through the main station in Wailuku," said Walter. "However, the majority of owners are people living in other states who keep vacation homes here. They may not even visit every year."

"How many total missing panels?"

"So far, one hundred ten, all taken from Maui residences. Again, some are multiples from big houses that are rarely occupied, and more than half were removed from arrays that were mounted next to the structure, rather than only on the roof. One property had ten panels taken from an array of thirty panels. Most, like your neighbor, didn't notice right away."

"So conceivably, there could be more. Maybe even a significant number, but they haven't been reported yet?"

"Exactly."

"First theft?"

"Initial report was a month ago."

"Okay. I'm on it." She paused. "Maybe," she added, the frustration evident in her voice, "if I'm distracted, it will shake some thoughts loose about the murder."

She phoned the Maui business and made an appointment to see the owner later that afternoon, explaining that she hoped to get some background information on the solar energy business. The hour-long drive led to the flat cement exterior of the Maui Solar Company, which was striking in its anonymity. The reception area was hardly an improvement, though Kali noticed that someone had made an attempt to soften the industrial setting with a stab at decor in the form of a potted bird-of-paradise plant and an outdated framed poster of an island music festival.

A young woman sat at a desk that was empty except for a computer and a telephone. Behind her was the entrance to the main area, what Kali assumed to be a warehouse where goods were stored until sold and transported elsewhere on the island.

The woman looked up as the door swung shut behind Kali, and smiled in greeting. "Aloha. May I help you?"

Kali smiled in return, looking around. "Aloha. I'm Kali Māhoe. I called earlier."

"Oh, right. You're the policewoman who wants to speak to Mr. Uru."

"That's right. It's Detective Māhoe. You are?"

"Vanessa. I'm Mr. Uru's assistant. I deal with the orders and purchase details."

"Does Mr. Uru have time right now?"

"Yes, absolutely," she answered, looking at Kali with open curiosity. "He's expecting you, but just let me tell him you're here, okay?"

Kali waited as the woman walked without haste through the wide doors leading to the warehouse. She returned soon with a middle-aged Japanese man behind her. He extended his hand in greeting, smiling in an open, friendly way.

"Detective Māhoe. I'm Harold Uru. I hope I can be of some help." He turned, gesturing for Kali to follow him. "Would you like me to show you around, and you can ask questions while I explain what we do here?"

"Sounds like a good plan."

Vanessa hovered near the entrance. "Can I be of any help?"

"No. I'll walk her around," said Uru. "If she has any questions about the sales process, she can stop by your desk before she leaves."

Kali watched as the woman walked away without saying anything further. She was wearing heels, and her shoes made a businesslike clicking sound against the floor. It was very un-Hawaiian to dress so formally during the day, and Uru seemed to sense Kali's unspoken thought.

"She's new to the islands. San Francisco business school graduate. I don't think she likes sitting inside at a desk all day."

"I get that," said Kali, feeling a rush of mixed embarrassment at her unspoken rash judgment, mixed with sympathy for anyone who was trapped indoors in Hawaii.

Together, she and Uru walked among the rows of solar panels. They were in two general sizes, the smaller measuring two by three feet, the larger three by five.

Uru paused beside a row of shelves that contained batteries.

"Is your home by any chance powered by solar energy?" he asked Kali.

"Yes." Kali shifted from one foot to the other, suddenly uncomfortable at her lack of knowledge about the technical aspects of the system installed on her house. "But I'll be honest with you. I don't really pay much attention to how the whole thing works."

Uru's voice became enthusiastic. "Not to worry. Most people don't. As far as they're concerned, the lights work, the refrigerator keeps their food cold, and when they switch on the television, *SpongeBob SquarePants* comes on to keep their kids happy, and that's all they want to know."

Kali nodded. "That's me, actually."

Uru pointed to the batteries. "They look like car batteries, don't they? Basically, that's exactly what they are—really expensive car batteries. Usually, they're stored in a small room or a garden shed, away from the main building they're powering. The array of solar panels is positioned on the roof of the house or business, or sometimes on a separate tower structure close by. The panels collect sunlight directly from the source, and the power is stored in the batteries."

Kali tried to hide her confusion. "Yes, but exactly how does the power get from the panels to the batteries, and from the batteries to the television?"

"Ahh," crooned Uru. "It's a beautifully simple process. You understand that household current, which powers everything from your lights to your toaster oven, is AC, which stands for alternating current?"

Kali nodded, lessons from her long-ago high school science class slowly surfacing in her mind.

"Well," Uru continued, "the power collected by the panels and stored in the batteries is in the form of DC, or direct current. An inverter unit turns the DC to AC, which is then fed via wires to a circuit box, and then on to individual appliances and the like."

That all seemed clear enough, but the panel-to-battery portion of the process still eluded her. Failing to perceive that she was still vague on the details, Uru continued.

"Then a very sensitive trace device within each panel maintains the power level in the batteries."

Kali nodded. "Right. This all sounds fairly high tech, though. Which usually translates to expensive."

Uru shrugged. "It can be, depending on the size of the building you need to supply energy to. For an average house of about fifteen hundred square feet, the setup is roughly twelve to twenty larger panels, plus the trace device and inverter, which run about ten to fifteen thousand dollars together. Then figure in up to twenty separate batteries, at two to three hundred dollars apiece, and there you are."

"Broke."

"Well, that's the problem—people get hung up thinking about the initial setup cost, forgetting that the source of the energy, the sun, is an infinite and completely free resource. A flame that never goes out. Once they've got their panels and other equipment, they're off the grid. Freedom from the utility companies."

"But the equipment still needs to be replaced now and then, doesn't it?"

"Batteries? Sure. They have to be replaced once in a while, but each one should be good for a minimum of a decade. The solar panels, unless damaged, can last indefinitely."

"Unless they're stolen."

Uru looked surprised. "Stolen? Yes, I guess that could be a problem, though homeowners' insurance would cover the loss. I like to think things are different here in paradise. More goodwill."

"There are people up to no good in every corner of the world," she said. "Hawaii's no different."

He looked suddenly uneasy. Kali watched his face, curious about the subtle change in his energy.

"Well, from what you've described about the business end of things," she said, "it seems that swiping the equipment and reselling it could be a potentially profitable little enterprise. Are there any identifying marks on the panels?"

"Manufacturer's marks, of course," he said. "But those are very small and not easily visible. There aren't any serial numbers, or anything like that. There are relatively few companies producing them for consumer purchase, so I can't see how that would be much help. And the batteries generally all look the same."

Kali looked around at the huge boxed inventory Uru had on hand. "Have you been approached by anyone trying to sell individual panels? Or had anything unusual occur?"

He shook his head, but again, Kali picked up on his uneasiness.

"Of course not. I would be immediately suspicious. I buy direct from manufacturers on the West Coast and in Japan. Someone coming in here with a panel under his arm would stand out as suspicious right away. Besides, what we sell is complete photovoltaic systems. We've very rarely had requests for a single panel."

"But you'd be likely to hear if someone was up to that kind of thing locally?"

"You bet I would. I wouldn't appreciate someone trying to undermine my business by selling stolen goods at better prices than I can offer."

Kali nodded. While her instincts were telling her that Uru wasn't the kind of person to get involved in anything sordid, she was interested in the change that had come over him.

"Is there something that's giving you concern?" she

asked, turning around in the vast cement-floored space. She took a few steps toward the door leading back to the reception area, which could be seen at the far end of the space, then paused, waiting for his response

He hesitated, walking up beside her in silence. A few steps from the door, he stopped. "It's nothing to do with solar panels. It's just . . ."

"Yes?"

"Well, there's been a stray cat hanging around. I've been feeding it. Put a box outside for it. You know, with an old towel in it." He looked embarrassed. "Yesterday I found the cat by the side door I use to get to my office. It was dead . . ." Again, he paused.

Kali scanned his face. She could see that he was both anxious and unhappy. "Maybe it was sick?"

He shook his head. "No, it wasn't sick. At least, that's not what killed it. It had been cut in half, like it had been sliced with something big and sharp. And then placed in front of the door, where it wouldn't be missed. Like it was deliberate. It felt like . . . well, as though it might be some sort of a message."

He looked sad. "Poor little thing. It was just starting to trust me." He turned to Kali. "Who on earth would do such a thing?" He shook his head. "And why?"

"That's unfortunate," she said. The thought of the cruelty was troubling, and the act that had taken the stray cat's life repulsed her, but she kept her voice even. "I don't see how it's related, though."

"No. I'm sorry. It's just that when you asked me if anything unusual had taken place, it made me think of the little cat."

"Have you received any threats? Complaints from customers, perhaps? If there's anything personal or professional that you think might be behind such an act, you should tell me."

He said nothing, and Kali could detect no subterfuge.

"I really don't think so," he finally said. "Perhaps just children acting out."

"With access to something large and sharp enough to slice a cat in half?"

Again, there was silence before he answered. "I don't know what to tell you. Like I said, I hardly think it's related to your investigation. Perhaps I just needed to tell someone about it, in an official sort of way."

"You need to let us know if anything else unusual like that happens," she said. "You can call me directly, or call the main line. Up to you, but if something else occurs, it needs to be looked into."

She handed him her card, and he looked it over carefully before placing it in his wallet.

"All right. I'll do that."

She thanked him and made her way to the reception area as he turned back to the door leading to his office. The receptionist was there, sitting at her desk. She looked up as Kali approached, and Kali noticed that she was wearing eyeliner and a tinted lip gloss, and that her hair had been carefully styled. She felt suddenly self-conscious and reached up involuntarily to shove a loose tangle of hair behind one ear.

"Mahalo for your time," said Kali, pushing at the heavy glass door. Just as she was about to step into the sunshine, she turned back, feeling as though there was something else she should have asked, a thought just out of reach.

"Mr. Uru told me about the cat," she said. "I don't suppose you saw anything or have any idea who might have killed it?"

The woman raised her eyebrows. "I imagine it was the ghost."

Kali looked at her in surprise. "Come again?"

The receptionist laughed. "Didn't he tell you?" She leaned forward. Her voice lowered, she explained, "Honestly, he's been going on about it. He didn't just find it by the door. He swears he saw a ghost running away just as he was walking up to the building." She made a dismissive sound. "A ghost carrying a dead cat. Have you ever heard of anything so insane?"

Kali kept her voice neutral. "Unusual, that's for certain," she said.

She turned and headed back into the warehouse. The story of the mutilated cat was disturbing, but she needed to know why Uru had left out the detail of the ghost.

When she confronted him in his office, he hung his head, mortified. "Really, I can't be sure of what I saw. A figure, moving away from the door. In my culture, there are stories about such things."

"Yes. The *noppera-bō*. I'm familiar with the legends."

He looked at her in astonishment, then in gratitude. "So you won't think I'm crazy when I say that when it saw me, it paused and turned to look at me, but there were no eyes."

"Was it an actual face?"

He frowned. "Now, I think perhaps it was a mask or a costume. It was all gray, like a shadow that blended into its surroundings. But it happened so quickly, and I was focused on the welfare of the cat. There was such a pool of blood, you see. I didn't realize until I was standing right over it that it had been mutilated. That there was nothing I could do to help."

"Was there anything else? Did you get a sense of height or weight or gender?"

"No." He looked away for a moment and then turned to her, his face without the slightest hint of guile. "I would say a slightly built person who moved quickly. I'm sorry I mentioned it to anyone."

"Is it possible someone was trying to frighten your receptionist and not you?"

He thought about it. "I would say that it's unlikely."

"If she moved here recently from the mainland, she could have left behind an ex-husband or lover, someone from her past."

"She's been in the islands for about two years, and I think she has some family here. If there had been something about this incident that struck her as being personal, I'm sure she would have said, or I would have noticed."

Kali had no idea why Uru had been targeted for such a bizarre act, but one thing was certain: There seemed to be an extraordinary number of spirits lurking around in the vicinity of solar panels. Too many, perhaps, to be coincidence.

CHAPTER 10

The harbormaster at Kona, on the Big Island, waved lazily from the dock beside the office as Kali motored slowly into the sheltered cove and brought the *Gingerfish* into an empty slip. She cut the engine power and felt the tense muscles across her upper back finally relax. She'd been in luck with the overnight channel crossing. Despite the torrential downpour, there had at least been no cruise ships to navigate around. The enormous boats were a necessary evil in the advance of tourism, she knew, but were quite intimidating from the deck of the aging *Gingerfish*, who'd left her youthful maneuverability far behind.

Even without cruise ships, the crossing had been daunting enough—the channel between the two islands was a notoriously perilous body of water—and as she completed the docking process, she silently decided to spend

the night here in the harbor before making her way back
in the morning. When she was younger, she'd made the
trip numerous times with friends and family, but the care-
free enjoyment she'd once felt had been replaced by a
more mature respect for the weather forces at play in the
wide strip of sea.

She'd had a lot of time to think about her final conversation with Uru about the cat. He'd been embarrassed,
she was sure of that. And also a little frightened, though
he had protested that he had no need of a patrol of the
area, or any worry that he was in personal danger.

The morning was clear and sunny, and the idea of
ghosts seemed out of place in the daylight. Walter had radioed ahead on her behalf to arrange with the Kona office
of the Hawaii County Police Department for the use of a
car for the afternoon. She realized that he must have suggested some sort of official interisland cooperation with
the solar panel investigation, because the harbormaster
told Kali not to worry about the time—she could use the
slip for as long as she needed, no fees necessary.

She took a folded blanket from the boat's storage chest
and stepped onto the dock. After nodding in thanks to the
harbormaster, she whistled for Hilo, who stood poised to
leap onto the dock, his tail up and his ears arranged in an
expectant half-mast position meant to convey willing-
ness, but not, at this stage, complete commitment. Kali
understood that this was in case he was left on board, at
which point the dog's ego would require at least the pretense that spending the day on the boat deck was exactly
what he'd hoped for all along.

Hilo sat back on his haunches briefly, then launched
himself from the boat deck to the dock. He loped along,
sniffing the ground enthusiastically. Fish, bait, other dogs,

humans he hadn't met, urine, dropped scraps of food—
each was significant and worthy of being explored before
moving on. It was, at least in canine terms, a marvelous
theme park of olfactory delights.

Kali shook her head as he nosed a fish head that had,
judging by its color and the rank fumes emanating from
it, already spent a considerable amount of time in the
rough grass of the parking area. When called, he came reluctantly to where she stood beside a slightly dented older
Prius. She checked the tag number against a slip of paper
in her pocket, then opened the door and reached beneath
the driver's seat. Her hand closed around the key that had
been left there, and she marveled for the length of a single
breath at the trusting—if sometimes misplaced—Hawaiian attitude toward life and theft.

She spread the blanket across the backseat and stepped
aside as Hilo clambered in. While he found a comfortable
position, she looked over the directions she'd printed out,
lowering the rear windows so that Hilo would have both
an unobstructed view and the pleasure of feeling the wind
pinning back his ears as she drove.

She was heading to a solar supply company located
just outside of Waimea, a small town in the northwestern
area of the Big Island. Compared to Maui, the roads here
were nearly free of traffic. She drove slowly from the harbor onto Highway 19, past two separate development
sites with rows of newly built homes and condominiums.
A few miles farther along, the hill on the inland side of
the highway showed various stages of yet another development—this time of larger, custom-designed houses. A
colorful billboard promised that the houses in the exclusive community of Secret Haven were now for sale, with
a variety of financing options available.

She slowed the car. The roofs of the custom homes all had solar panels angled to face the south. The development was extensive and looked as though it would have around several hundred houses when it was complete. Some company, thought Kali, had likely made a good profit supplying solar arrays to that many structures.

On impulse, she pulled in and parked next to a large flatbed truck loaded with pallets of ceramic floor tile. There were several workmen moving between the two houses closest to the truck. Another man was checking the tile delivery, ticking off items listed on a clipboard. He paused, and waited as Kali approached.

"Aloha," Kali said. She nodded toward the pallets. "The tile for the bathrooms?"

"Kitchens," said the man. "Can I help you?"

"Just stopped to look. These places are huge."

The man looked toward the buildings. "Too big," he said. "Who needs that much space?"

She nodded, agreeing. "Can't imagine what it will cost to cool off those places," she said. "And the mainlanders have to have air-conditioning while they're in their vacation houses, right?"

"Don't think they can live without it," the man said, grinning in agreement. "Give me an open window and a tropical breeze any day."

Kali smiled and looked up, then scanned the rooflines. "Does the utility bill cost less in a housing development with the solar electricity?"

The workman shrugged. "Not my department. I just lay the tile. But if you're interested, there's a guy in the office over there who can give you a brochure with some contact information on it. The builder has a Web site that tells all about how it's good for the environment."

"Thanks," said Kali. She walked in the direction the man had indicated. There was a small trailer that had a sign by the door reading SALES OFFICE. She knocked, and a voice inside told her to come in and close the door.

Inside the small space was a table doing double duty as a desk and a filing cabinet. There was a stack of brochures on one side, and Kali picked one up.

"Mind if I take one of these?" she asked.

"Help yourself," said the man behind the desk. "If you want rates, you'll need to call the builder directly. The units vary in size and finishes, so the prices are all over the place. He's got a couple of different developments in progress. Not all the houses are as expensive as these."

"Are they all solar powered?"

"Most of them. This builder is competing with a lot of other local developers, and his big marketing tool is the renewable energy angle."

"Thanks," said Kali. She left the trailer and closed the door carefully behind her. She studied the brochure as she walked back to the car. The builder's business address was listed as in Honokaa, which was past Waimea. She folded the brochure and put it in her pocket, thinking it might be good to speak to a couple of general housing contractors, who might be able to give her a different perspective than the actual suppliers of solar equipment.

She followed the highway north, past a collection of five-star resorts positioned along the coast, spread out to such a degree that each one seemed to be its own oasis amid the arid lava-rock landscape. For miles on either side of the road, tourists and locals had spelled out private messages with pieces of white coral, which stood out in sharp relief against the ancient black lava stone. The messages were a mix of declaration and longing—*Marci loves Jonathan 4-Ever*, *We Miss You Papa*, *Will You Marry Me, Brett*?

She made her way at a leisurely pace, relishing the views to the east of the lush Kohala Mountains and the long-dormant volcanic hump of Mauna Loa. North of the mountain range was the rich Waipi'o Valley. When she was a teenager, Kali had spent more than one season working for her mother's cousin Brian in his taro fields. Every morning had begun with Brian and the other workers chanting, invoking the demigod Kamapua'a, also called Pig Boy, to help them by burrowing in the watery earth, making it more malleable and easier to work. The laborers, cooled by the ocean breezes, had moved through the mid-knee water, planting and weeding. The sound of their conversation and friendly banter had been a soothing sound track.

For long hours, Kali waded through the muddy water with them, picking snails off the plants and dropping them into a bucket. She simply couldn't understand how she could collect so many snails and still find so many more the next day.

"Do you bring the snails back out here at night and sprinkle them over the plants?" she asked Brian one particularly frustrating snail-filled day.

Brian laughed, then called out to some of the others. "She thinks we're planting snails," he said.

Kali frowned. Planting taro—or, in this case, making sure the snails didn't consume the crops before they could be harvested—was as Hawaiian an activity as surfing and fishing. The crooked, knobby roots were believed in island mythology to be the original source of the Hawaiian people. The old legends told how the union of the son and daughter of Wakea, the Sky Father deity, had resulted in the stillbirth of a malformed infant. The following day a taro plant arose from the place where the child's body had been laid to rest. According to the legend, the plant was the forefather of all Hawaiian people.

The taro plants that were spread out before her in the shallow water, concluded the young Kali, deserved more respect than she was currently showing them. For the rest of the season, she dutifully picked off the snails, filling bucket after bucket, each snail making a small, dull clunking noise at it fell atop the others. An ignoble fate, and hardly worthy of their remarkable perseverance, she decided. In the end, she felt sorry for the small, determined snails and was unable to enjoy eating taro, in any of its various incarnations, for years afterward.

Traffic remained light, and Kali reached Waimea about twenty minutes before her first appointment. She pulled off onto the side of the road where the long fields of Parker Ranch ran east toward the island's interior, rising slowly beneath the ancient lava cones that ascended in ever smoother bumps across the cattle grazing grounds. She looked again at the address she'd been given and at a page that Hara had printed out from a Web site, advertising Sunshine on Your Shoulders Solar Energy Company, Inc. The one-page flyer featured a poor-quality image of a roof boasting a covering of solar panels.

Hilo sniffed at the air through the open rear windows, enticed by the aroma of distant cows. He whimpered, pushing his nose against Kali's shoulder.

"Not a chance," Kali responded, eyeing the many visible piles of dung that the cows had left behind. Hilo, given the opportunity, would proudly cover himself in muck. Kali knew from numerous past experiences that it would take several energetic baths to remove the scent, and covering the interior of the borrowed car with Eau de Hilo à la Cow would not win her any favors with her colleagues on the local police force.

She pulled slowly away from the road's shoulder and followed the detailed directions just north of the town, where what looked like an old garage had been brightly decorated with enormous painted sunflowers. A hand-lettered sign above the wide double roll-up doors identified the building as the correct address. Kali parked next to the building in the shade offered by a stand of palms. As she opened the car door and slipped out, Hilo pushed past her, positioning himself close to her hip.

At the edge of the building a second door, largely camouflaged by the giant sunflowers, bore a sign that read OPEN FOR BUSINESS. Kali turned the handle and entered, setting off a jangle of bells and metal chimes shaped like surfboards that hung above the doorframe. Inside, sitting at a long, scuffed wooden table, his feet slung across a surface littered with papers and food wrappers, was a young man in his early twenties. His long hair was pulled back into a ponytail, and he was wearing a faded shirt covered with hula dancers and denim shorts that had frayed at the edges. He glanced up as Kali and Hilo entered, his eyes slightly unfocused. He yawned, confirming her suspicion of sleep.

"Many alohas, dude," he said, then covered his mouth with the back of his hand as he yawned a second time.

"Sorry to interrupt," said Kali.

"No prob. Just catching up on a few REM cycles." He caught sight of Hilo and did a double take. "Whoa. That's one seriously large dog."

"He won't bother you. He already ate today."

The boy grinned. "That's cool, then."

Kali took a deep breath. "Are you the owner?"

"Me?" The young man laughed, swinging his legs off the table and onto the floor in front of him. "Nope, just the hired help. I'm Matt. This is Randy's business. He's the solar dude." He caught sight of the flyer in Kali's hand. "You're looking for some sun fire, right? Well, this is the place."

Kali waited, but Matt just continued to smile.

"Is Randy anywhere nearby?" she finally asked.

"Yeah, sure. He's around here somewhere." Matt looked suddenly doubtful. He eyed Kali closely, his gaze resting on the edge of a tattoo just visible below the short sleeve of her T-shirt. He nodded, as if in approval. "I mean, I think he is."

Kali looked out the window. There wasn't any real reason to hurry. The sun was shining, no one expected her back in Maui until they saw her, and Kali suspected that Matt wasn't deliberately trying to be annoying. He didn't impress her as the type that thought that far ahead.

She glanced more closely around the office, targeted a plastic chair in the corner, and turned toward the make-shift table-desk. She walked over to the chair and sat down. Immediately, Hilo dropped to the linoleum at her feet and spread his long length across most of the available floor space.

"Sounds good," she said. "I'll just wait, if you don't mind. Maybe you could see if he's around?"

Matt nodded helpfully. "You bet. I'll be right back."

He exited through a door to the rear of the room, and Kali could hear him whistling as he moved away. She looked at the chipped linoleum. Sunshine on Your Shoulders Solar Energy Company, Inc., didn't appear to be an especially prosperous enterprise, judging from the collection of mismatched furniture and rusted file cabinets. But it was hard to say. Casual was definitely the governing principle in a lot of the smaller towns, and recycling office furniture was certainly an environmentally responsible thing to do for a company with an eco focus, whether or not it was aesthetically pleasing.

The sound of whistling returned, and the back door opened. Matt, still grinning, came in, followed by a second man, also dressed in shorts, sandals, and a worn Hawaiian shirt. He was only a few years older than Matt, and Kali detected the possibility of a slight family resemblance.

She rose to her feet, extending her hand. Hilo reluctantly pulled himself into a sitting position, his head clearly visible above the table's surface. "You must be Randy."

The man smiled, nodding. "Randy White. Matt tells me you're in the market for some solar panels. And that you have an enormous dog."

"Hilo. Keeps me company." Kali waved the flyer. "Mostly, I suppose, I have some questions about solar panels."

Randy turned to Matt, and nodded toward the door. "Go ahead and take a break. I'll help Miss . . . ?" He paused as Matt gave him a thumbs-up and headed out the front door, and waited for Kali to give her name.

"Kali." She hesitated. "Detective Kali Māhoe. I'm making some inquiries on behalf of the Maui Police Department."

Randy's face collapsed, a look of panic washing over it. "Oh, crap."

Without another word, he turned and bolted through the rear door. Kali watched, slightly amazed, as the door slammed shut. Then she walked over and pulled it open, whistling to Hilo. She snapped her fingers.

"Hilo!"

The dog raised his head, then scrambled toward the door. Kali pulled it open a little wider.

"Fetch, boy," she said.

Dutifully, Hilo bounded forward, his tail pointing in a straight line behind him.

She settled back into the chair, leaving the door propped open. Half a minute later, she heard a bark, followed by a terrified human yelp, and then silence. She pushed back the chair and walked out the door, then along the edge of a path leading back across the lot behind the shop, following the sound. She could make out a small storage shed just on the other side of the trees. Rounding a curve, she came upon Randy, sprawled facedown in the underbrush on one side of the path, with Hilo half sitting, half lying across his back and head.

"Good boy, Hilo," she said, scratching the big dog behind his ears. "Good boy."

Hilo closed his eyes and panted in acknowledgment, thumping his tail against Randy's upper legs. The only sound coming from Randy was a muffled whimper. Kali snapped her fingers again, signaling to Hilo to move and allow Randy to get up.

He turned over onto his back, shaking his head. "What the hell, man? He could have killed me! He weighs, like, three hundred pounds. This is clearly a case of undue use of force."

"I didn't sit on you. The dog did. And he weighs only about a hundred twenty. I hate it when people exaggerate."

Randy scowled and pulled himself into a sitting position, running his hands through his mass of hair, made worse by the bits of twigs and grass that had become tangled in it during his encounter with the ground.

"And I'm not selling, anyway, whatever you heard. I just grow enough ganja for myself. I have a medical marijuana license, I swear! Seven plants, that's all!"

Kali shook her head. The last thing she was worried about was a little herbal *pakalolo*. "Good for you. I don't care what you're growing, pal. I'm here to find out where you get your solar panels and equipment."

Randy looked at her blankly. "What?"

"Where you buy your solar panels," she repeated patiently.

Randy shook his head. "My solar panels? For crying out loud, that's why you're here?"

Kali waited. When Randy did not elaborate, she said, "Not the answer I'm looking for."

Randy got to his feet, then brushed off his shirt and shorts. He turned without a word and made his way unsteadily back to the office, followed by Kali. Inside, he walked over to a large gray filing cabinet in one corner. He ran his fingers across the tops of the files, selected several thick ones, and pulled them out. After slapping them onto the table, he gestured for Kali to take them.

"It's all right there, man. Japanese company outside of Tokyo, cheaper than the ones on the mainland in the States. Orders, shipments, invoices, canceled checks, the works. Knock yourself out. The blue file has records of the sales I've made this year and last year—which is when we opened—along with the dates of installation that the insurance companies want documented. And my license. My ganja license, too."

Kali picked up the folder nearest to her and began to

thumb through it. On the surface, at least, it all appeared to be in order. Randy was organized, if nothing else.

"You got a copy machine?"

Randy pointed to a copier half buried beneath a stack of papers.

"Good. Make copies of these for me, and I'll be on my way."

Sputtering at the injustice of it all, Randy did as he was asked, while Kali sat back down in a plastic chair by the window.

"Aren't you supposed to have a subpoena or something like that?"

"Something like that. But it's always better to volunteer information than to have it dragged out of you. Unless, of course, you have something to hide."

"Yeah, thanks for the philosophy lesson."

Her phone rang, and she saw that it was Walter's number. "News?" she asked him when she picked up.

There was a grunt. "Funny you should choose that particular word. Your friend the actor-blogger, or whatever the hell he calls himself, posted a podcast with a local psychic about an alleged string of attacks on Maui that have . . . Let me quote this to you . . . 'left a wake of bloodied bodies targeted by a malicious spirit.' The phones have been ringing off the hook."

"Chad." She scowled even as the name passed her lips. "Have Hara pick him up and toss him into a cell for the night."

"Right. On charges of being a jerk? Fake news is all the rage, as you well know. And he's the local pretty-boy celebrity. If you ask me, he's nothing more than a highly recognizable pain in the ass."

"That's a stretch. Nice teeth and a part on a forgettable series hardly make him a celebrity."

"Only your point of view, I'm afraid. It was pretty popular. Even my wife and kids watched it. But regardless. Free speech, et cetera."

"Yeah. I still think we should pick him up."

"Neither the time nor the energy, I'm afraid." He paused. "Anyway, I called to let you know that Grace Sawyer hasn't come around yet. No sign of any change."

"Okay." She glanced over to the copy machine, aware that Randy was listening. She ended the call and waited as he slipped the stack of copies into a large envelope and handed it to her.

He waited, fidgeting. "That's it?" he asked, looking nervously over his shoulder at the back door leading to the path and the storage shed.

"That's it. Course, I could do a quick search of the grounds if it would make you feel any better."

Randy shook his head energetically. "Not necessary. Really."

"Well, then, have a good day. And remember that over-watering never did anything any good." She half smiled. "At least, that's what I hear."

Randy looked at her in surprise, but Kali didn't elaborate. She walked back out to the car and opened the door for Hilo. She settled herself behind the wheel and slowly pulled out, waving. Hilo stuck his head out the open window and barked. She could see Randy watching from the doorway. He looked, she thought, a little worse for wear.

CHAPTER 11

After stopping for a quick lunch, she found her way to the Secret Haven builder's business address in Honoka'a. It was a small office in a row of colorful old buildings fronting the main street, near the People's Theatre. The historic cinema had been a centerpiece in the town for decades, and she pulled up along the curb next to the old, familiar marquee.

The office door was open. Inside, two men were seated across from one another at a glass-topped coffee table, talking earnestly. She walked up the front steps and along the narrow porch, then paused in the doorway and knocked lightly on the frame. Both men turned in her direction.

"Looks like I might be interrupting," she began.

One of the men stood up. He was smiling, but she didn't

like the way his eyes raked up and down her body and paused a little too long on her T-shirt.

"Please, come in," he said. He turned to the other man, who also rose to his feet. "I believe we were just finishing up, weren't we?"

The second man nodded, but Kali sensed that he was displeased. "Sure. I'll catch up with you at the building site tomorrow. Just remember my wife hates those floor samples. All of them. We need to see something completely different."

"Understood." The builder reached out and slapped the other man on his shoulder. "Last thing I want to do is get on the wrong side of the little lady. Especially since now I know who wears the pants, right?"

Kali winced, biting her lip. The man's voice was arrogant, condescending. She felt herself take a strong and immediate dislike to him. The second man, who appeared to be a customer, frowned and headed for the door, nodding curtly to Kali as he passed. She watched as he got into a car parked on the street outside, slamming the door as he got inside.

As she turned around, she saw that the other man had stepped up beside her and was standing quite close.

"Well, now. How can I help you?" He thrust out his hand. "Billy Shane. And you are?"

"Kali Māhoe," she said, ignoring the hand and displaying her badge. "Actually, that's Detective Kali Māhoe, Maui Police Department."

There was a nearly imperceptible narrowing of his eyes. She watched him closely, estimating him to be in his late fifties or early sixties. There were streaks of silver in the well-groomed hair framing his face, and significant lines around his mouth and across his tanned, leathery forehead, which indicated a cavalier attitude toward sun-screen.

"My goodness. Should I call my attorney?"

"You're assuming you'll need one?"

He threw back his head, laughing. "No, but that's what they always say in the movies, right?"

She tried to hide her annoyance. "If you say so, Mr. Shane."

He sat back down, clearly at ease. "Have a seat. Make yourself comfortable. Let me sell you a house."

"I already have one, thanks." She ignored the offer of a chair, enjoying the effect of looking down on him. "I'm here as part of an investigation and would like to ask you a few questions related to solar homes."

He looked at her blankly. "Come again?"

"You have a number of building projects here, I under-stand. Can you tell me what the costs are for configuring them for solar power, along with a few other details? For instance, at what stage are the panels added?"

He shrugged, losing interest. His eyes played across her T-shirt again, deliberately lingering, as though he was challenging her to react. She made direct eye contact with him and stared at him without blinking. He smiled.

"Depends, right? Bigger the house, the more energy it needs to run. Some of these babies are over six thousand square feet, not counting the pools, terraces, and outdoor buildings. Course, a lot of them in some of the smaller developments average only around twelve hundred square feet. So a wide range. But not all of them are solar homes—that's an option offered to the buyer at an additional cost. You understand?"

She felt her stomach tighten with distaste. "Yes, I under-stand."

He grinned. "Great!" He pulled himself out of his chair. "Care for a cocktail? I was going to mix up my afternoon margarita, and I'd be happy to whip one up for you, as well."

"Thanks, no. I'm on the clock." She smiled, her lips tight. "You understand?"

He laughed, slapping his thigh. She speculated about how annoyed he'd be if she asked him to document all his purchases, and decided it would be worth it just to inconvenience him.

But when she asked, he merely smiled in agreement.

"Happy to help. I use suppliers in Minnesota and Japan. They all give me a great discount based on sheer volume. As for installation, they go up after the framing and roofs are complete."

He poured ice from a bucket into a blender resting on a small table, where bottles of expensive liquor were displayed on a glass tray.

"Sure I can't talk you into a drink? My margaritas are pretty famous in these parts. Small-batch artisan tequila here, better than sex." He held up a sparkling glass bottle. "Men give their lives for beauty like this."

Once again, she ignored his attempts to control the conversation. "What about used panels?"

He paused in the act of pouring the tequila into the blender. "I don't follow."

"Surely there would be significant cost savings if there were a reliable source of used panels."

"You're saying customers wouldn't notice? Besides, I don't think I've even heard of a supplier dealing in used panels. Have you?"

"What about your competitors?"

"What about them? The only builders I'm aware of who are offering renewable-energy homes are small-scale contractors. A few houses a year. Nothing like what I've got going on."

"I see. Building empires?"

His smile turned suddenly cold. "If you like." He switched on the blender, and the noise prevented her from making an immediate reply. He lifted a glass and turned it upside down, deftly spun the rim in a plate of salt, then poured the frosty contents of the blender into the bowl of the glass. Gazing at her over the rim, he took a long sip from his drink. "I must say, this is beginning to feel a little bit like harassment."

"My sincere apologies, Mr. Shane." She returned his gaze. "You're not from Hawaii, are you?"

"Don't mistake me for a malihini, please. I'm no newcomer. I've been in these islands for twenty years."

She noted his use of the Hawaiian word for "recent arrival." He watched her, smiling slightly, a look of satisfaction on his face. After turning away, she walked toward the shelves along one wall, where a few books and photographs were displayed. She stopped in front of a framed photo of an expensive-looking sailboat. A young woman stood on the deck, her unsmiling face obscured by sunglasses and the brim of a large, soft sun hat. Beside her stood a slender man in swim trunks and a white T-shirt. The man was clearly Hawaiian and wore a strained look on his face, as though the photographer had caught the couple on the edge of an argument.

Shane followed her with his eyes. "Late son-in-law. Untimely death, but he managed to teach me just enough Hawaiian to annoy the locals."

She kept her voice neutral. "Where are you from originally?"

He raised his glass in a toast. "Why, the fine state of Texas, since you ask. But the real estate market is here. I'm a businessman, Detective. I go where the business is."

"And to date, none of the panels from your new homes have gone missing?"

He raised the glass to his lips haltingly and turned to her, a look of surprise on his face. "Well, now." He looked suddenly thoughtful. "Heavens. Actually, that's an interesting question. Can't say that anyone on my team does any sort of formal assessment on whether or not the houses have the same number of panels we install as they do at the point of sale."

He put his glass down and walked to a small desk in the corner, then leaned over a computer while he pulled up a spreadsheet on the screen. "However, it sounds like something I should maybe be doing."

"Let me know if your numbers don't add up, Mr. Shane. So far all reported thefts have been on Maui, but with all the second and third homes spread across the islands, it's highly likely some owners may not be aware yet that anything's gone missing from their roofs."

He nodded, still looking preoccupied. "It will take me a few days to compare our installation records with a visual check of roofs."

She smiled and turned to leave. "We'll have someone do it for you. I'll need copies of all your records, of course, going back to your first purchases. Unless you'd like to go a more official route and have them subpoenaed. I'm sure you understand."

He looked up from the screen. "Touché, darlin'. I'll have them sent over first thing tomorrow. E-mail okay for you?" He focused his gaze deliberately on her chest. "Or I can hand them over in person. Maybe over breakfast?"

She placed her business card on the glass coffee table and turned and left without a word. Sometimes, she reminded herself, saying nothing at all was all that needed to be said.

CHAPTER 12

A trio of seagulls settled on the rail of the lanai, squawking noisily. Kali rolled out of her porch hammock with great reluctance and placed the sand-toughened soles of her feet onto the scratched, worn floorboards of the lanai. She'd missed the sunrise again.

Looking across the wild, overgrown lawn toward the ocean, she considered with some disgust the undeniable fact that even though she hadn't been awake to perform the morning sunrise chant, the sun had nevertheless managed to make it into the sky without her assistance. *Just as well*, she thought. If it were up to her to get the day started, the world might have to exist in perpetual darkness. She closed her eyes, letting out a small sigh. Her mood grew even gloomier as she considered that she'd made an equal lack of progress moving forward in the murder investigation.

The light across the surface of the ocean changed, and the sky grew increasingly brighter. The view was good from here, exactly as she'd intended it to be. When she'd decided to make some renovations to the small house that her grandmother had left to her, her first project had been to repair the long, wide lanai, deliberately positioned to make the most of both the sea views and the shade provided by the tall palms and dense fruit trees that grew on the property.

The lanai had quickly turned into the place where she spent the majority of her time when she was home. There was a hammock on one end, where she frequently slept; several comfortable, well-worn chairs that allowed her to stretch her legs out to their full length; and an old, polished table made from koa wood, where she could eat her meals and enjoy the views of the sea. She considered the indoor table and bedrooms to be the equivalent of storm quarters: a dry place of retreat, but only when absolutely necessary. In truth, she loved the storms that periodically swept through the islands, and could often be found outside in the rain, walking the steep paths into the uplands, wet leaves clinging to her clothes, Hilo at her side, and a peaceful expression on her face.

She preferred her solitude and was used to living alone. None of her long-term relationships to date had lasted, though she'd tried to find a reason to invest in them emotionally. Mike Shirai had been the only exception. She'd met him after earning her degree from the University of Hawaii and had decided to change gears and train at the police academy in Honolulu. Still a rookie, she had been called in to help with a case involving a series of assaults that seemed to be rooted in an old

Hawaiian legend, and had met Mike, the detective inspector in charge of the investigation.

She'd known, without doubt, that this was love. Mike was smart and kind and funny, and they'd been instant friends. Eventually, they'd moved in together, and she'd done her best to establish a positive relationship with his sullen teenage daughter, Makena, his only child from a brief previous marriage.

Kali looked across the surface of the sea, now glittering in the growing sunlight, and remembered the feeling of being absolutely content, and of being deeply loved. She believed that she and Mike would have been happy together, but the universe had intervened. On an evening filled with starlight, after a morning that had begun with making love, Mike had been shot and killed during a police raid on one of the growing number of meth labs being established on the island.

Kali closed her eyes. It did no good to feel guilty.

No one held her responsible for him being in the line of fire. No one, that is, except herself.

Perhaps because of the details surrounding the event, or maybe because of how the future had changed with the abrupt cessation of one single, singular heartbeat, she'd found herself living in a kind of limbo. Without Mike, the wide beaches and the tall, swaying palm trees had felt judgmental: Who was she to enjoy their beauty, when Mike's soul had been so brutally wrenched from the world?

She had thought about leaving, had spent countless hours perusing ads for jobs on the mainland. Instead, she had stayed on in Honolulu, with its bustle and lights and its year-round masses of tourists. The calm southeastern shores of Maui spooling out along the coast had seemed to be part of a dream—a memory from someone else's life. The rhythmic break of ocean waves rolling ashore had receded in the noise of traffic, becoming no more than a half-remembered story played out in a distant childhood.

From her vantage point on the lanai, she recalled the feeling of disconnection that had followed the shooting, how it had grown stronger each day, as she had struggled for sleep in her small city apartment. She realized now that she'd been waiting for a sign, something to tell her it was time to move on.

Finally, one had arrived. As she was drifting off into another night of restless sleep, her phone had rung. It was her grandmother, insisting that she come home to help with a healing ceremony. It was high time, her grandmother told her, that she accepted her place as *kahu* in her own community.

"Who is the ceremony for?" Kali asked, a sudden wash of apprehension descending on her.

"It's for me," her grandmother had answered, and then, before Kali could respond, she'd simply hung up the phone.

CHAPTER 13

After her grandmother's call, she'd arrived back on Maui, racked with guilt. Walter had met her at the airport, and they'd made the long trek along the narrow, winding road to Hana, trying not to express their mutual annoyance at the slow crawl of sightseeing drivers, who had seemed to find nothing wrong with leaning out of their rental car windows to take snapshots.

The road had more twists and turns than Kali had recalled, punctuated with narrow bridges, which forced the cars into a single, disgruntled lane. It had taken over four hours to reach the small town of Nuʻu, and she had been sick at the thought that she might be returning home too late to be of any use.

By the time they'd reached the dirt driveway sloping up from the sea to her grandmother's house, years had fallen away. Suddenly, it seemed that Honolulu was the dream; Maui was the only reality. Everything was exactly as she'd last seen it: the thick, tall grass; the old mango tree at one end of the yard, bent beneath its load of heavy fruit; the faded yellow paint peeling away from the house's exterior. She took the five sagging wooden steps leading to the front door with a single leap and then stopped. The main door was open, with the old interior screen door on its crooked hinges closed to keep out the sun-warmed, sleepy flies. She took a deep breath, then gently pulled open the door and walked across the kitchen.

"You took your time," came a voice from the single bedroom.

Pualani Pali lay in her narrow wood-framed bed near an open window in her book-filled room, propped up against the headboard by a half-dozen soft pillows. She looked up as Kali leaned over and kissed her forehead.

"So," she said, her eyes looking over her granddaughter carefully. "This is what it takes to bring you home, is it?"

And then she laughed, a deep, happy laugh, like the one Kali remembered from the days they'd spent traipsing slowly up the mountainsides while her grandmother taught her how to locate the healing herbs and plants that grew in abundance on the island. She'd taught her the protocol for their use and instilled the importance of honoring the spirit of each plant, teaching Kali how a plant's living energy was an essential component of its ability to provide healing.

"What's this, child?"

"Noni, Grandmother."

"And what is it good for?"

"To make a tonic when you don't feel hungry for a long time."

"And what about the ripe fruit?"

"It makes a poultice to put on cuts and bruises."

"And the bark?"

"It helps when your muscles hurt."

"And what do we ask of the plant before we take it from the earth?"

"We thank the living spirit in the plant and ask it to sacrifice itself to help someone heal."

"Good, child. You must remember this."

"Yes, Grandmother."

There had been many such lessons as Kali memorized the hundreds of plants that made up the Hawaiian pharmacopoeia. Most of them had multiple uses and more than one recipe for their proper preparation, all depending upon the specific needs of each case. She'd memorized them all, and the ceremonies that were part of their use. She had learned by heart the creation myths of the Hawaiian culture, the genealogies of the sun and moon, the sacred chants and songs that called the day and night into being. Eventually, it was this extensive knowledge of Hawaiian lore and botanic life that had earned her top honors at the university.

As she gazed at her frail elderly grandmother, resting so patiently in the tiny room, Kali knew instinctively that there wasn't a single plant that would restore her to health. Another failure, she thought, to add to her ever-lengthening list.

"What seems to be the trouble, Kali? You don't have much to say. Did you leave your tongue behind in Honolulu, or did the drive here give you a headache?"

Kali exhaled slowly, surprised to realize she'd been holding the air in her lungs. She smiled wryly, reaching out to squeeze her grandmother's hand. "It was a long trip. But you know I'd swim across the ocean just to be beside you."

That amused Pualani. She laughed again and then patted the soft, worn quilt beside her, gesturing for Kali to sit down.

At first, Kali was hesitant, not wishing to tire the older woman. But Pualani began to ask questions, and Kali's answers came flooding out: Mike's death, the loneliness she'd felt in the city, the deep lost feeling of being separated from who she really was. They talked for hours, until the shadows grew long across the sloping green of the yard. Eventually, Kali heated a pot of fish stew, then sat in the chair beside the bed while she and Pualani slowly sipped the smooth, rich broth.

They were silent as they ate. When they were through, Kali collected the bowls and rose to take them to the kitchen. Her grandmother reached out, took Kali's elbow, and gently held her. She smiled.

"There is a beautiful proverb in our culture, Kali," she said. "It is said that the lehua blossom unfolds when the rains tread on it."

Outside, the coastal wind kicked up a notch. Kali heard the scratch of tree branches on the outside of the house. She regarded her grandmother solemnly, with respect. "I wonder sometimes if I will simply drown in the rains instead."

Pualani's eyes swept over Kali's face, and she perceived the remnants of sadness and longing. "Never forget who you are, granddaughter. You are the next *kahu*, and someday you will be a great and much-loved healer.

Your struggles and disappointments, they're just rain. Only rain, necessary for the flower to be born."

Kali sighed and shook her head. She forced a smile. "I don't know what's true and what's not."

"You know. It's inside, where no one can take it from you, deep in your bones."

Pualani laughed again, this time very softly, sounding for a second like a young woman. Then she told Kali to find something to do outside, so she could sleep.

The next morning Kali asked her grandmother to describe her illness, hoping that she might offer some relief. Pualani merely shook her head and smiled.

"You've been living in the big city too long, breathing in all that dirty air. It's eaten a hole in your brain. What does being *cured* have to do with being *healed*? Nothing. If I have a heart attack and you perform surgery, does that make me well? Not if my heart is filled with anger, jealousy, or grief. Maybe those are the very things that caused my heart to fail. Remember, Kali, it's not the quelling of symptoms that should be the goal. It is true spiritual balance, the state of *pono*, that we should strive for. Now that you are here, I am whole and in harmony, and ready to join my ancestors when they come to take me with them."

Kali was startled. She noticed now the thinness of the skin stretched across the backs of Pualani's hands, the crepe beneath her eyes and along her neck, the fine white strands of hair. Surely this kind, powerful woman was not going to die for long years. Kali felt her heart lurch, suddenly desperate to do something, anything, to keep that from happening. She would arrange a particular ceremony, called *Ho'oponopono*, which meant to "make right," "to restore the essential equilibrium to one's existence."

Silently, she made a list of details, remembering what had been involved in conducting the ceremony during the times when she had accompanied Pualani on her healing rounds to homes in the surrounding community. The ancient ritual was intricate and involved and would take some time to arrange. There were prayers and chanting, and the members of the ailing person's family were all asked to attend. As part of the ceremony, they would be asked to release any feelings of anger or ill will they may be harboring against others from past or current transgressions, whether imagined or real, in order to clear all negativity from the setting. It was a tall order, and Kali felt overwhelmed at being thrust into the role her grandmother believed she was destined for.

Being home on Maui had left her feeling distracted, and the preparations for the ceremony took longer than she'd planned. She had hesitated too long by her grandmother's side; she had wasted years in the city, away from those she loved. While she wrestled with the clash of inexperience and the knowledge lodged inherently within her, Pualani drifted away, falling asleep in the cool, sweet evening, never waking. Kali was paralyzed by the conviction that the role of *kahu* bestowed upon her was a simple mistake, that she occupied a place of honor in the world she had never really earned or been meant to assume. Her expanding list of monumental personal failures simply seemed too great.

Now, from the shade behind the hammock, Hilo stirred slowly and stretched his front legs outward, only slightly more enthusiastic than Kali about beginning the day. She took a deep breath and bent over slowly, touched her toes, then jogged unhurriedly down the porch steps and across the lawn. Hilo followed a few paces behind, hesitating until he was completely sure that Kali intended to continue this ridiculous and needless display of physical movement, and that he—large, faithful companion that he was—had no options but to accompany her. At the point where the ground began to slope downhill toward the water's edge, Kali paused. The gray dog collapsed gratefully by her feet, turning his body to face the direction of the house, the suggestion anything but subtle.

Kali turned back toward the house and picked up her pace, her muscles loosening in response to the rhythmic movement. Maybe, she thought, it was finally time to embrace her heritage. Maybe she could, at last, leave the past behind and consider what the future had to offer. She'd been back on Maui for long enough now, and it was probably time she started to remember what it meant to be a native Hawaiian. The trouble was, she wasn't completely sure where to begin.

CHAPTER 14

W alter stretched his legs beneath the picnic bench in the outdoor seating area at the Ranch Restaurant. He'd just enjoyed an exceptionally tasty pulled pork sandwich and a bowl of coleslaw mixed with bits of fresh pineapple, and he was feeling uncharacteristically benevolent toward the rest of the world.

Across from him, Hara smoothed the well-pressed collar of his uniform, smiling at someone that Walter couldn't see. This was due entirely to the fact that whoever the recipient of the smile happened to be, she—and Walter knew that it was most definitely a girl—was positioned out of sight, somewhere behind his back.

Seconds later, a very pretty blonde, who appeared to be about eighteen or nineteen years old, materialized beside their table, a sweating plastic pitcher of iced lemonade held aloft in one hand.

"Hi! Umm, Carla—she's your waitress—just went on break, so I'm taking her tables. Would you like some more lemonade?" she asked eagerly.

Walter noticed immediately that though the invitation for refills seemed to be directed at both him and Hara, it was at Hara that she was busily fluttering her eyelashes.

"Indeed I would," Walter said, noisily pushing his empty glass across the table toward her.

The girl ignored him. Still smiling, she reached forward and took Hara's glass instead, which was still nearly full.

"Thank you," said Hara, smiling at her in return.

"Sunny day," she offered.

Walter pushed his empty glass a little closer to the waitress. "It most certainly is," Walter said.

"Day like this should be spent on the beach," the girl said to Hara.

"Or on a shady porch, with a tall, cold drink," Walter continued, not giving Hara a chance to respond. The girl was oblivious.

"You ever go to the beach when you're off duty?" she asked Hara, her voice sounding hopeful.

"Sure. I usually head down to—"

"Have you got any more lemonade in that pitcher?" Walter interrupted.

The girl glanced at him briefly, seemingly surprised to find another person at the table. She looked down into the pitcher, where the ice had begun to melt.

"Yeah, sure, plenty," she said. She turned back to Hara, her smile nearly blinding in its intensity.

"That spot just north of the waterfall, where the rocks make a cove," Hara said, finishing the thought.

"Oh, wow! I know exactly where you mean. I go there,

too," she said. "I love to dive off the rocks right into the waterfall."

Walter leaned forward and tapped the bottom of his glass on the table to get her attention. "Excuse me, miss," he said, his voice beginning to betray the edges of combined annoyance and thirst. "I would like you to pour some of the lemonade from that pitcher into my very empty glass." He paused for effect. "If, of course, it isn't too much trouble."

She looked astonished. "What? Oh, sorry. Be right back."

After picking up his glass, she swung around and headed toward the kitchen, Hara following her with his eyes as she bounced away. Walter merely sighed and shook his head.

"I don't get it. It's almost spooky how women react when you're around. Like you put a spell on them or something."

Hara looked slightly embarrassed. "I don't know. I guess it's just because I try to be nice to them, you know? When you're nice to people, they're just nice back."

Walter snorted in disgust. "Oh, yeah. Right. You learn that in Sunday school?"

Hara's cheeks began to flush. "Well, it's just good manners, isn't it?"

Walter lowered his voice, leaning across the table slightly. "Hara, if you told that girl to take her clothes off and dance for you right here, right now, with a coconut balanced on her head, she'd do it without even asking you your name."

Hara drew himself up as though trying to give at least the impression that this sort of talk was an affront not only to him but also to the island's population of women.

"I hardly think that's the case. I think she's new here, anyway. Probably just trying to meet people. You know how it is."

Walter rolled his eyes. "Oh, I know how it is. I've been married for twenty-eight years, Hara. Three daughters, all of whom I want you to stay away from, incidentally. Mortgages, dental bills, riding lessons, cold dinners, and a wife who thinks romance means a computerized washing machine. Sure, I know how it is."

The girl came back to the table, Walter's glass in hand. She placed it in front of him, her glance clearly saying that she'd just done him an enormous personal favor. "Here's your glass, sir."

Walter noticed immediately that somehow, during the short trip from the table to the kitchen and back, the top button of her blouse had managed to come undone, strategically revealing a section of very tanned collarbone.

Walter drained his glass and grinned across the table at Hara as he stood up. "Lunch is on you today, Officer. I'll wait for you at the car."

Walter headed for the spot where the patrol car was wedged as far beneath a sprawling banyan tree as possible, which wasn't a lot. They'd left the windows rolled down, but it was still too hot to get inside. He opened the doors and walked behind the car to where the roots of the banyan spread in a wide parameter from the tree's trunk. He was about to sit down on the edge of one when he saw a girl. She was curled up on the ground, her dirty dress pulled up along her thighs, her feet bare. Makena Shirai. It took him just a minute to recognize her, and when he did, he felt the beginning of a migraine tighten up directly behind his eyes.

Sighing, he moved closer, then reached among the roots and shook the girl's arm.

"Makena, get up."

The girl swore under her breath and tried to roll away from him. Walter swore back, shaking her harder.

"Leave me alone," she snapped.

"I will not leave you alone. Get up, or I'll pull you out of there. And I don't care if I break your arm in the process."

"Yeah, yeah," she growled, pushing herself upward into a half-sitting position. "Police brutality. I keep forgetting that's your specialty."

He said nothing, instead surveying the girl's state. At nineteen, she could pass for thirty-five. Her matted, unwashed hair and filthy clothes reeked. Her eyes were sunken, with dark circles still clearly evident beneath them, despite the soft brown of her skin.

Walter pulled out his cell phone and punched in Kali's number. At the other end of the line, her voice answered, sounding more than a little annoyed.

"I'm trying to write a class synopsis, Walter."

"Working hours, Detective. And I've never even seen you finish writing a shopping list, so don't give me any grief."

"That's because—"

"I've got Makena here. That's got to be worth at least a book on its own."

Silence. Then the sound of a deep breath.

"Conscious or unconscious?" she asked.

"Somewhere in between, I'd say."

"You want me to come down?"

"Not necessarily. Just wondered if you had any clever ideas."

Walter waited, knowing that she was considering the available options. Having him deliver the girl to Kali's doorstep was not one of them.

"Bring her over to the park entrance. I'll meet you there. And if you don't mind, let's keep it from being official."

"No problem. Just giving a local a ride."

"Yeah. Thanks."

Walter slipped his phone back into his pocket. The girl looked up at him, glaring.

"Did you call Mommy?"

"She's not your mother, Makena. Now get out of there."

Hara, finished with bill paying and the gathering of phone numbers, walked up and looked curiously to where Walter was standing and, to all appearances, having a conversation with himself. As he drew closer, he caught sight of Makena.

"Need some help there, Captain?"

Makena crawled out from beneath the roots, straightened the grimy skirt of her dress, and eyed Hara with growing interest.

"Drunk, sir?"

She scowled. "I'm not drunk. I was sleeping, until Sir Lancelot here decided to wake me up."

Walter turned to Hara. "Yeah. The poor thing was just trying to come down from her latest meth spree without anyone bothering her. Terribly sad."

Hara looked at Makena with growing disapproval. "Did you search her?"

Makena scowled more deeply, then lifted her dress up over her shoulders, revealing tattered panties and bones protruding sharply from emaciated hips. "Nothing here, sweetie. See?"

Hara looked away, clearing his throat.

"Put your dress down, Makena," said Walter. "Your father would be ashamed of you. I'm ashamed of you."

"Oh, the whole world's ashamed of little old me," she mimicked sarcastically. "And my father's dead, remember?"

"I remember. Probably a good thing he died when he did. Seeing you like this would have no doubt killed him."

Makena pushed past him, attempting to cross into the parking lot. Walter grasped her firmly by the shoulders, bringing her to a halt.

"Let go of me, you creep."

"We're giving you a ride up to the park."

"Am I under arrest?"

Walter tightened his grip. "Not yet. But we can do it that way if you prefer. Hara, cuffs please."

That caught her attention. She stopped struggling and scowled at Walter. "Fine. Whatever."

He released his grip, pointed toward an open car door. "Get in."

She climbed into the backseat, slumped against the upholstery.

Walter looked at Hara and gestured toward the area beneath the tree where he'd found Makena. "See if there's anything of hers down there, would you? Some shoes, maybe."

Hara climbed among the roots and emerged finally

with a pair of cheap, cracked plastic sandals. He tossed them into the backseat then joined Walter in the front and closed the door.

They made the drive to the park entrance in silence. When they pulled in through the gate, Kali was already there, leaning against the hood of her Jeep.

Kali nodded in thanks to Walter, watching as Makena extracted herself ungracefully from the back of the police car. Ignoring Kali, she walked around to the passenger seat of the Jeep and climbed in. Kali regarded her without enthusiasm, then turned back to Walter.

"She clean?"

"Hardly," said Walter. "You can smell her an island away. But she doesn't have any drugs on her, if that's what you mean."

"Okay. I'll deal with it from here."

Walter shifted the police cruiser into reverse. "I'll be over at the station. Got some paperwork to catch up on, and Hara needs to re-wax the patrol car."

At this, Hara looked up, dismayed.

Kali nodded. "Right. Thanks."

The police car slowly pulled out, and Kali slipped into her seat behind the steering wheel.

For a minute, the two sat in silence. Makena stared straight ahead, with a sour expression.

"Thought you'd stopped using, Makena."

The girl continued to stare out the windshield. "Yeah. So did I. So what?"

"So if you want to kill yourself, why don't you just go ahead and do it? Throw yourself off a cliff. Slit your wrists. Show a little dedication. Put some real effort into the project."

Makena turned her head so that Kali could no longer see her face. "What's it to you?"

"Nothing, anymore. I've tried to help you. I don't think you want to be helped."

"Uh-huh. 'Cause you were in love with my father a million years ago. Big deal."

"Yes, because I loved your father. That is a big deal."

"And he broke your heart by getting killed, and you think you have some kind of obligation to me because he was going to marry you, and blah, blah, blah."

Kali gripped the wheel. "I don't think I have any obligation to you at all. You're just an ungrateful, self-indulgent addict, as far as I'm concerned. Worse, you're a contributing factor to the drug problem on this island, and you don't even have enough of a conscience to know or care that it was meth dealers who shot and killed your father."

"So? Everybody dies. This is your big crusade, not mine. You know, I'm getting sick and tired of you showing up all the time with your crappy philosophy. And your crappy Jeep."

Kali shrugged. "Someday I won't. Or someday I'll show up just long enough to identify your body and wait while someone writes up a case report that explains how you overdosed or how some dealer raped you and then beat you to death for not paying your bill. I guess until then, you'll have to put up with me. Maybe I'll buy a new car, just to see if that's what it takes to make you happy."

"Don't bother. What makes me happy is to be high. To be someplace else, even if it doesn't last."

"So now you have your own philosophy. I guess that's progress."

She started the engine.

"Where are you taking me?"

"To the shelter."

"Good. I need a fix. That's the best place to get one around here."

When she got no response, Makena put her feet up on the dashboard and leaned back against the seat.

Kali said nothing. She eased the Jeep as far as the park's entrance, then waited as a line of rental cars slowly wound past on the legendary Hana Highway. She could see the tourists craning their necks out the windows, determined not to miss a single sight. They stared at her, and a few snapped pictures. She wondered briefly what stories they'd tell once they were home in London or Philadelphia or Connecticut to explain the Hawaiian with the long dark hair and the string of ceremonial talismans around her neck and the warrior tattoo wrapped around her upper arm. Chances were, not a single one would identify her as a respected detective with the Maui police.

Not that she cared. At the moment, she had bigger issues to consider—one of which was sitting beside her in her crappy Jeep.

CHAPTER 15

Walter stood looking over Hara's shoulder at Hara's computer screen, where an angry-looking house-wife was delivering her version of instant karma on the head of a would-be thief.

"Where did this come from?"

"Chad Caesar's *Ruler of the News Podcast*. He picked it up after a couple of teenagers recorded it on their phones at the Kmart and blasted it all over social media. Apparently, it's been all over for the past twenty-four hours. Also . . ." He hesitated.

"What?"

"Well, Caesar had the teenagers on his show for a brief interview and insinuated—rather strongly, in my opinion—that not only is our department not doing its job, but that we're also deliberately keeping information from the public."

Walter closed his eyes and took a deep breath. "I think I'm getting a migraine."

"Would you like me to get you an aspirin, sir?"

"This headache is going to require more than an aspirin." Walter frowned, then suddenly leaned forward and peered more closely at the screen. "Back up."

"Sir?"

"The video . . . Can you rewind it a bit?"

Hara clicked on the time bar beneath the video window, then dragged the tab backward a few seconds. Walter watched intently until the camera footage of the thief showed a closer view of his face.

"There. Stop it right there."

Hara did so, then backed his chair away from the computer to give Walter a better view.

"Well, I'll be a damned shell collector," said Walter, smiling slightly. "If I'm not mistaken, that's our old pal Polunu Hausuka."

Hara looked at him expectantly. "I don't follow, sir."

"Mr. Hausuka is one of Maui's more successful small-time crooks. You haven't been here long enough, I suppose, but he's a familiar face."

Walter crossed to his own desk and sat down. He turned his computer screen slightly to avoid a shaft of sunlight coming through the office window and typed Polunu's name into his file search. A few seconds later the printer hummed, indicating that it was ready to deliver the pages that Walter had selected for printing. He leaned back in his chair, gesturing to the printer.

"Have a look."

Hara reached toward the printer and retrieved the pages. He gave a low whistle as he read the long list of minor offenses that Polunu had racked up over the years.

"Looks like his career—if you can call it that—started when he was in grade school."

"Indeed it did," agreed Walter.

Hara shook his head. "Seems like after you've been caught shoplifting for the tenth time, you'd figure out it's a bad idea."

Walter shrugged. "Or it's become such ingrained behavior, such a familiar way of life, that it's the default option. Why buy a candy bar if you can slip one in your pocket when no one's looking?"

"Except someone was looking."

Walter laughed. "Don't kid yourself. For every time some shop owner's called us in because Polunu Hausuka's sweet tooth got the better of him, there are probably a hundred times that he walked away without anyone ever knowing."

"Interesting, I suppose, that he never made the jump to anything bigger."

"Well, it's not as though Maui has an organized candy crime syndicate to speak of."

"Drugs."

Walter nodded. "True. Plenty of that."

He looked out the window. On the other side of the partially opened louvered glass, a group of parrotbills had gathered in the thick vegetation. He could hear their song and thought briefly of how beauty was so often confined to the surface of things. The birds' songs belied the scratchings and battles, the hunting and small deaths that made up so much of their existence, just as the island's lovely face hid its share of darkness and despair.

He turned abruptly back to Hara.

"This guy is kind of a master pickpocket. Our very own Hawaiian Fagin, if you will. Specializes in the tourist trade. Right now, he's working at one of the resorts. We get ongoing complaints of disappearing wallets and purses after every luau performance there. Not coincidentally, our hero has a role as a warrior in the show. Never been able to catch him in the act, but I'd be willing to bet my breakfast that he's behind it all."

Hara looked alarmed. "If we know what he's up to, shouldn't we station someone there to catch him? Maybe plant someone on the hotel serving staff or something?"

"Hardly worth the effort."

Hara looked unconvinced. "Well, shouldn't we at least bring him in and scare him a bit? Tell him we know what he's up to? And what about this Fagin? Is he Hausuka's mentor or some kind of fence?"

Walter stifled a groan. "His *mentor*? Yeah, I guess you could say that's exactly what he is." He eyed the younger man with a degree of curiosity. "Where did you go to school, anyway?"

Hara seemed surprised at the question. "Honolulu."

"They have a library there?"

"Of course they do." He paused. "Sir."

"You ever go there?"

"The library? Sure. Sometimes."

"Glad to hear it, Hara. Glad to hear it. I'm going to go out and get some lunch. Find out where Polunu is holed up these days, and I'll pay him a visit later on."

He left, letting the door slam shut behind him. He passed the tree where the parrotbills were still engaged in happy song, and turned toward the parking lot, wondering as he walked how any kid could get out of high school without at least a passing knowledge of Charles Dickens or *Oliver Twist*. Then he thought of his own kids, whose literary interests seemed increasingly limited to shortening words and phrases to text to their friends. He didn't like what was happening to so much of the world, but realized he had very little control over any of it. What he could do was what he did best—find out who was committing crimes on his beloved island, and make sure they were held responsible for their actions.

CHAPTER 16

The crackling in the underbrush turned suddenly to silence. There was a strange whiffling sound, followed by a snort, and the bushes erupted into a panorama of thrashing movement. Close by, Hilo stood poised, frozen like a statue, one front leg bent and saliva dripping from his muzzle.

Pig in the brush.

With a single, fluid movement, the dog launched his enormous body into the air and landed on the far side of a ring of palm scrub. The pig squealed, fleeing, bent on escape. Hilo thundered across the earth, his thoughts of food, sleeping, being scratched behind the ears, and riding in the Jeep coalescing into one obsessive goal: catch the pig.

The chase was good—far more so for Hilo than for the pig. An interloper had been discovered, pursued, and punished for trespassing. When Hilo emerged from the underbrush, he was sweating and his muzzle was covered in blood, but he was wagging his tail in absolute contentment.

On the way to her car, Kali saw him trotting toward the porch and shook her head. *Damn dog.* The feral pigs that populated this part of the island had become a fixation with him, and he'd been known to career across the road in front of traffic while in hot pursuit. Last winter the sight of his huge gray body hurtling in front of their rented convertible had caused two astonished tourists to run off the road and slide down an embankment, narrowly avoiding having the remainder of their tropical vacation take place in a Maui hospital. Kali had not only arranged for a tow truck but had also bought the tourists dinner to make up for the event. Who would have guessed, she wondered—and not for the first time—that the scent of a wild pig could be such a powerful aphrodisiac?

She climbed behind the wheel of the Jeep and removed an old hand towel from beneath the front seat, ready to wipe Hilo clean. The Jeep was an old Willys model left over from the post-Vietnam shipments of used vehicles dumped off in Honolulu. Makena's description of it wasn't completely unfair. There was nothing wrong with the engine, but the transmission was on its last legs. Despite a seemingly endless round of maintenance and repairs, it wouldn't stay in gear unless she held it there, making hard turns a challenge.

Hilo, oblivious to mechanical issues, jumped into the passenger seat, bits of blood-flecked saliva still visible on his lips. Kali cleaned him to the best of her ability with the towel, then studied the printed list she'd brought with her. It showed the names and addresses of Maui residents

who'd reported a loss of one or more solar panels. Whoever the thief was, Kali gave him or her credit for being
industrious. Rarely had a neighborhood or property been
targeted more than once, and the thefts were spread all
over the island.

Many of the residences were winter or vacation homes
occupied for only short amounts of time each year, making the exact time of a theft difficult to pinpoint. The fact
that the thefts had occurred across different districts also
meant that they were being reported to different police in
different jurisdictions. And, as she'd come to learn, what
happened in one official backyard may or may not ever
make it into any shared pool of island knowledge.

She'd spent the morning and the entire previous day
reinterviewing the off-island theft victims by phone and
the local theft victims in person. She'd just left the last
person on the list. No one had seen anything, and no one
had noticed their panels missing until a flux in power out-
put had finally prompted them to call one of the various
maintenance companies responsible for servicing their
systems. Her gentle inquiries as to any strange events or
unusual sightings coinciding with the disappearance of
panels had been met with blank looks and confusion. No
one besides Mr. Uru and Birta had seen a faceless entity
darting about in the darkness.

It was now 3:00 p.m., and she was completely frustrated. She folded the printed list and placed it in her day
bag, then sat for a moment, staring out of the windshield.
She felt tired and in no mood for the long drive ahead.
While it was growing late in the afternoon, the Hana
Highway—though less crowded—was still an arduous
undertaking. A few miles along the road, she decided to

make a detour into the village of Paia for a late lunch. She swung the Jeep onto Baldwin Avenue, then parked in front of the Octopus Café.

As a child, she'd lived in this neighborhood. Her mother's cottage had been a few blocks away on one of the winding side streets leading off of Baldwin, but in those days, the quirky, brightly painted café, with its image of a grinning orange octopus wrapped around an exterior wall, hadn't been here. She dimly remembered an empty lot with a makeshift basketball hoop hanging dejectedly from a palm tree. The building that now housed the café had been built years later and had been at various times a laundry, a gift shop, and a beach sports shack where surf-boards and snorkeling gear could be rented by the day.

With Hilo at her side, Kali went in and found a table. She liked to sit with her back to the wall, where she could watch people without them necessarily realizing they were being watched. It was a habit she'd developed long ago, one that had grown out of all the times she'd dined alone in Oʻahu. She told herself the habit of memorizing useless details about strangers she most likely would never see again kept her skills of observation both sharp and dependable. Someone else might think she was sim-ply bored or lonely; in truth, she was simply curious.

"Howzit, Kali? Haven't seen you down this way in weeks."

The man who'd spoken was Simon Carver, proprietor, dishwasher, and backup waiter at the Octopus. It was a popular stop for tourists making the long drive to Hana, and Carver was known for the sumptuous take-out picnic lunches he always had at the ready. Kali liked the food and the atmosphere and usually enjoyed a conversation with Carver, who paid attention to what was going on in the area, and who was often a good source of local information. While Carver was fully aware of Kali's status as both a detective and an authentic *kahu*, to him she was just an interesting local who happened to like fresh fish sandwiches and the occasional scoop of pistachio ice cream.

The Octopus hadn't yet begun to fill with the evening dinner crowd, and Carver grabbed two chilled bottles of soda, then pulled up a chair next to Kali.

"Hot day," he said.

Kali nodded in agreement, taking one of the bottles and clinking it against Carver's. "*Okole maluna!*" she said, offering the island version of "Cheers."

"Anything interesting going on in the deep, dark underworld?" Carver asked, grinning. "Better yet, any more tourists up in Hana reporting sea monsters near the beach?"

Kali smiled, relaxing against the high wooden back of her chair. "Not this week."

"Too bad. It's good for business."

She looked at him appraisingly. "Something you're not telling me?"

Carver laughed. "You'd be the first to know. Right after I sign a contract with HBO or the *New York Times* for an exclusive."

"Yeah. Good luck with that." Kali took a long drink from her bottle, then set it carefully on the table. "You heard any talk around here about anybody starting up a solar supply business out of their garage?"

Carver considered for a moment. "Can't say I have." Then his face lit up, as if he had suddenly remembered something. "I did hear about the old woman over in Kihei getting beat up and her solar panels being stolen, though. Some kind of connection?"

"Maybe. There have been reports all over the island of panels going missing."

Carver watched as a couple entered the restaurant. A waitress came out of the kitchen, smiling, and showed them to a table. He turned back to Kali.

"You think someone's taking up a collection or just keeping them for themselves? They're pretty expensive."

"No idea. Seems like too many have been taken just to supply power for one home."

"Well," said Carver, "maybe there's a do-gooder collecting them for his whole family. Or some *kolohe* just making trouble."

"Might be." She hesitated. "There's also been some talk of a ghost."

Simon looked at her in surprise. "A nightwalker?"

"No, something moving around in the dark that doesn't have a face."

Carver was quiet for a moment, then shook his head. "I got nothing. But I'll keep my ears open."

Kali finished her soda, and rose, ready to leave. Hilo stretched and sat beside her, waiting. "Don't suppose you got a mahimahi sandwich back there I could take with me?"

"You bet." Carver slipped through the beaded curtain blocking off the kitchen and returned minutes later with a wrapped sandwich and a bottle of cream soda.

"Mahalo, Simon." Kali took the food and slipped a few bills onto the counter. "You hear anything interesting, give me a call, okay?"

"Sure."

Kali stepped out of the egress, then took a deep breath

of the warm, salt-tinged air. Hilo followed, sniffing at the bag. They were about to walk away when Carver appeared again, then held out a burger to Hilo.

"This solar thing . . . ," he said as Hilo swallowed the food. "Isn't there some old Hawaiian legend about the sun and the demigod Māui? Wonder what the elders would think of how long it's taking us to get behind the concept of renewable energy."

Kali nodded slowly, an idea, half formed, darting through her thoughts. "Māui trapped the sun with his ropes and pulled it out of the sky, then made it do exactly what he wanted it to do. You're right."

Carver nodded, and Kali grinned at him.

"You know, you're pretty smart. For an old guy, anyway."

Kali looked at her phone, checking the time. She'd promised to meet Walter at the Wailea Palm Harbor Resort while he talked to his candy thief. She headed down the street toward her car, with her sandwich and soda, Hilo close beside her. Carver's laughter followed them both into the light.

CHAPTER 17

The slow drive back to Hana gave Kali plenty of time to think. Prompted by Carver's remark, her mind wandered to the legend of Māui and how he had snared the sun. It was one of the Hawaiian origin tales taught to her by her grandmother. The story chronicled the exploits of the clever demigod Māui, who pulled the islands up out of the sea, lassoed the sun, and wrested the secret of making fire from a selfish brood of mud hens that were intent on hoarding the knowledge for themselves.

The colorful and often violent creation myths had been a constant source of frustration to the missionaries who set up local schools in the islands in their quest to convert the native population to their beliefs. Most of the Hawaiian children had grown up with the stories as part of their lives: the tales explained the order of the universe in a way that made sense to them. As far as Kali was concerned, they were no more fantastic than tales of turning water into wine or parting seas. She'd never understood the issues that arose between people when it came to religion, or why adherents of every denomination had to insist that only they could truly explain the riddles of the universe. Personally, she preferred a little mystery.

Like most creation legends, the Hawaiian stories were riddled with acts of cruelty and ferocity. While she recognized this, they were still part of who she was, and a powerful source of connection between her and all the other life and environmental forces that made up the planet.

In the Hawaiian stories, Māui wasn't always a positive figure. He shared many characteristics with the Native American figure of the Trickster Coyote, who was engaged in constant acts of mischief. At least in the legend that told of how he'd captured the sun, Māui began with good intentions, based on deep familial concern for his mother's well-being. Each day he watched as the sun rose and fell within the space of mere minutes, leaving his poor mother unable to finish her daily tasks before darkness washed across the landscape.

Intent on finding a way to provide her with more daylight, he made his way to Mount Iao, then struggled up the steep ridges and climbed to the top of the sleeping volcano. From here, he could see the peaks of Mount Haleakalā, recognized by the Hawaiians as the House of the Sun. He pondered the sun's exhausting schedule and became convinced that even a force that powerful must require some degree of rest. He considered the possibilities and formed a theory that this must be the very spot where the sun found a few moments of respite between its rapid excursions to and from the heavens.

After descending Iao, Māui lay down, resting in the

fragrant fields near the volcano. For days, he paid careful attention to the arrival and departure of the sun, carefully observing the route the blazing golden orb followed in its continuous path around the island world. As he rested, Māui planned and plotted, determined to find a way to capture the fiery and uncooperative star.

Carefully, he traversed the dense, pathless countryside and arrived at the foot of Mount Haleakalā. He ascended to one of its peaks, then studied the landscape of the quiet crater, which stretched nearly twenty miles across. He walked to the edge and looked into the depths, some twenty-five hundred feet below. Within the crater, two gaps could be seen from which molten lava had spewed during the volcano's last eruption.

On the eastern side was the deep gap of Koolau. This, Māui told himself, was the place where he would hold the sun prisoner. But first, he must capture it and subdue it, and then he would release it only after he'd taught it not to run so quickly through the sky.

Māui returned home and told his mother of his plan. She gave him a length of powerful woven rope, from which he fashioned a strong lasso. He returned to the crater at the top of Haleakalā's brow. As the sun slowly came into view, he cast his rope over and over and caught each of the sun's rays in turn, then bound them to the trunk of a strong wiliwili tree. The sun resisted, fighting vigorously with Māui, but was unable to break free from the demigod's lasso.

Exhausted but still tethered to the tree, the sun decided that the best way to deal with this powerful warrior was to bargain with him. When Māui demanded that the sun move more slowly through the sky each day, the sun agreed, but only if it was freed.

Satisfied, Māui released the glowing sun and returned home to his grateful mother. Ever since, there had always been enough daylight to gather crops, to fish, and to cook food, and the Hawaiian people had never had to hurry to finish their tasks before darkness enveloped them at the end of each day.

A job well done, reflected Kali. Having the luxury of light was something the Hawaiians had grown used to, and the flicking of a wall switch to bring the light about worked only if the fire of the sun was harnessed by the solar panels that provided electricity to so many of the islands' homes. Whoever was stealing those panels was effectively robbing the victims of the sun's potent flames.

Perhaps, thought Kali, it was time that she reflected on Māui's lesson with regard to her own life. Māui had had a lasso, but she had a detective's badge. She hoped, fervently, that that would be enough.

CHAPTER 18

Kali slipped into a seat next to Walter on the hotel's stone lanai. Around the perimeter, tall bamboo tiki torches flickered in the dark. The sound of rustling palms was part of a larger sound track that included the murmuring of the audience and the clinking of glasses and cutlery. She looked around, curious. Most of the tables were filled, occupied by happy tourists sipping bright tropical drinks.

"Have you seen this show before?" she asked.

Walter nodded. "Couple of times. Pretty average." He nodded to the crowd. "Not that they'll care. They're in Hawaii, having a good time."

Kali nodded in affirmation of Walter's review. She'd never been impressed by any of the hotel luau shows she'd seen over the years, and she suspected his "average" review was likely generous. Her view on the whole topic was conflicted: on onc hand, it seemed like a good idea to expose others to the culture of the islands, but part of her was put off by the commercial facet of the luau shows, an aspect that somehow felt disingenuous.

There was the mournful wail of a conch shell being blown like a trumpet, followed by the sound of beating drums. Walter touched her arm, and pointed to the performance area. The show had begun. A group of hula dancers came onstage, swaying to the music. The crowd watched, rapt, as the dancers gracefully lifted their arms and moved their hands fluidly, mimicking the flow of waves and the fall of rain.

Once they'd finished, the lighting changed. Two men moved into the open space. A slim, dark-haired actor spun nimbly to one side of the stage, dodging the spear of the actor facing him. One of his eyes was framed by a swollen black-and-blue area.

"That's him," said Walter, his voice low. "Polunu Hausuka. Small-time thief extraordinaire."

Kali studied Polunu's figure, frowning. "How come I don't know him?"

"We used to get calls on him about once a month, but he's laid pretty low the past few years. I thought he'd retired, to be honest. He's getting a little long in the tooth." He looked at her sideways. "Remember I told you about the guy who fell into the koi pond at the cultural center while trying to run away with some poor tourist's camera?"

She grinned. "And then jumped the wall into the street and got run over by a kid on a bicycle?"

It was his turn to smile. "That's him. A broken arm, a broken camera, and about thirty stitches, if I remember the details. The kid on the bike was fine."

Kali shook her head, then settled back in her seat and sipped from a tall glass of chilled mango tea. For the next half hour, she watched Polunu pretend to be a chieftain from Tonga fighting for the hand of a thick-legged princess in a grass skirt. The humid evening air carried the sour aroma of perspiration, and a brief spasm moved across Kali's face as it wafted toward her, mingled with the cloying scent of jasmine flowers.

Finally, the attacking actor stabbed upward, and Polunu feinted, bringing the point of his fake weapon down against the man's neck in a choreographed kill sequence. The other actor fell, the crowd clapped and cheered, and Polunu stepped forward to claim his bored-looking bridal prize. Collectively, they bowed, and as the drum music reached its crescendo, Polunu slipped away and moved into the dressing room behind the stage.

Kali and Walter were already on their feet, moving between the tables toward the door to the dressing room. Backstage, Polunu had just tossed a light spear made from coconut wood onto a table holding the various debris of the performance—headgear, cheap ceremonial robes, and the stiff bikini tops made from coconut shells that were worn by the dancers at the beginning of each show.

They stepped back, out of the way of the actors. Walter leaned against the doorframe. Polunu appeared to be unaware that he was being watched. Finally, he looked up, and his eyes darted briefly across Walter's face and then away. He looked at Kali. There was a slight dilation of his eyes as he realized who they were. While Kali blended more easily into a crowd, Walter didn't have to be in uniform to be spotted as a cop, even if he was a block away.

"Nice evening," Walter said, smiling.

"Nice enough," agreed Polunu, his voice carefully neutral.

"Haven't I seen you around here lately? Your face looks familiar. Or maybe it's your eye."

Polunu shrugged, clearly not interested in engaging in conversation.

"I'm pretty sure," Walter insisted.

Polunu looked steadfastly down at the floor and fished his shoes from beneath a counter that held snacks and a cooler filled with juices and bottled sodas.

"Could be, I guess," he said.

Walter pretended to study the other man's face in earnest. Kali looked at Walter.

"Walter . . ."

"I've seen you somewhere," Walter said, ignoring her. "I'd swear to it."

"Good for you," said Polunu, slipping his feet into a pair of worn tennis shoes. "Maybe I'm just lucky to have one of those faces." He reached into the glass-doored cooler, selected a small bottle of papaya juice, and placed it on top.

Walter's hand slipped in front of Polunu and lifted the juice off the cooler. He turned it with feigned curiosity, then read aloud from the label. "Water. Papaya. Plus sugar, of course. And whatever garbage they put in here to fill the bottle. Odd, though. Doesn't say anything about bestowing superpowers on people who drink it."

Polunu looked at Walter in amazement. "Do you mind? There's more in the cooler if you want it, but this one's mine." He paused as Walter's words registered more fully. "Superpowers? What are you talking about?"

"Well, you know. Like being invisible or seeing through

steel," said Walter, his voice serious. "Or running really fast and fighting off middle-aged lady tourists."

Polunu's eyes narrowed. He turned to Kali. "You like working with a bully?"

"It's worse than that," she said. "I'm related to him."

Walter nodded. "Under the right law-abiding circumstances, I'm actually a pretty nice guy," he said.

"True dat," Kali affirmed. "He's buying me breakfast in the morning."

Polunu crossed his arms over his chest, the gesture both defensive and protective. "I remember you, too, come to think of it. Captain Something." He looked pointedly at Walter's waistline. "Captain Cookies?"

"Hilarious," said Walter. "Afraid we're here in an official capacity. To offer you some friendly advice, of course." He turned to Kali. "Isn't that right?"

"That's right. Stealing is naughty. Bad for the island image. Leave the tourists alone."

Polunu spat on the ground. "Tourists. What do I care about them? They can all sink into the sea and take this backward island with them."

Kali raised her eyebrows. "Aren't you local?"

"For the moment," he said. "But I'm out of here as soon as possible."

"Big plans?" Walter's voice was innocent, but Kali could see that he was interested in what Polunu had to say.

"Damn right I have big plans. Las Vegas. Civilization."

"Sounds like you've got it all figured out," said Kali.

"You'll see. Going to buy myself a pair of handmade snakeskin boots and dance the night away at the biggest casino in town. Then I'll get the respect I deserve."

He snatched the bottle from Walter's hand and turned toward the back door, through with talking. Walter sauntered after him, followed by Kali. They watched as Polunu climbed behind the wheel of a beat-up delivery van and pulled quickly out of the parking area and out onto the road.

CHAPTER 19

The first thing Kali saw as she and a very wet Hilo trudged up the porch steps out of the downpour was that someone had pinned a note to her front door. She hesitated before taking it down. Chances were it was from someone at the shelter, who didn't want to leave a phone message, warning her that Makena was back out on the streets. If that was the case, she didn't have the energy tonight to deal with it.

When Makena had first shown up on Maui a year ago, Kali had mixed feelings. On one hand, Makena was a direct link to Mike and a whole world that had vanished in a brutal stream of gunfire. On the other hand, she was a dedicated meth addict who'd long since crossed the threshold from confused kid to full-blown trouble. She had been arrested for petty theft on three separate occasions and had been picked up multiple times at the local resorts for prostitution.

She'd come to Kali for money, appealing to her on the basis that Kali had nearly become her stepmother. Kali had tried. She paid for counseling, took Makena to the clinic to be checked for every possible needle and sexually transmitted disease, bought her some decent clothes, and helped her get a job as a receptionist at a local gallery. As thanks, Makena chose not to show up for her counseling, quit her job the same day that the gallery's on-hand cash disappeared, and sold most of the clothes purchased by Kali to a used clothing store.

Kali was well aware of the crowd Makena ran with, because two of its members were under ongoing surveillance by the Maui police for suspected crystal-meth production. Makena seemed bent on self-destruction, and Kali had been alive long enough to know that you couldn't force someone to accept help. They had to want it.

She sighed and looked down at the note, expecting the worst. Instead, there was a moment of intense relief. The note was from Elvar, asking for her help in locating some materials he needed to construct a handle for the new weapon he was working on.

Kali felt a sense of pleasure at the prospect of getting up into the high country to stretch her legs. And she could count on Elvar to be pleasant company. She'd guided him up the mountain paths once before when he was searching for a particular plant, needing a sample in order to produce an accurate carving on a knife handle for a competition. He'd asked her to tell him some of Hawaii's history, and they'd spent hours discussing the similarities and vast differences between the legends from Kali's store of knowledge and from his own Icelandic lore.

She went inside and picked up her phone to call him back. Elvar answered within a few rings, which suggested that he'd already stopped work for the day.

"Hi, neighbor," he said. "Feel like going for a nice long walk?"

Kali looked doubtfully outside the window. It was long since dark, and the rain hadn't slacked off in the least.

"Now—" she began, but he interrupted, laughing.

"Not at this exact moment."

"Sure. What are you looking for?"

"I got a commission today for a knife, but the buyer wants a handle made from sandalwood, with a carving of an awapuhi flower. You'll know where the healthiest plants are growing, of course."

"Probably at the botanical gardens," she said.

There was silence on the other end of the line, and she mentally kicked herself.

His voice sounded serious when he said, "Ahh. Afraid to go off into the wilderness alone with me?"

"Of course not, I just meant . . ."

"It's okay if you're busy. I don't mind hiking alone. I've been going into the uplands or down to the shore along the park beach a couple of times a week and think I can find my way."

"No, really, I'd like to go. I wasn't trying to put you off. It's just that gardens might be easier if you're in a hurry."

Elvar laughed. "You know me, Kali. No captive, domesticated plants allowed in my work. I need them wild, in their natural habitat, free and happy."

Kali closed her eyes, hoping she hadn't offended him. "I only meant . . ."

"Great! Is there any chance you'd have some time tomorrow morning? We could go at daybreak and catch the sunrise. Maybe we can locate a good piece of sandalwood from a branch, too . . . something that came down during the last storm."

There was more silence. This time, hopeful.

"Sounds like a plan," she said. Finally, a sunrise. "See you in the morning. And if Birta happens to have left any muffins lying around . . ."

"Deal."

Kali put down the phone and began to tidy up the kitchen table and its jumble of papers. She was already looking forward to the morning excursion. Elvar never complained that the paths were too steep or too rocky or too muddy. He wasn't fussy or demanding and seemed to be sincerely interested in her island stories. He was, in fact, pretty good company.

The sound of her phone's text alert interrupted her thoughts. The message was from Jamie Tagert, the boy she'd interviewed at the high school. She read it, frowning. **Something I didn't tell u. Kekipi said he saw a ghost. Told me to keep it secret. Sorry.**

She replied immediately. **Call me now, please.**

The phone rang a moment later.

"It's all I know, I swear. He told me he saw something on the hill path, back in the trees. He said it was a ghost, and that he was telling me because we were really tight and he could trust me. He said he was going to go back there to see if he could find it. I laughed at him, and he got angry and wouldn't say anything else."

"Did he describe it to you?"

"No."

She could hear the distress in his voice.

"When did this happen, Jamie?"

"Two days before the cops found him in the water."

"Can you think of—"

"I told you. That's seriously all he said. He didn't tell me what it looked like or if it was doing anything."

She heard him catch his breath.

"He was really mad at me for making fun of him, so he wouldn't talk about it. I feel sick about it now. I don't know if it means anything or not."

"It's okay, Jamie. Thank you for getting in touch. This is very helpful."

She hung up, staring at the ceiling. *Ghosts.* Someone else had seen a ghost.

CHAPTER 20

The morning mist still clung to the ground as Kali and Elvar made their way up the twisting paths leading toward Mount Haleakalā's crater. This was one of Kali's favorite walks and, in her opinion, the ideal time of day to be making it. There were no sounds other than the rustling of small creatures in the brush and the first notes of birdsong. This was what it must have been like, she thought, before the islands were populated with people, when there was nothing to distract from the natural beauty of the planet.

It didn't take long for Kali to locate the plant that Elvar was after. She knew from past excursions with him that he would insist on leaving it intact and unharmed. She also knew that he would quickly become completely immersed in his sketches and would forget that she was anywhere nearby.

They had located a healthy clump of awapuhi, more commonly known as bitter ginger. She watched as Elvar pulled out a notebook, pencils, and a large magnifying glass from his knapsack, then settled down cross-legged on the ground in front of it. For the next half hour, he made rough sketches, all while checking the intricate vein patterns in the leaves and examining the flowers closely beneath his magnifying glass. It was what made him so much in demand for his beautiful knives, Kali thought, this obsessive attention to detail.

She relaxed on a nearby pile of boulders, their edges worn smooth by thousands of years of exposure to rain and wind. She hadn't realized she was drifting off to sleep until Elvar gently shook her shoulder and abruptly brought her back to full wakefulness.

"Hey, you. I found a piece of sandalwood and have all the sketches I need."

She sat upright, grazing her arm against the surface of the stone. She winced, and Elvar frowned.

"Sorry. I tried not to startle you."

She pulled herself to her feet, stretching. "No problem. Just a scrape."

"You'll need to rub some aloe on that," he said, smiling.

Kali laughed. "You're a good student."

They walked a few minutes along the mountain path in companionable silence. It was Elvar who finally broke the silence, his voice thoughtful.

"It's funny how some plants sort of become commonly accepted, isn't it? Aloe's a good example, and I've noticed you can find it everywhere. It's like our Icelandic moss, which we use as a tea or an infusion. When Birta and I were still living back in Iceland, even her husband, who was a no-nonsense kind of doctor, used to recommend it for everything from an upset tummy to skin irritations."

Kali tried to hide her surprise. In the years she'd been neighbors with Elvar and Birta, she'd never heard either of them make more than a passing reference to their personal lives before Maui. She'd certainly never heard any mention of an ex-husband for Birta. She had a hard time imagining her as anyone's wife, and a silly image came to mind unbidden, of Birta standing at a stove, stirring a pot of soup, dressed in a frilly apron, looking out a window over a snow-covered landscape.

"Fascinating," she said hesitantly. She didn't know whether to comment any further or not, or whether the dozens of questions that were flooding her mind would offend Elvar.

Elvar seemed to sense her thoughts. "Yes, that's right. Birta was Mrs. Doctor. For a long time, in fact."

She took a deep breath. "But . . . ?"

Elvar didn't seem offended. "Well, I guess we've all been friends for some time now, haven't we?"

"Longer every day," she agreed. "But you don't need to tell me . . ."

"Well, I'm going to. And I'll tell you why. I know you're scared to death of her, and I know she can come across as, well, a little grim sometimes. But she's not, you know. She's wonderful and caring and funny." Elvar corrected himself. "Okay, maybe not funny. But she'd do anything for anybody, regardless of any inconvenience or cost to herself."

Kali began to protest. "Scared of her? I'm not—"

"Oh, of course you are." He grinned. "It's okay. You don't need to be embarrassed. Most women have the same reaction. Most men, too, come to think of it. It's just that the good doctor took off with a pretty, much younger intern at the hospital when it turned out that Birta couldn't have children. Didn't seem to matter to him at all that it was every bit as devastating for her."

He looked up at Kali and smiled. "It's why she's such a great teacher. She really loves kids. They can tell she cares about them."

Kali's face must have registered the combination of skepticism and surprise she felt. "That's nice," she said, then quickly corrected herself. "I mean, it's nice that she likes kids and gets to work with them. But it's a sad story. That's what I was trying to say."

Elvar nodded. "Well, our mother was obsessed with Hawaii, with all the similarities between your warm islands and our cold one. Volcanoes, legends, isolation. The divorce gave Birta a great excuse to move here and explore some of the stories we'd grown up listening to. I thought I'd come along and keep her company. It was a good idea. And she's happy enough, I think."

Kali thought about his words as they made their way slowly down the mountain path in the growing heat. *Happy enough. Is that all that we should hope for, to be happy enough? Perhaps.*

This morning, she thought, *I am exactly that.*

CHAPTER 21

*P*ele stood on a pile of lava rocks jutting out of the sand. She towered above Kali, at least twelve feet tall. Her fierce eyes were slits of sparkling black against her skin.

Kali knelt, dropping her gaze. It would do no good, she knew, to challenge a goddess of this stature. She stayed as still as she could while Pele balanced on her bare feet and swayed gently from side to side, her thick dark hair glinting in the moonlight.

"Speak," Pele roared, and the waves rose and crashed against her.

Kali remained motionless. She'd forgotten why she was here. The presence of Pele was overwhelming. Her body trembled, and her lips refused to form the words to her forgotten question.

"Have you dared to summon me?" Pele asked, her voice rising above the sea, above the wind.

Kali tried to gather her thoughts. *"Why did the shark god kill the boy?"* she finally managed to ask, but even to her own ears, her voice sounded faint and muffled.

Pele threw back her head, and flames rose behind her, framing her in the darkness. Kali shook. She realized too late that she had accused Ka-moho-ali'i, the shark god brother of Pele, whom even the volcano goddess knew to fear.

Again, Pele spoke. But the wind drowned her voice, and Kali couldn't make out the words. Then she was gone, the rocks empty, the sea a tumult of spray, the moon revealed full and without shadow. There was another figure there now: a man with a shark's head, standing knee-deep in the sea, holding something in both arms. It was the still figure of a boy, who seemed to be sleeping. Kali knew the boy's face. The shark man turned away from the shore and slowly waded deeper into the water until he was submerged, lost from view, the sleeping boy clutched close against his breast as they disappeared together.

Kali sat bolt upright, suddenly fully awake. The moon was high, just like the one in her dream, and a wide path of light broke the darkness, spilling across the sofa and the gleaming wooden floor. She tried to swing her legs over the edge, but her feet were asleep, and she could see by the moonlight that Hilo was lying across them. She lay back, not up to the task of shifting Hilo from his position. She needed to shake off the night terror brought on by the dream.

She lay there for hours, falling fitfully in and out of sleep, until the pale waking dawn began to lift the night.

Through her open window, she could smell the faint scent of a wood fire burning somewhere not too far away, most likely on the beach. Campers, perhaps, who couldn't afford the astronomical hotel and resort room prices, or teenage lovers, wrapped in one another's arms.

The scent was plainly that of driftwood, an unmistakable and oddly comforting aroma of old wood melded with salt and bits of seaweed, all blending perfectly to stir a series of familiar memories. Not one perfumer in all the world, she thought, had been able to replicate it, to pour it into a bottle.

For several more minutes, she lay quite still, savoring the scent and trying to decide what had woken her. It was the dream, of course. She pushed at Hilo, rubbed the sleep from her eyes, remembering in vivid, sudden detail the dream image of the shark god. She slipped off the sofa, shaking the numbness from her feet and ankles, and walked to the kitchen. She switched on the low light over the counter and filled the coffee press with some ground beans from the day before, kept in a small ceramic pot that was stamped with the clear message COFFEE, a gift from one of Walter's daughters.

She switched the kettle on to boil, then waited for the soft whistle that always preceded the automatic shutoff. She poured the steaming water over the ground beans in the coffee press, a trendy glass object that seemed far fancier and much more unnecessary than a standard automatic coffeemaker. Mike had brought it home one day, had enthusiastically told her how it would always brew the perfect pot of coffee, and she had found herself unable to part with it.

She poured the fragrant coffee into a mug and carried it to the lanai to watch the day come fully into focus. A small breeze moved the already warm air. Her thoughts turned, ever so briefly, to how she'd considered moving to Colorado following Mike's death. She'd shown Walter a Web site of the Rocky Mountain countryside near Denver, with its line of tall, craggy mountains to the west of the city, nearly always topped with snow. Some of the photographs on the Web site had shown people in the city bundled up in heavy boots, wool hats, thick gloves, and fur-rimmed jackets. Walter had been appalled at the idea and had offered to take her to see a psychiatrist.

Maybe she needed one now—someone to help her decipher her disturbing dreams. She drained her mug and went inside to dress. Time to start the day.

CHAPTER 22

Kali checked one last time to make sure Hilo was securely anchored to the front deck in the shade of Elvar and Birta's house, and made her way to the small airfield several miles outside of Hana. She wasn't especially fond of air travel, though she'd always liked the idea of planes and the long-faded romance of airports—the kind portrayed in old movies, where everyone was elegantly dressed for the excitement of an air journey. Those were the days, she thought, when flying still carried an air of excitement and possibility, rather than stress and inconvenience.

At least she didn't have to go through the song-and-dance routine required of passengers at the main airport in Kahului, where the combination of tourist throngs and convoluted—and, in her professional opinion, mostly useless—security procedures usually resulted in an intense migraine that lasted for days. Larry Mahuka, a retired Hawaiian Airlines pilot and longtime friend of Kali's, kept a private plane in Hana and made several trips each month to the other islands. Today he was headed to Oʻahu and had agreed to let Kali tag along for the ride.

She parked and made her way to where Larry was doing a final exterior check on his blue-and-white Cessna. He looked up and waved, his weathered face splitting into a welcoming smile beneath a shock of thick silver hair.

"Making sure everything's still attached to whatever it's supposed to be attached to?" Kali asked, her voice clearly indicating that this was of major personal concern.

Larry grinned. "Appears to be, but don't worry, Kali. I've got an extra roll of duct tape, in case a wing comes loose. Of course, I'll be busy keeping us level, so I'll have to send you out with the tape to make repairs."

Kali narrowed her eyes, an unbidden image flashing through her mind, one of her clinging to a piece of wing as the roll of tape plummeted toward the surface of the Pacific far below. She shook her head and followed Larry as he checked the air level in the tires and ran his hand over the lower part of the struts. He turned to Kali, gestured that it was time to board.

"Where's that half dog, half rhinoceros of yours? I wondered if you were going to try to pass him off as a colleague."

"Last I saw of him this morning, he was pretending he'd been abandoned and was howling at the top of his lungs about being left behind. The neighbors are babysitting him for me."

Larry shook his head. "Spoiled right down to his giant feet. You need some kids. Take your focus off that dog."

Kali grunted. "No thanks. I think I prefer the howling."

"Really? No secret longing for dental bills and college funds?"

"Not a single one. You always know where you stand with a dog."

They strapped themselves in and donned their headsets, and Larry proceeded with his instrument check. Satisfied that all was well, he started the engine, then smiled at the steady purr.

"Just giving you a hard time. It's how I feel about planes, I guess. Everything straightforward and simple. Not like relationships."

Kali said nothing, remembering a rumor she'd heard that Larry's wife had left him years ago, taking their kids and moving to the mainland. Somewhere in New Jersey, if she remembered correctly.

The plane's somewhat bumpy taxi down the runway turned suddenly smooth as the Cessna lifted into the clear, brilliantly blue sky. Larry seemed content to fly, and Kali relaxed against the seat and let her gaze drift out the window. They'd been in the air for about ten minutes when he gestured downward and turned the plane in a wide, lazy circle. Below, a pod of whales was moving south. She watched as a young whale pushed through the surface, arced through the air above the waves, then dove out of sight. Larry smiled, as did she.

The flight was short, and soon the coast of Oʻahu was plainly visible. Kali wasn't looking forward to the traffic of Honolulu, an unavoidable nuisance given that it was one of the largest cities in the United States. Her first destination was right in the thick of the Waikiki Beach scene. Traffic central, in fact.

She'd timed the trip to Oʻahu to coincide with an alternative-energy conference being held at the Hawaii Convention Center, in the hope that it might arm her with some useful information before she visited the solar companies on her Oʻahu list. It was still early by the time she'd picked up a rental car and made her way from the airfield to her hotel adjacent to the convention center. She checked in for two nights, planning to meet up with Larry on Wednesday for an early lunch and the flight home. This afternoon she'd talk to a solar power expert at the conference. The next day had been set aside to visit the local Oʻahu solar suppliers on her list.

Since none of the exhibits at the conference center could be accessed until after ten o'clock, she had a few hours on her own. She followed the curving sidewalk of Kalakaua Avenue to the corner where it intersected with Saratoga Road. It was about quarter past nine by the time she'd strolled the distance, and already the sidewalk at a popular restaurant across from the Waikiki post office was lined with tourists, who sat on the edges of curbs and walls, waiting to be seated by the cheerful, smiling staff in their handmade aprons.

Bemused, she made her way through the throng and down the street, then turned the corner and walked to where a small, less advertised coffee shop was tucked between a day spa and an insurance office. She'd come here often with Mike, and as she pushed through the door, the older woman who owned the café and who waited on tables looked up and smiled.

Once she was seated, she waved away the menu and ordered coffee, juice, a stack of coconut pancakes, and a side of Spam. Two young men sitting at the next table heard her as she placed her order, and snickered when they caught the mention of tinned meat. Kali turned, and the neckline of her loose T-shirt slipped down her shoulder, revealing her tattoo. She raised an eyebrow, making deliberate eye contact with one of the boys. He was probably only eighteen or nineteen, Kali decided, eyeing his casually hip clothing and expensive haircut.

There was an unmistakable air to privilege, she'd learned long ago. The boys' deep tans and the bleached streaks in their hair suggested that they were spending time relaxing at their mainland family's vacation home or had embarked on a post–high school, precollege surfing adventure. *Probably both*, Kali thought, scowling involuntarily. A boy like Kekipi Smith was worth a thousand of them, she decided. She caught herself before the thought went any further, realizing its unfairness and assumptions.

Her reactive scowl, however, had been ferocious enough to make the boy facing her jerk in his seat, look away, and mumble something under his breath that might have been an apology. Or not.

Kali nodded at him, deciding to give him the benefit of her doubt.

"Ever try it?" she asked.

The boy looked back, still a bit nervous. Kali was usually oblivious to the effect her appearance had on other people, but today she was secretly pleased that the bands of traditional tattoos on her lean, muscled upper arms seemed to have a subduing effect.

"Try what?" the boy responded, his voice cautious.

"Spam," answered Kali.

The boy shook his head.

Kali swung around in her chair, considering the often dismissive attitude of the young toward anything they hadn't directly thought of themselves.

"Do you even know what it is?" she asked.

Both boys shook their heads, looking slightly repulsed at the very idea.

"Some kind of fake meat?" ventured one.

"Back when the islands were crawling with servicemen in World War II, Spam was part of the food rations given to soldiers," she said. "It's pretty much just pressed seasoned pork. And as far as I'm concerned, it's pretty damned tasty."

The two boys looked supremely uninterested, which just served to spur Kali on.

"You've heard of World War II, right?"

The boy facing Kali rolled his eyes. "Of course we know about it. And we know what Spam is."

"Or isn't," offered the second boy. "Like, it isn't food. And it's not organic."

Kali shrugged, losing interest in her game. Her juice and coffee had arrived, and she turned her attention away from the boys and toward the selection of sweeteners available to her on the tabletop. As she was stirring sugar into her mug, the boys pushed back their chairs and got ready to leave. On their way out, they stopped beside Kali, who looked up, waiting for them to speak.

"Are you, like, a real Hawaiian?" asked one of them, his voice a bit hesitant.

Kali tilted her head, considering. "You bet," she answered. "Just like Elvis Presley."

Again, the two boys looked completely blank.

Kali sighed. "The singer? *Blue Hawaii*? *G.I. Blues*?"

"Yeah, sure. Whatever," said the boy who had asked the question. They continued on their way toward the door, shaking their heads.

As they disappeared into the sunshine outside, the waitress returned with Kali's food. The Spam had been fried on the grill, and steam was rising from it. She leaned over her plate, breathed in the familiar, slightly sweet fragrance.

"Enjoy," said the waitress, smiling.

"That I will," said Kali, picking up her knife and fork. "Every single bite."

CHAPTER 23

Hara had been assigned the task of researching the conference host, a group called Green World America, and had prepared Kali with a wealth of information for her trip. The group had turned out to be part of a larger worldwide network of environmentally sensitive businesses organized by country—besides Green World America, there was also Green World Germany, Green World Portugal, and Green World Australia. It was a dice role that wandering through the displays and speaking with the exhibiters might add any useful information to the investigation, but she knew that too much information was always better than too little.

More information came as she walked along the waterfront back to the hotel after her breakfast: an unwanted text from Walter. Grace Sawyer had died that morning, without ever having a chance to tell her story. An autopsy had been scheduled. Kali shoved the phone back into her bag, filled with a combined sense of anger and sorrow.

When Kali arrived at the conference center later that morning, events were well under way. The lobby entrance was jammed with earnest-looking individuals dressed in Hawaii business casual—jeans, open-neck cotton shirts, sandals and loafers, and the occasional linen jackets or Hawaiian shirts. She found her way to the registration desk, where a young woman was handing out badges and name tags, checking them against a list of registrants. Kali explained who she was and why she wanted entrance. The woman at the desk looked interested and suggested that Kali would probably save herself a lot of time if she went directly to the exhibit being hosted by NREL, the National Renewable Energy Laboratory. She got directions, pinned her temporary badge to the shoulder of her shirt, and began weaving through the crowds milling about on the exhibit floor.

The exhibit being presented by NREL was made up of a lot of high-tech computer screens displaying an assortment of images and data. On the walls of the main booth, charts and graphs were on view, along with photographs of wind turbines and solar arrays that showed installations at famous locations. A series of poster-sized images showed fields of wind turbines in California and Germany. Kali paused in front of them, amazed by the scale of the tall towers with their spinning blades and by the variety of designs.

"Pretty impressive, aren't they?" said a friendly male voice. She turned, startled, and saw a man in his early thirties standing beside her. His bright blue eyes were framed by hair that was nearly the same shade as copper. Kali glanced quickly at his shoulder. His name tag, which read JACK BADER, PH.D., included a ribbon with the word *Presenter* written in gold lettering down its length.

"Very impressive," she agreed. "I guess I didn't know there were so many types of turbines."

"More than you'd imagine. There are even design teams around the world producing turbines that look more like huge art installations than windmills. In the renewable energy field, we're always tweaking to see if we can come up with more efficient models, or ones that integrate less intrusively into various landscapes or that can function offshore on floating platforms in distant locations." His hands moved as he spoke, as if he were illustrating some vital point. She noticed that his jacket fit poorly over his wide, rugged shoulders.

"Are you one of the designers?"

"Actually, I don't work in wind at all." He smiled. "My field's geothermal energy. Volcano research, specifically."

Her face betrayed her disappointment. "Not solar, then?"

Jack smiled. "No, though I know a few of the solar researchers at NREL. Is that what you're interested in?"

She nodded and introduced herself, then explained that she was at the conference as part of an investigation.

He looked surprised but extended his hand. "Well, Detective Māhoe, maybe I can be of some help, anyway. My name's Jack, by the way. Jack Bader, but I guess my badge already gave that away."

She took his hand and did her best to smile in return.

"Nice to meet you, Jack. And it's Kali, please." She glanced around, trying to quell her impatience. The floor of the conference center was becoming increasingly crowded, and with it came a definite and corresponding escalation in the din. "To tell you the truth, I'd be grateful if I could ask you a few questions. Is there somewhere a little less noisy where we could talk for a few minutes?"

He looked down at his watch, frowning. "I actually have to speak pretty soon and should really go and make sure everything's ready. The last time I had to present at a conference, my assistant—well, my ex-assistant—put the wrong notes on the podium, and I wound up looking and sounding like a complete idiot. I'm afraid I'm not much good at winging it."

Kali tried to look sympathetic but was secretly appalled at the idea of standing in front of an auditorium full of strangers and speaking into a microphone.

"That's okay," she said. "Maybe you could point me in the direction of someone who could answer a few questions about solar panels."

Jack thought for a moment and then pointed down a row of booths.

"Myra—Dr. Myra Wilson—is down there with the Pure Sun folks. She'd be perfect." He smiled, hesitating. "Of course, I'd be happy to spend some time later on telling you anything you don't already know about volcanoes."

She laughed. "I know when one's about to erupt, I suppose. Most native Hawaiians have an intuitive sixth sense about that kind of thing."

"Really?" he said, sounding intrigued. He hesitated again, his cheeks flushing with sudden embarrassment.

"Well, then. Maybe, instead, you could tell me everything *I* don't already know about volcanoes."

Kali was startled. Was he flirting with her? Surely not. She looked at him closely, at his earnest gaze, which appeared to be sincere. Was it her tattoos? Perhaps he was simply overcome with the exotic sense of being far away from home on a tropical island for a few days, confronted by a bona fide native? Lots of things, she reflected wryly, could interfere with the judgment calls made by attractive men.

"Well . . . I can't say that I know that much about the science end of volcanoes. But I could tell you a legend or two," she said, watching closely for his reaction. He seemed pleased, and she relaxed, suddenly realizing that she'd actually been holding her breath. She spoke again quickly before she had time to think long enough to change her mind. "Coffee later? Perhaps after the floor closes?"

Jack's face widened into a broad smile, and she noticed how even and sparkling white his teeth were.

"Sounds great. I'm staying at the hotel next door, at the Ala Moana," he said. "Seemed easier than trying to find my way around a city I've never been to."

"I'm staying there, too." She hesitated, so out of practice when it came to anything even close to social interaction that she had no idea what to say next. "We could meet down in the lobby later, if that works for you. Say, six o'clock?"

"Perfect." Jack suddenly looked shy. "I'm looking forward to it already," he said, then added in a slightly flustered tone, "The volcano legends, I mean." Kali noticed how his face flushed so brightly, it nearly matched the shade of his hair. The effect was strangely charming, and she grinned.

"Okay. So, see you later, then," she said, then made her way down the exhibit aisle toward the Pure Sun display. From the corner of her eye, she saw Jack hurrying toward the conference rooms, his coppery hair glinting beneath the harsh lights of the room.

CHAPTER 24

Dr. Myra Wilson turned out to be a tiny woman with oversize glasses and a serious, earnest expression on her pale face. For someone who worked in sun energy, Kali thought to herself, she didn't seem to be exposed to it very often. She introduced herself, and Wilson grasped her hand with the overcompensation of the physically less endowed, then pumped it energetically while quickly scanning Kali's face.

"Last time I was approached by anyone connected to the cops, it was for being criminally boring," she said, then laughed at her own joke.

Kali tried to smile encouragingly. "I guess I've never thought of scientists as being particularly funny," she said.

"Oh, we're not."

Refrain from commenting, Kali told herself. She

leaned over and looked closely at a chart pinned to one wall of the display, which showed the percentage of solar power being generated in various areas of the world. She was surprised that Hawaii didn't rank very high.

"I guess we don't get as much sunshine as I thought," she said, gesturing toward the chart.

"Ahh," said Wilson in response, nodding her head knowingly, "the United States in general is pretty far behind the curve when it comes to alternative-energy generation and use, even in obviously suitable locations like Hawaii. It's unfortunate but true nonetheless. Relationships between oil companies and politicians have a lot to do with that, of course. There's a lack of incentive to find other sources if your perks and funding come from oil companies."

"But interest is picking up, isn't it? My own home is completely off the grid, and pretty much the entire area of the island where I live is using solar power."

Wilson looked back at her chart. "Yes, interest is picking up, and the funding for research and development has definitely improved over the past few years, but it still isn't where it should be. But the politics of renewable energy probably isn't what you wanted to discuss with me, is it? Is someone holding the sun for ransom?"

Kali tried to hide her surprise. "Not far off the mark," she said. "Solar panels are disappearing off the roofs of houses on Maui, and we're trying to figure out what's happening to them."

"Being resold, most likely," said Wilson, shrugging. "Until pretty recently, they weren't being manufactured with easily distinguishable registration marks or other identifiers. That's changing, but most of them look pretty much alike, and if they were bought before two thousand seven, chances are they'd be difficult to track or identify as having been removed from a specific location."

"So I've discovered," Kali agreed wryly. "Perhaps you could tell me if you've heard of any kind of black market for them? We don't think they're leaving the islands, but the distributors we've checked out so far all seem to be legitimate dealers."

Wilson picked up a small model of a photovoltaic array that was part of her display.

"Maybe," she said slowly, "you're looking in the wrong place. I'd talk to some of the independent builders. Could be someone is selling directly to them. Bypass the dealer entirely, sell for cash, and everyone looks the other way. There's so much new building going on around the country—including over here—plus enough of a growing demand for solar power, that some smaller contractors could be dealing in the back room, without a prospective home buyer ever knowing." She returned the model to the display. "And," she added, grinning, "from what I know about you Hawaiians, no one says anything unless they're sure there's no possibility of a distant cousin being involved."

Kali ignored the culturally inappropriate comment and tried not to groan out loud at what Wilson was suggesting. First, she was absolutely right that the natives and locals didn't necessarily look favorably on the influx of outsiders and their money. This was especially true—and, she admitted to herself, understandable—when it involved buying up island land and constructing obscenely large and pretentious houses that flaunted wealth in the face of near poverty. Especially the enormous, flashy vacation homes, which might be occupied for only a few weeks each year. More practically, and of far more immediate concern to Kali, was that while interviewing the handful of distributors doing business in the islands was one thing, tracking down every building contractor and verifying their supply sources would be a nightmare of monumental proportions.

She thanked Wilson for her time and walked slowly through the other displays and back out into the cool quiet of the convention center lobby. At least there was coffee to look forward to. But first, a long walk. The news about the attack victim's death had been in the back of her mind all day. And something during her encounter with Wilson had stirred a vague feeling or memory. She couldn't quite put her finger on it, but it was there nevertheless, submerged, waiting to take full form and rise to the surface of awareness.

CHAPTER 25

At the exact moment Kali was speaking with Wilson, Walter was making his way slowly along the Hana Highway, caught between a couple in a convertible who kept slamming on their brakes to take photographs and a pickup truck being driven by a hearing-impaired woman with curlers in her hair. At least Walter assumed she was hearing impaired, as the volume was turned up so high on her radio that he could feel the seat in his wife's car vibrating. He mentally kicked himself for not being in his police car, but his wife had asked him to fill her tank for her next day's trip to the west side of the island, and he was trying to avoid having to deal with her expression of matrimonial disappointment over dinner if he didn't make the trip to the gas station.

He blasted his horn again, knowing even as he did so that it was a pointless action, and his effort got the zero reaction from the cars ahead that he'd expected. He sighed, took his foot off the accelerator, and crawled along with the rest of the traffic, before finally pulling in with relief at the pumps in front of George's Island Market. He filled the tank and walked inside to say hello to George Tsui, who was, as usual, sitting behind the cash register, reading the day's tabloid headlines. He kept his eyes focused on the paper but nodded to Walter in acknowledgment of his presence.

"Says here they've found out the queen of England has an illegitimate daughter hidden away in an Australian prison, and that they found another flying saucer back on the mainland. Someplace in Nevada. You hear any news of that over the police scanner?"

Walter shook his head, slipping a couple of twenties from his wallet and pushing them across the counter to George. "Nope. Not a word. Seems a shame, though, that Nevada would be the first impression intelligent beings from another planet might get of the earth."

Both men were silent for a moment.

Finally, George nodded in agreement. "Seems like Bali or Rome or Honolulu would be a better choice."

"Maybe not Honolulu."

"Okay, maybe not, but you get my drift. Course, maybe they'll come from someplace where sand doesn't exist, and Nevada would seem like an interesting place to take pictures for the family travel album."

George pushed the buttons on the cash register, and the drawer opened. He slid the money in without looking at the slot, his eyes peering over the top of his reading glasses at Walter. "You be sure to let me know if you hear about anything intergalactic heading this way, Walter. I'll need time to stock up on those disposable cameras."

Walter smiled and turned toward the door. He was about to leave when another man entered, brushing against Walter's arm as he passed. Walter was annoyed—there was plenty of space, and it seemed almost as though the other man hadn't even noticed the contact. As the man turned to walk toward the refrigerated cases in the back of the store, Walter saw with surprise that it was Polunu Hausuka. He opened the door of one of the cases and selected a sandwich, then made his way toward the cash register.

George looked up curiously and took note of Polunu. Walter winked at George, who immediately turned his attention back to his newspaper.

Polunu's face twisted in a mixture of anger and embarrassment. "You again. You following me around?"

"I was already here. Thought I'd stop in for a candy bar."

"That's really funny." He eyed Walter's considerable girth with contempt. "You always pick on people smaller than you?"

Walter suddenly looked serious, as if considering the question carefully. "No, not always. Just when the other person is a thief."

"That's true," said George from behind the paper.

Polunu hesitated. He looked poised for sudden flight, shifting his weight rapidly from one foot to the other. He put the sandwich down on the counter. "Keep it," he said to George.

Walter turned and watched as Polunu walked out of the door, empty-handed.

Behind him, George coughed gently. "Any desire to explain that little bit of action?" he asked, his voice betraying his interest. "I believe you just cost me a sale."

"That's one of my favorite pickpockets," Walter answered.

"Really? I thought his talents were limited to small food items."

"Has he been stealing from you, too, George?"

George shrugged. "Sure. I imagine he steals from everybody."

"You don't seem too concerned."

"Didn't say I like it. But it's his nature. It's who he is. Getting that guy to stop stealing would be like telling the birds to stop singing. It's what they do. It's what he does. Sometimes you have to accept the nature of others, even if it's disagreeable."

Walter looked at George with surprise. "That's all very philosophical."

George thumbed his chin, considering. "I suppose so. But if I ever actually catch him in the act, I'll break his arm with this," he said calmly, lifting a wooden baseball bat from where it was hidden behind the counter.

Walter laughed. "That might leave an impression. You'd really hit him with that?"

George replaced the bat, then looked at his friend solemnly.

"Of course I would," he said. "It's my nature."

CHAPTER 26

On the stage, Polunu stumbled. His face was pale, beaded up with perspiration, as though he had suddenly been swept with a bout of nausea. There was a familiar man sitting on the corner barstool, watching him. It was the agreed-upon signal for an early morning face-to-face meeting the following day.

When the lights came up at the end of the show, Polunu took his time changing out of his costume. His message delivered, the man on the barstool had disappeared. As he left the resort parking lot, Polunu's expression reflected a sense of defeat. There was no energy for the tourists' pockets this evening.

In the morning he dragged himself out of bed before daybreak, exhausted from tossing and turning through the night. He loaded his van, then made himself a cup of coffee but left it on the table, untouched, worried about being late. He drove carefully to the wooded track leading to the drop-off. At the base of the hill, the lights of a fifty-four-foot Sunseeker cabin cruiser flickered in the harbor against the still-dark sky.

He backed the van carefully and stopped at the top of the narrow path leading to the cove where the man would have moored the large dinghy that served as the intermediary between the van and the boat. There was movement at the base of the path, and he saw the man's stocky figure coming to meet him.

"Morning," he said.

The man nodded, a half smile on his face. "Morning. Sorry for the extra run and the short notice."

Polunu's face relaxed in relief. Maybe the video hadn't found its way to the entire world, after all, and his long, sleepless night had been for nothing. Maybe his public indiscretion had gone unnoticed, and he wasn't about to be fired from his lucrative side job.

"Not a problem." He gestured toward the dinghy with his head. "Do you want me to get started?"

"No time like the present," the man answered, his voice still friendly.

This was the difficult part. The transfer to the rocking dinghy and onto the larger boat's teak swim platform, then into the saloon and staterooms, had to be negotiated carefully and as quietly as possible. The cove where the dinghy was anchored was very secluded, but there was always the chance of being seen by a camper or hiker.

The morning's enterprise took the better part of an hour, and by the time they'd finished, the first streaks of sunlight were well over the horizon, orange and warm. Polunu heaved a sigh of relief. The man had still not referenced the far too public YouTube video of the shopping battle he'd had with the woman tourist.

Standing on the expansive deck of the Sunseeker next to Polunu, the man gestured for him to sit down. "Unbelievable how fast the heat comes up in the morning," he said. "I've got some juice and soda in the galley. Can I offer you something? If you want something hot, there's coffee."

Polunu was surprised at the unusual friendliness of the gesture. "Sure," he said. "Coffee would be great."

The man made his way toward the hatch leading belowdecks. "Be right back," he said. "Make yourself comfortable."

Polunu settled onto one of the cushioned benches that lined the sides of the aft cockpit of the powerboat. He looked around curiously. The boat was opulent, with shining brass and plush textiles.

The man returned a few minutes later, a mug in each hand. He handed one to Polunu and sat down opposite him. He was relaxed and smiling, one arm thrown casually over the back of the seat. He took a sip from his mug and sighed in satisfaction.

"This should take care of the immediate problem," he said.

Polunu sipped his coffee. "Glad to have been of help."

The man was watching Polunu as he relaxed into his seat and gazed out over the water. The man tilted his mug back and finished the last drop, then placed the mug carefully into a holder built into the corner of the seating area. He leaned forward, then gazed closely at Polunu.

Polunu lifted his own mug to take another drink but was suddenly unable to raise it all the way to his lips.

He looked across at the other man and tried to speak. "I think . . ." He stopped, frowning. His face showed he was confused. He began to speak, but only a jumble of sounds emerged. He tried again, but this time nothing came out at all. He was peering intently at the man facing him but seemed to have difficulty focusing. He passed one hand unsteadily in front of his face, as if trying to push away cobwebs.

The man watched carefully. After a moment, he reached down and took Polunu's arm, then pulled him upright.

"Time to go, pal," he said.

Polunu looked baffled. He struggled to gain his balance but lurched forward and nearly fell. The man caught him by the arm and led him to the edge of the boat and the access point for the dinghy.

"Careful," he said, helping Polunu over the side and into the smaller watercraft. The man climbed in after Polunu and looked around. He scanned the shoreline and hillside. There was no movement, no indication of anyone else being around. Instead of starting the small motor that powered the dinghy, he picked up the set of oars lying along the bottom.

Polunu sat down in the small wooden boat, fumbling at the boat's edge with one hand. His muscles didn't seem to be cooperating. His eyelids drooped, and he appeared to be on the verge of falling asleep. As his eyes began to close again, the man reached out and grabbed his shoulder, then shook him vigorously. Polunu's eyes flew open briefly, then began to close completely.

The man maneuvered the dinghy from the side of the boat, but instead of heading toward the shore, he turned the prow and headed toward the deeper water in front of the cruiser. The dinghy stopped. The man listened carefully, his glance sweeping the shoreline as he searched for the slightest movement. After a few minutes, he laid the oars in the bottom. Reaching under the wooden seat, he pulled out a length of rope. He moved carefully to the space on the seat next to Polunu, who was listing to one side. The man grinned, then reached down, half kneeling, and began to loop the rope around Polunu's ankles.

Polunu looked down, his face slack with confusion. He tried to shift his feet, but they wouldn't move. He reached down with one hand and fumbled with the weight now firmly tethered to his feet.

"Sit still, you idiot," said the man. His voice had lost its false friendliness and had taken on a hard, impatient tone.

Polunu reached down again, this time with an air of urgency. His eyes had widened, as some sense of awareness had crept through to his consciousness.

The man sighed and stepped carefully behind the bench where Polunu sat. He reached beneath Polunu's arms, then half lifted and half dragged him to the edge of the dinghy, his breath hot against Polunu's neck.

"Big mistake turning yourself into a social media star, loser. Can't have a famous face like yours pointing any attention my way." His face was close to Polunu's. "Just be grateful it's me taking you on this little cruise this morning. You'll just have to take my word for it, but this could have been a whole lot worse."

He adjusted his grip around Polunu's upper body and heaved him partially upright. The dinghy rocked dangerously. Polunu's limbs flailed uselessly. There was no resistance. The half-dozen muscle relaxers that the man had slipped into his coffee had gone directly into Polunu's system, and though he seemed to be making an effort to say something, his face and body were growing increasingly limp.

There was a brief moment of falling, when Polunu was neither fully in the dinghy nor completely in the water. His eyes, now wide open as his subconscious grasped the realization of what was happening, stared upward at the sky, warm brown pools filled with the cloudless blue above. He seemed to float upon the surface for just a second before the weight pulled him silently into the depths.

The man waited as Polunu disappeared beneath the water, then rowed back to the cruiser and securely fastened the dinghy to its mooring. He gathered the two coffee mugs from the aft cockpit and rinsed Polunu's carefully in the seawater, then let it fill and sink. He looked at his watch, an expensive diver's model belted to his thick wrist with a gold band.

The engine of the cruiser started up with the push of a button. He engaged the electric windlass to haul in the anchor and pointed the prow of the Sunseeker toward the open water, motoring slowly along the coast. He left the boat at the end of a private dock and followed the wide path leading to the landscaped pool and garden complex of his daughter's home, then let himself in through the back door.

He went into the kitchen and opened a cupboard door, then reached in and removed a mug. Time for a second, more leisurely cup of morning coffee. His face was completely void of worry. But even he didn't know everything. He hadn't noticed, for instance, the thin, filthy girl sitting huddled in a small clearing above the place where the cruiser was moored, watching with interest as he helped Polunu get ready for his early morning swim.

CHAPTER 27

The hotel air-conditioning was chilly and uncomfortable to Kali, who preferred an open window. She lay stretched across the queen-sized bed, which was covered by a quilt printed with a cheery pineapple motif and which was definitely more comfortable than her porch hammock.

Of course, if she were to invest in a bed of these proportions for her own house, she'd have to take out a wall. Her grandmother's space requirements had been modest, and Kali had seen little reason to expand or make any substantial renovations beyond the porch additions and a few updates. She had replaced the stove when it finally stopped responding to her efforts to resuscitate it, had hung new screening around the back porch, and had torn up the old linoleum kitchen tiles and put in bamboo flooring, but that had so far been the extent of her remodeling efforts. As far as she was concerned, she had everything she needed. Still, there was no denying that this bed was comfortable.

Struck by a sudden awareness of her solitude, she got up to shower and dress. She felt weary from perusing the endless exhibits on the convention center's show floor, and instead of reviving her, the nap she'd just taken had left her feeling bleary.

The possibility of a coffee date hadn't occurred to her when she'd packed, but she supposed a fresh pair of jeans and a clean shirt would be acceptable. She had brought her favorite white T-shirt, with its embroidered Hawaiian petroglyph symbol, and shook it out to smooth a few of the wrinkles that had formed from it being jammed into her small duffel bag. She pulled it on, then untangled the collection of talismans that hung from a leather cord around her neck. There was a small shell among them, and she fingered it, recalling the morning that Mike had handed it to her after finding it on the beach during one of their daily runs. Now, she gazed at her reflection in the mirror over the bathroom sink as she combed the sleep tangles from her hair and brushed her teeth, wondering, suddenly, what others saw when they looked at her. Perhaps she simply blended in with the scenery—just one more unremarkable feature on a tropical landscape.

A few minutes before she was due in the lobby, she took the elevator down. She'd expected to be the first to arrive, but Jack was already there, sitting in one of the overly deep chairs to one side, his back very straight, his hands resting casually in his lap. He didn't see her step off the elevator, but as she walked toward him, he sprang to his feet, his face all smiles. He was wearing jeans that looked freshly ironed, as did his short-sleeved Hawaiian shirt with an abstract pattern of blues, greens, and purples. Despite the creases, he looked slightly more comfortable without his blazer. She managed not to smile.

"Hi," he said, as she drew closer.

"Aloha," she answered.

The lobby area was packed, with a line of people snaking toward the coffee-bar counter, where two baristas were frantically trying to fill orders. She looked toward the lobby doors, suddenly ravenously hungry.

"I don't suppose you'd like to grab a bite to eat?" she suggested, her voice hesitant. "There's a place nearby that has great seafood."

He grinned. "Good idea, or my lack of willpower to resist the tray of brownies and sweets at the coffee bar might be really embarrassing."

"Wonderful. The place I'm thinking of is about three blocks from here. Do you mind walking?"

"Not at all. It's really nice out right now. I saw the sun starting to go down from my window while I was getting ready. Maybe we'll see the moon later."

"Ahh," she said. "That's where Hina lives."

Jack raised a brow. "Hina?"

"The goddess of the moon," she said.

Jack stepped aside, allowing her to exit through the lobby doors in front of him. Once surrounded by the warm early-evening air, she continued her story.

"Our ancestral stories explain that Hina spent her life taking care of her husband and her family, none of whom appreciated her. Every day she labored to make kapa cloth out of the bark of the mulberry tree, pounding it for long hours until it was soft and pliable."

Jack turned to her expectantly as they made their way down the sidewalk. "And?"

"One day she got sick and tired of it, chucked the kapa making, left her ungrateful husband and kids, and climbed to the moon, where no one could bother her, and she could rest in the cool silvery light." She laughed. "Can't say that I blame her."

Jack smiled. "Is there a legend for everything?"

"Pretty much. Sometimes more than one."

They walked along in companionable silence. A few blocks along, Kali stepped off the curb and led Jack toward a pathway lined with tiki torches, their flames moving gently in the soft sea breeze.

"I don't eat here that often, but it's always good—even if it's a year between visits," she said. "It's owned and run by a local family. Here's hoping nothing's changed and the same cook is still in the kitchen."

A young hostess dressed in a flowered sarong seated them at a table on the restaurant's outdoor patio, then handed each of them a menu. Tall, thin palms in deep ceramic pots on one side of the table made it secluded and romantic.

Jack grinned—a lopsided, easy smile. "Oh, dear, she probably thinks we're lovers out for a romantic night on the town."

"Do you think we should tell her we're here only to discuss volcanoes?" she asked.

He seemed embarrassed.

"Oh . . . I'm sorry. I didn't mean . . ."

"It's okay. I was just joking. She was just being nice, I'm sure." Jack picked up the menu and began to study it.

"Seafood is what they do best here," she offered, trying to be helpful.

He looked closely at the list of seafood, then looked at her, surprised. "Wow. Dolphin? You eat dolphin here?"

She could see that he was appalled. "Dolphinfish," she said, her voice reassuring. "Not Flipper. It's a completely separate species, a green-and-yellow fish with kind of a mean-looking face."

"Oh," he said, his voice low. "Things I don't know. I just thought for a minute . . ."

Kali smiled. "It's okay. A lot of people have the same reaction. Which I guess is a good thing, if you think about it. Most of the time, you'll see dolphinfish on the menu listed as mahimahi. They do a good job with it here, pan roasted with local tomatoes and sweet Maui onions, or crusted with coconut."

He looked noticeably relieved.

"And the ahi? What kind of fish is that?"

"Tuna, but ahi sounds more interesting, doesn't it?"

He laughed. "Damn. This is all very confusing. The power of marketing, I suppose. Though I'll be the first to admit that crème brûlée does sound a lot more tantalizing than baked custard with a burned top." He pondered in silence for a moment. "I remember an article I saw in a magazine a while ago. The writer had interviewed a couple of psychologists, who said we tend to enjoy our food more and think that it tastes better if it has an interesting name and it's served on beautiful plates."

Kali considered this bit of information, thinking of the paper take-out containers that usually constituted the major contents of her refrigerator. More often than not, she ate directly from them, rather than transferring the food to a plate or bowl. It was more efficient than dirtying a few dishes, and somehow less depressing than sitting down at the table by herself.

"I suppose I can see how that might have an effect, especially if you're in a fancy restaurant, paying a lot of money for a meal," she said, her voice doubtful.

"Yes, maybe it adds to the overall experience, and if you feel like you're being pampered and given special attention, and you're in a beautiful setting with crystal and china, it doesn't really matter how good the kitchen team actually is. Or what the bill is."

"Hmmm. I like to think I'd know an overcooked steak, regardless of how beautifully it was presented."

The waitress arrived to ask if they'd like cocktails, and Jack nodded. He glanced at Kali, grinning. "You'll probably think this is the height of silliness, but I'm dying to try a Lava Flow. I heard someone ordering one at the bar in the hotel the night I got in, but I was too tired to stick around to find out what it was. And it does seem like the only choice for a volcano expert with any degree of self-respect, don't you think?"

"I think you're required to have one," she said. "They're actually pretty tasty—a lot like a piña colada, with pineapple juice, coconut cream, and rum, but with a streak of strawberry puree running through it." She nodded to the waitress. "Two Lava Flows, please."

When they arrived, he took the glass with obvious delight, then turned it in his hand to look closely at the strawberry mixture running in trickles and streams through the creamy drink.

"Wow! It really does look just like a lava flow, but without the temperature," he said, sipping through his straw. "Umm . . . it's delicious."

Kali felt herself being oddly moved by the innocence of his pleasure. She looked across the table at his smile and found her own mood lifting. Jack was easy to be with.

"I take it this is your first time in Hawaii?"

He winced. "It's that obvious?"

"Yes, but not in a bad way."

He considered this carefully. "It's one of those places I figured I'd see eventually, especially from a work perspective. I guess I'm a bit of a volcano chaser. My research has to do with the amount of geothermal energy generated in the vicinity of a given volcano and how far that extends geographically. I'm particularly interested in active volcanoes and how that kind of energy can be collected or utilized to generate clean energy."

"You travel from volcano to volcano?"

"When possible. I work mostly out in the field, not in the lab. I've spent a lot of time in Italy and in the Azores, where there's ongoing activity. It's exciting. I like being close to the source, knowing that somewhere beneath the patch of earth I'm standing on, there are ancient forces at play."

"Sounds a little bit dangerous."

"Not as dangerous as being a detective, I'll bet."

The waitress returned to take their food order. As Jack made his choice, Kali considered his comment about danger.

"I guess being an accountant could be risky, given the right circumstances." Kali hesitated, then decided to share a little more. "Being a detective is only part of what I do, though. My degree is in cultural anthropology. It comes in surprisingly useful. A lot of crimes are connected to or driven by things that are culturally significant."

He looked at her with genuine interest. "Fascinating," he said. "You know, I lived in Florida for a while and made a couple of short trips to the Caribbean. I guess I thought Hawaii would just be more of the same—sand and palm trees."

He looked toward the swaying trees on the edge of the patio with appreciation.

"And?"

"Well, it's not really like that at all, is it?" he said slowly. "I mean, it's all of those things, of course—the beaches and sunsets and a more relaxed approach to daily life. But . . . it's also as though the colors here are deeper and richer, the air is more fragrant, and everything seems to exist on a more vibrant level." He stopped, fingered the stem of his glass, looking at her intently. "I must sound like just another goofy tourist."

"No," she said, her voice serious. "What you said is exactly true. Not many people get that. And you haven't even been out of Waikiki yet, have you? It's pretty touristy here. There are places in Hawaii, even on this island, that are still close to the way they used to be. I hope you get a chance to experience some of that before you go home."

"Actually, I may be coming here for a while. I'm on the list for a research transfer to the Big Island to study Kilauea Volcano while it's still in its active stage. There are several other people being considered, but I have my fingers crossed."

Kali was surprised but tried not to show it. "Have you asked Pele for permission?"

"Ah," he said, smiling. "In the Azores I had to watch out for disgruntled saints with names I couldn't pronounce. But I think I actually know who Pele is. The goddess who lives in the volcano, correct?"

"Exactly," she said. "Though there's more to the story, of course. Are you interested?"

Jack nodded, then listened intently as Kali spoke.

"Well, there's more than one version of the Pele story, but she's regarded as one of our most important and powerful deities. She had a constant stream of lovers, including the husband of one of her sisters, Na-mako, who was the goddess of the sea. In one story, Pele was of Tahitian origin and was banished by her father both for her destructive, foul temper and for constantly fighting with her sisters."

Kali stared off in the distance, to where the band of sandy beach held the island together. "She was put into the ocean aboard a small boat, and eventually it drifted ashore at a tiny mountain-covered island in Hawaii. She tried to make her home there, but the resident snow goddesses who lived in the mountain peaks had other ideas. They pummeled her with blizzards and ice storms, trying to drive her away."

"Hmm. That all sounds very un-tropical."

"Well, not really, if you think about the fact that Mauna Kea, on the Big Island, has snow on it for a good part of the year. But Hawaiians know that Pele eventually wins every argument with fire. So if you're going to go poking around where she lives, you should be properly respectful, or you'll have to deal with her temper."

Their food arrived, and Jack took an enthusiastic bite of his mahimahi. He chewed thoughtfully, then smiled. "When you say 'show respect,' you're serious, aren't you? I mean, aren't there spiritual ceremonies and things that people do to keep the gods and goddesses happy?"

Kali nodded. "Sure. Lots of them. I practice a few myself, but probably not as often as I should."

"What do you mean?"

She hesitated. The last thing she felt like doing was engaging in a discussion of spiritual practices with a scientist. Part of her reluctance, she guessed, no doubt stemmed from her own lingering sense of guilt. Wherever her grandmother's spirit was right now, she was probably shaking her head in disappointment.

"Just that it's part of being Hawaiian," she offered. She decided it was time to change the subject. "Tell me something I don't know about volcanoes."

Jack tapped his upper lip with two fingers, thinking. "Well, over eighty percent of the planet's surface was originally volcanic, and the volcanoes here in Hawaii are part of a much larger system, called the Ring of Fire. It includes all the coasts that enclose the Pacific Ocean."

She was impressed. "Good to know, I guess. Probably not something real estate agents in those areas like to emphasize."

Jack laughed, and they settled back in their seats, enjoying their meal. And though Kali wasn't ready to explore too deeply what it meant, she was enjoying the company, as well. This smart, funny man, with his uncomplicated laugh and hair like a volcano burst, was making her feel as though she was in exactly the right place, at exactly the right moment. It was a new feeling, but it was good.

CHAPTER 28

The next afternoon, driving her rental car along the H-1 west past Pearl Harbor Naval Base while listening to the Hawaiian music station, Kali thought about her meal with Jack. She'd enjoyed herself more than she'd expected, and he had seemed to have a good time, as well. They'd exchanged business cards, and he'd said she should let him know if there was anything else he could contribute to her investigation.

Now, driving alone through the countryside, she regretted that she hadn't rung to ask if he'd be interested in a drive out to the north end of Oʻahu and its famous surfing beaches.

She swung north and slightly west onto Highway 99, which she preferred to the busier and more crowded H-2 running parallel to it. Here, there were still open spaces free of massive hotels. She drove through the small town of Wahiawa and continued on toward the coast, where 99 ended and became 83. It was at this juncture, she'd been told, that she'd find the last solar supply company on her list. Earlier today she'd made the trek to the harbor at Ko Olina, where enormous luxury resorts filled an area close to the water. It had proven to be a waste of time, as she was sure this last call would also be.

The owner of the company in Ko Olina, after expressing an understandable level of outrage at the suggestion she might have knowledge of stolen goods, had grudgingly shown Kali around her facility and explained that the photovoltaic systems she dealt with were based exclusively on a new technology that allowed the user to track the amount of energy collected by each individual panel. The homeowner was even able to track their own energy collection and energy use via a personal Web site.

The last company was, indeed, an equal waste of her time. The husband-and-wife team that owned it also did their own installation and maintenance. They seemed genuinely surprised at the idea that someone was actively engaged in stealing panels, and willingly offered to provide documentation of their sources and customers.

The only thing that seemed to tie any of it together was the fact that all the dealers in Hawaii seemed to be buying their panels and supplies from two companies. One was located in Japan, and one was based in the States, on the mainland. Other than that, there seemed to be absolutely no connection of any kind.

She was frustrated and had finished far earlier than she'd planned. The clock on the car's dashboard showed that it was just past lunchtime, and she wasn't due to show up for her flight home until 11:00 a.m. the next day.

On a sudden impulse, she pulled the car over onto the side of the road and pulled out her small day bag.

Jack's business card was tucked inside the interior pocket. She retrieved it and stared at it for a moment, her hesitation to ask him if he'd like to see the other side of the island fading in the warm afternoon sunshine. She looked out the car window at the ragged line of the Ko'olau Mountains, a world away from the traffic and congestion of Honolulu. It would be a shame, she told herself, if she let him leave with his only impression of Hawaii being Waikiki Beach, but she knew that she was also curious about whether her vague attraction might have lasted overnight.

She told herself she'd let the phone ring three times and then give up if he hadn't answered by then. She punched in the number, and on the third ring, he answered.

"Hi Jack. Kali here. I was just wondering if you might have any interest in watching some of Hawaii's famous big-wave surfing?"

"Surfing? I'd love to see some in person," he said, sounding delighted. "As long as you don't expect me to try it."

She reassured him that the expedition would be purely observational in nature and arranged to pick him up in front of the hotel in a half hour. She filled the gas tank in the rental car and then headed back to the city. He was there when she pulled up, his tall figure leaning against the hotel's exterior wall in the shade. He waved and walked over to the car.

"Hi there," he said, smiling. "How's your investigation going?"

"I'd say less than satisfying," she answered as he opened the passenger door and climbed inside. "But I've finished what I came to do on Oʻahu, so I might as well enjoy the rest of the afternoon. And I thought it only hospitable to show you the other side of the island. It's a lot different from what you've probably seen so far."

She glanced over at him, trying to gauge his interest level. He had picked up a folded map from the pocket divider between the front seats and was studying it carefully.

"That's very kind of you," he said without looking up. Instead, he followed the road line with his fingertip, then turned to her. "Are we headed for the North Shore? There are lots of little surfers drawn there on that part of the map."

"We are. That's the area that's become so famous for the big sponsored professional surfing competitions. It isn't the right time of the year for the really huge waves, but there's always a good crowd of locals out there. If you've never seen it before, it can be pretty exciting. Of course, if you'd rather go somewhere else . . ."

"No," he said quickly. "That's perfect. I can't really go home and tell people I was in Hawaii for three days and never saw anything beyond the hotel. Too embarrassing."

Kali's music caught his attention, and he reached forward toward the volume dial of the car radio.

"Do you mind if I turn it up a little? The music here is so beautiful."

She tried not to show her pleasure. "Be my guest." She listened. "That's the Kaʻau Crater Boys."

He turned the knob and began to hum along to the song. Fresh air rushed through the open windows, and Kali made a decision.

"If you've got the time, how would you like me to give you a crash course in Hawaiian history and culture?"

His face showed interest but also a certain amount of suspicion. "Is there some sort of ritual involved?"

She shrugged. "There's music. And a fire dancer."

That got his attention. "I'm listening."

"There's a really great show at the Polynesian Cultural Center that's sort of become a local institution. There's a really decent luau, and the center is set up with villages that represent the different islands of Polynesia, showcasing their arts, crafts, foods, and culture. There's some hands-on stuff, and the show is outstanding. If you don't have to get back to the hotel at any certain time, we could head there after you have your surfing lesson."

Jack laughed. "Afraid I'm staying firmly on the beach," he said. "But a show that involves food and fire? Right up my alley."

Her body relaxed. His smile seemed to reflect genuine pleasure.

They drove along, listening to the radio and enjoying the cool breeze. When they reached the North Shore, the beach was thick with locals and surf pilgrims. She pulled the car over along the verge, and they walked across the street to a spot on the sand where portable stadium seating had been erected.

"This is kind of odd," he said, climbing up a few rows. "Bleachers on the beach?"

"They leave these up for most of the year," she said. "This is one of the most popular competition spots when the big-wave season hits, and it makes it easier to accommodate the crowds that show up. It can be a real circus, between the competitors, spectators, sponsors, and television crews."

Today, however, the view was peaceful. The surfers—ranging in age from teenagers to a few older people who looked as though they could easily be in their eighties—paddled and rose with the waves in seeming harmony, with the battles over wave territory blissfully nonexistent on this quiet, competition-free afternoon.

"It can get pretty cutthroat out there when there's a contest going on," Kali explained. "Today, looks like everyone's at peace with the island gods who have dominion over the sea."

Jack turned to her, his curiosity evident. She explained that to traditional Hawaiians, being at one with the water and the spirits who made their homes there wasn't an outlandish thought at all. Until the Calvinistic missionaries descended on the island, introducing their foreign beliefs to an ancient culture that was already thriving, surfing was almost a religion of its own.

The practice of balancing on the crests of the waves was approached with a mixture of joy and solemn reverence. Elaborately fashioned, hand-carved boards were chanted over and blessed before they found their way into the deep, rolling waters. Both royalty and commoners perfected the art of riding the tops of the waves, though strictly observed class distinctions meant that they never surfed together or even on the same beaches.

Jack was quiet, considering what she'd told him. Kali went on, taking it as a sign of his interest, and told him how surfing had enjoyed an enormous revival in the 1960s.

"It was thanks to the Gidget movies that a whole new surfing culture emerged," she said. "Surfing spread its own message of peace, love, and beaches via films, magazines, and the makers of mass-produced boards. Icons like Woody Brown and Anona Napoleon became huge celebrities. Even now, Hawaii is a mecca for surfers, who travel to the islands from every part of the world just to surf the same beaches that their heroes have."

She stopped, her mind switching to darker thoughts. Boys like Kekipi Smith lived and breathed a mix of the old Hawaiian spiritual approach and the present-day passion for bigger waves and better boards. Surfing, thought Kali, was alive and well, even if Kekipi no longer was.

Oblivious to her thoughts, Jack smiled, leaning back against the seat behind him, content. The sun glinted off the water, and a soft breeze blew across their shoulders and faces, lifting their hair. Kali felt herself relaxing.

"So, I'll stop talking for a while so you can tell me about yourself. Why the fascination with volcanoes? Which one do you find most interesting? And what's your favorite color?"

He looked thoughtful. "Hmmm. Let's see . . . Volcanoes fascinate me because of their fierce, raw power and the way they connect directly to the ongoing act of creation. I'm a little obsessed with Pompeii, but maybe it's because that's the very first one I was ever aware of, back in middle school." He looked at her appraisingly. "And right now, without a doubt, my favorite color in the whole world is the shade of blue in the sky above this beach."

He smiled. "Your turn. Why a career with the police instead of pursuing anthropology?"

She didn't say anything for a minute, deciding it was too early to talk about her status as a *kahu*.

"My grandmother was a pretty famous historian. I always loved listening to her talk about the history and culture of the islands, and I guess it got under my skin. But academia is too much sitting inside, doing research, instead of being out in the world. Though with the police . . ." She trailed off. "You see things. There's a lot of dirt out there, covered up by pretty things. Drugs, domestic violence. Makes me wonder if anything good has a chance of making the long haul. I don't want that to be the only thing I wake up to every morning, so I keep one foot in anthropology."

"That's kind of pessimistic, don't you think?"

Jack watched the water for a few minutes, his eyes following a young woman in a bright pink swimsuit who had risen to her feet on her board and was coasting along a wave, all tranquility and grace. The sunlight flickered on the surface of the turquoise water, making it sparkle.

"Look at that," he said, pointing toward the girl. "Such beauty. Do you really think that it's all bad out there?"

She thought carefully before answering, recalling Mike's optimism, remembering the barrage of gunfire that had ended his hope and his life.

"Some days, I guess I do." She smiled suddenly, wanting to dispel the heavy mood that seemed to have descended, unbidden. It was pleasant sitting here in the sunshine, next to an interesting man who appeared to enjoy her company. "Job hazard, I suppose. Most of the time, I'm a lot more fun to be with. Just ask my dog."

His face broke into a wide smile. "Oh, you have a dog? I'm kind of nuts when it comes to dogs. My sweet old retriever passed away last year, and I guess I'm still not over him. He was twelve years old. I raised him from a puppy. I still really miss him."

She nodded. "You don't need to explain. I get it. If something happened to my Hilo, I'd be pretty lost."

She reached into her bag and pulled out her phone, then scrolled through her camera images until she located a photo showing Hilo sitting proudly in the passenger seat of the Jeep.

"That's him. My second-in-command. I don't have kids, so you'll have to put up with animal photos."

He looked at the image on her phone screen and smiled. "That may be the biggest dog I've ever seen." He studied the image closely. "And he has happy eyes."

Kali glanced again at the image of the big gray dog looking happily into the phone's camera lens. She hoped that by now, he'd stopped howling and that Birta and Elvar weren't regretting their offer of dog sitting. Strangely pleased with Jack's reaction, she slipped her phone back into her bag, and then glanced at her watch.

"If you've had your fill of surfing, we could head over to the cultural center now. There's a lot to see before the luau performance actually begins. By the time you get back to the hotel tonight, you'll know everything there is to know about Hawaii."

He looked unconvinced. "I doubt that." Grinning, he added, "But I've always been a pretty good student."

They drove south along Highway 83 to the outdoor theater and show complex that made up the Polynesian Cultural Center. There were already a considerable number of people wandering about, taking in the demonstrations and displays, trying their hand at various traditional crafts.

"Ever started a fire all by yourself?" she asked as he looked around, impressed.

"No, can't say that I have. I nearly got kicked out of the Cub Scouts for deliberately tipping over a canoe with a scout leader in it before we got to the campfire part of things. Kind of put a damper on my scouting career."

"Then here's your big chance," she said, laughing.

She steered him toward one of the thatched-roof huts that served as stations for the various activities that were offered, each showcasing a Polynesian skill or historic cultural element. Inside, a young man in traditional Samoan dress was demonstrating to a half-dozen onlookers the art of rubbing two sticks together to create a flame. He rubbed the sticks rapidly against one another at an angle, and small wisps of smoke began to rise from the spot where the wood met. The small crowd listened as he explained the process.

"For this to work, the two pieces of wood must be the same type. You can't rub wood from a coconut palm against a stick from a banyan tree. You'll never get anywhere."

The presenter looked around, smiling at the watchers. "Would anyone like to try?"

Jack waited a moment to see if there were any volunteers. When no one else made a move, he raised his hand. "I'll give it a try," he said.

The young man gestured to Jack to come stand beside him. He demonstrated the proper technique, then handed Jack the two sticks he'd been working with. Jack took a deep breath and began rubbing, his face creased in concentration, the muscles in his neck and shoulders engaged. In a few short minutes, his face was red from the exertion. He paused and examined the sticks.

The small crowd began clapping, urging him on. He took another breath and resumed the rubbing motion. Smoke began to curl upward. In a moment, there was a sudden spark. The Samoan presenter leaned forward and blew gently on the smoking wood, and a small flame burst forth. The onlookers cheered, and Jack looked up triumphantly, catching Kali's eye.

"Are you going to tell me that's pretty good for a mainlander?" he asked her, smiling.

Kali shook her head. "No. I was going to tell you that if I get stranded on a desert island without a lighter, I hope you show up so that I don't have to live off raw fish."

He laughed and pushed his hair away from his brow, perspiring from the exertion of rubbing the wood together in the hot, humid air. They left the Samoan hut and wandered through the rest of the exhibits, pausing to watch demonstrations of stick games played by New Zealand's Maori, Tahitian lei weaving, and Tongan spear throwing.

Soon enough, it was time to gather for the luau. As they made their way with the flow of the crowd toward the theater seating, Kali explained the historic cooking method of the underground oven, used to slowly roast the kalua pig, which was central to the feast.

"The base of the oven—called an imu oven—is made of hot stones," she told him. "Hot stones are also stuffed inside the pig, and layers of shredded plants are used to create the steam that actually cooks the food. The whole thing gets covered with thick woven mats, and then dirt is shoveled on top. The trick is to cook everything very, very slowly, which is what makes the pork especially tender."

"Very impressive," he said. "So, if I show up on this desert island with my fire skills, you'll offer to do the cooking?"

"I'm afraid we might starve," she said, thinking wryly of her refrigerator, with its bowls of leftover rice, take-out containers, and old fruit.

"Listen," he said, interrupting her train of thought. "I hear drums."

He turned along the pathway, where a line of performers had begun to pound passionately on huge carved drums. Jack stood, transfixed, as the sound reverberated throughout the space. It seemed as though the very air were pulsing with the raw beat of the massive instruments.

Kali closed her eyes. Yes, this was Hawaii. This was the heartbeat of the islands that she loved so deeply. She felt her pulse quicken, and a sudden sense that she was part of the music overwhelmed her.

They found their seats as the show began. Night had settled around them, and Kali was content to let the dancers, singers, and actors carry her from one island to the next as they traced out the history of Polynesia through song and dance. This, she thought, was a true performance, not the sad effort made by the actors at the Wailea Palm Harbor Resort.

By the time the final performers came onstage, the entire crowd was caught up in the drama. A group of skilled fire dancers wielded lit spears, which they moved in intricate patterns through the darkness. Even Kali was exhilarated by the sheer magic of it all.

One of the dancers was carrying a traditional war club in each hand and was moving them in an elaborate choreography that was nearly impossible to follow. Kali watched as the glow from the fire flickered off something embedded along the edges of the clubs. She sat bolt upright, struck suddenly by a thought that she knew instinctively was correct.

She leaned over to Jack, then whispered in his ear. "I'll be right back," she said, her voice distracted. She pushed herself out of her seat and nudged her way down the row, past the seated spectators, most of whom were clearly annoyed that this sudden exodus was interrupting the grand finale.

Kali made her way to an area away from the music, where it was relatively quiet. She pulled her phone out and dialed Walter's home number, then waited impatiently as each ring went unanswered. Finally, Walter's voice came over the line.

"Alaka'i here," he said, sounding less than enthusiastic.

"I know what the murder weapon was."

"Kali? Where the hell are you? Is that drumming I hear?"

"It was a war club. With shark's teeth embedded along the edges. And if the lab got the age right on the wood fragment, there's a good chance it will be an authentic collector's item. Not a replica."

There was silence on the line, then a long whistle.

"Why didn't I think of that?" Walter finally asked.

"Well, it's not as though you see a lot of people walking around these days carrying ancient weapons, is it?"

"Why was Kekipi Smith in the company of someone holding a war club, for crying out loud?"

Kali was growing impatient. "I don't know, Walter. But it narrows things a bit, doesn't it? Find out if there are any collectors or any collections missing a club. And then find out if there's anyone in or around Hana, including his school and surfing friends, or friends of the family, who might have something like that in their possession."

"You still haven't said where you are."

"O'ahu still. At a show with Jack, which is how I figured this out. I'll be back tomorrow, midday."

"At a *what*? With *who*?"

She disconnected without bothering to answer and made her way back toward the theater. The crowd was already dispersing, and she waited until she saw Jack stand up and look around, slightly lost. She waved to get his attention and stood out of the way of the other guests until he'd made his way to her side. He looked at her enquiringly.

"Is everything okay?"

"Sorry about that," she said. "It's one of the cases I've been working on. Suspicious deaths of a teenage boy and an elderly lady. I had an idea and needed to call it in."

"Oh," he said, watching her. "That's a good thing, right?"

"It is," she agreed. She tried to focus on Jack, but her mind was miles away, turning over a million different scenarios, none of which made any sense at all.

They drove back to Honolulu in near silence, and it wasn't until Kali had collapsed into bed that it occurred to her that she probably had offended Jack with her preoccupation.

On Maui, Walter was also still awake, but he wasn't thinking about the war club. He was trying to decide if he'd heard Kali correctly on the phone. It had sounded like she said she was at a show with someone named Jack. To him, it had sounded like she was describing a date. Walter rolled over in the dark, mentally shaking his head. Either it had been a bad connection or there was something seriously wrong with his hearing.

CHAPTER 29

The flight back to Maui was unpleasant. The weather had taken a turn for the worse during the night, and rain pelted the small plane for the entire trip, which was slowed considerably by a buffeting wind that never seemed to be blowing in a favorable direction. The plane rocked back and forth, dropped suddenly, and pitched from one side to the other while Kali gripped the edge of her seat and swore, trying not to let Larry see how terrified she was. By the time he'd eased the Cessna to a stop on the runway, close to the private plane hangars, she had resolved never to fly anywhere ever again, for any reason.

She had tried to distract herself by thinking about work and about the farewell at the hotel with Jack. He had mentioned again the strong possibility of his transfer to the Big Island's volcano research facility, and they'd agreed that if that proved to be the case, there would be another dinner to share. *But not*, Kali had thought to herself, *if I have to fly to get there*.

She drove from the airport to the police station, feeling queasy. Her mood wasn't improved by Walter's greeting. It was clear that he'd been awaiting her arrival, as he didn't waste any time saying hello or asking how the flight had gone.

"Did you tell me you were on a date?"

Kali gave an exaggerated sigh and sat down at Walter's desk, then tucked her feet beneath her. When she gave no response, he continued to question her.

"With a man, right? Not some oversize, homeless hound dog that you rescued and took out for a burger? And get your filthy feet off my chair. Hara just cleaned the upholstery."

Kali swung her feet onto the floor and tried to look nonchalant. "Abusing the trainees? And yes, I was with a man. A source for the investigation, that's all. But he does happen to like dogs."

"Explains what he was doing in your company, I suppose."

"Oh, that's hilarious. Men don't hate me."

Walter snorted. "Yeah, I know. Mysterious tattooed tribal babe. Irresistible. You and Hara should open a dating service." He looked up, not even close to being through. "He have a name? An arrest record? Any connection at all to the work you were sent over there to do?"

"As a matter of fact," said Kali, "he was one of the speakers at that renewable-energy conference."

"And a name?"

"Dr. Jack Bader," Kali said, emphasizing the academic title.

Walter raised his brow. "Well, la di da," he said. "That should last all of two minutes. I suppose you corralled him into dinner as part of the investigation so you can write it off as an expense."

"Yes," said Kali. "And also because he's got the most stunning red hair I've ever seen. Like a burst of lava."

"Great," said Walter. "Moving on to things that actually matter, I talked to Stitches first thing this morning about the autopsy results for Grace Sawyer. Death was caused by a blow to the skull from a heavy object, which may or may not be the same weapon used to kill Kekipi. Regarding the wood splinter and your war club theory, she says it's completely consistent with the boy's wound, and that if the club was old and a bit unstable, a forcible blow to the skull could certainly have dislodged one of the shark's teeth and left it in the wound."

"And?"

"She's running some additional tests to determine the precise type of tropical wood. I don't know exactly how we can leverage this information, unless, of course, we can come up with a collector or a dealer who's missing a specific piece. We don't have any theft reports for anything resembling a club. Hara checked back over a ten-year period island-wide, but there's nothing even close."

Kali got up and walked toward the window. From here, she could see the stretch of ocean close to where Kekipi had been discovered. So many secrets would always be hidden by the dead, she thought. She turned back to Walter.

"There could be dozens of clubs like this in people's homes, hanging on walls," she said.

"True dat," Walter agreed, "but here's the good news, if you can call it that. There are only two actual collectors in Hawaii who specialize in ancient weapons. That includes the buying and selling of. And, as good fortune would have it, both collectors are located on Maui."

He reached across his desk and retrieved a single-page printout showing two names and addresses. "This is them. One's a retired professor from the University of Hawaii who has a pretty well-respected collection. He guest curates a lot of the historic exhibits that get loaned out to major museums in Asia and on the mainland. Name's Kinard, and he lives alone over in Lahaina. The other guy is Franklin Josephs, and he's in Kahana, north of Lahaina. So you should be able to get to both of them today."

"What's the background on Josephs?" asked Kali.

"Seems to be more of a dealer than a dedicated collector. Acquires pieces from estate sales and the like. Probably reads the obits religiously and approaches the families of multigenerational locals to sift through their leavings. He's on our books because a complaint was made against him by a seller a few years back, an older woman who claimed she'd been bullied into selling."

"Or was pissed off when she realized that she should have held out for more," said Kali sardonically.

"That's what we figured at the time. She dropped the charges, so it never got to court, but we still have the record of the complaint. And I did you a favor . . . We've got a search warrant for both properties already. Hara will meet you later on at the Josephs residence. Just give him a call when you're through talking to the professor."

Kali took the copies of the search warrants and the paper with the names and addresses from Walter and moved toward the door. "Okay. On my way."

"While you're taking care of that, I'm heading back out

to do another door-to-door," he said. "Unlikely that any of the locals saw anything and haven't stepped forward, but there aren't a lot of options. We're also re-questioning Kekipi's friends about war clubs and historic Hawaiian artifacts. His mother says she never heard mention of anyone having one, but you never know whose granddad might have one in a closet somewhere. If they were playing warriors on the beach, no one's likely to admit they took a swing at Kekipi."

Kali agreed. She tried not to let herself feel too hopeful. The possibility that they'd at last come up with a plausible theory regarding the murder weapon didn't mean they'd necessarily find it or the person who'd used it.

She drove by her house to retrieve Hilo from Elvar and Birta. She planned to use the less busy southern Pi'ilani Highway later on. Part of that road was a glorified dirt track that led to the western area of the island and the towns of Lahaina and Kahana. It was one of the reasons she was so attached to her battered Jeep, which never seemed to mind the unfinished surfaces, some filled with potholes that were difficult to negotiate following heavy rains.

As she pulled into the yard, Hilo, alerted by the familiar sound of the engine, came galloping through the path opening in the trees in greeting. As she climbed from the Jeep, he jumped up on his hind legs and knocked her to the ground.

"I think he missed you," said a voice. Turning, Kali saw Elvar sprinting along the path, in pursuit.

"I missed him, too," said Kali, laughing.

"How was O'ahu?" Elvar asked, helping her up. "Did you have a chance to enjoy yourself at all?"

She turned her head slightly, feeling her face flush.

She clapped her hands and pointed to the Jeep. Hilo, understanding, sprang instantly into the passenger seat.

"It was mostly work," she said. "Lots of traffic. The usual mass of tourists."

Elvar smiled. "Well, we're all glad you're home, safe and sound. Birta says to come by later if you like. She's making up a batch of that seafood stew from that recipe you gave her a while ago. And I can show you the sandalwood knife handle with the awapuhi flower we hunted on our hike. It turned out pretty well. I've also got a couple of weapons finished for the film people. I wouldn't mind getting your opinion on their authenticity. I even managed to get hold of some really old wood."

She nodded slowly. "That'd be nice." She took a small step away, feeling a chill along her spine, like icy fingers tracing a path. "It might be late when I get back, though. Right now, I've got to go to the other side of the island to do some interviews."

"Well, no one here's in any hurry. Stop over when you get home."

He waved and turned back down the path, then faded into the shadows. She watched him as he disappeared, then turned slowly toward the Jeep. Hilo barked in encouragement, and she slid behind the wheel and absently scratched the dog's head.

She turned the key and headed down the driveway. *Surely not*, she thought. Of course he was concerned about creating the most authentic weapons possible. She pushed the thought out of her mind, concentrating on the road. Maybe she was completely wrong about the significance of the war club and its possible connection to the island's legends. Even as the thought flitted through her mind, she felt the skin on her arms prickle, as if in warning.

The drive to Lahaina took the better part of two hours. It had once ranked as an important fishing port, but the small town now served as a tourist magnet, with rows of shops, art galleries, and restaurants. She checked the directions that were printed next to the addresses and found her way to 21 Beach Lane. The house turned out to be a small bungalow with a wide shaded porch. She parked and warned Hilo to stay put, then made her way up the shallow set of steps onto the porch and to the front door.

A surprisingly fit elderly man wearing wire-rimmed glasses and an old Rolling Stones T-shirt over faded black jeans answered her knock.

"Aloha. Professor Kinard?"

The man nodded, smiling in a friendly manner. "One and the same," he said. "Can I help you?"

Kali smiled in return. "Kali Māhoe. I'm a detective with the Maui Police Department. Do you have a few moments? I have some questions about traditional Hawaiian weapons, and I'm told you're the man to talk to."

Kinard's gaze swept over Kali, and he took in the tattoo visible beneath the edge of her sleeve. "My. Detective. That's interesting," he said, standing back and holding the door open. "Come in, come in. I'd be pleased to talk story with you."

Kali noted with approval the older man's use of the Hawaiian phrase "talk story," which meant to have a relaxed, respectful conversation.

"Thank you, sir," she said, entering the coolness of the house. Kinard's interest in Hawaiiana was evidenced in the decor of the living room. Bamboo floors were covered with woven mats, and a number of old framed kapa cloths were displayed on the walls.

"May I offer you something cold to drink?" Kinard asked politely.

"I'm fine. Thanks," said Kali.

"Then please . . . sit down and make yourself comfortable."

She sat down in one of two wide bamboo chairs that faced each other near the front windows. The light was good, and Kali imagined the professor sitting here, reading and enjoying the sunshine. He chose the chair across from her and nodded gravely.

"Welcome to my home."

Kali nodded in return, then glanced toward the kapa cloths. "Those are exceptionally fine pieces of work," she said.

"Yes, early examples. The bark used was soaked and pounded repeatedly over a period of weeks to attain that level of pliability. Those particular pieces were most likely items of ritual clothing for a chieftain's family, worn only for important occasions. No one today spends the proper amount of time in the cloth preparation."

Kali peered at the one closest to where she sat. The beautiful bark cloth had been painted with images of fish, each finely detailed.

"I'm told you also have a collection of war clubs, which is actually why I'm here."

"Yes, I have several. It's not a large collection, but each of the clubs is authentic. Would you care to see them?"

"If it's not too much trouble."

"It's not," said Kinard. "I keep them under glass in my

workroom. Do you mind following me? I assure you it
will be much faster than carrying them all out here."

"Of course," said Kali. She walked behind Kinard as
he made his way down a short hallway and into a large
room overlooking the back garden. It was obviously used
primarily as an office, but there was a long glass-covered
case running along one of the walls. Kali walked over to
it, then looked in with curiosity. The case, which was
locked, was lined with a length of dark red velvet. On its
surface, two daggers and four war clubs of varying
shapes and sizes had been deliberately placed to show
their carvings to the best advantage.

Kinard took a key from a small drawer in his desk and
unlocked the case. He reached in and extracted a hook-
shaped club that had been fitted with a rim of shark's
teeth and handed it to Kali.

"A fishhook club," said Kali, studying it closely. "Koa
wood, with teeth from a tiger shark."

Kinard smiled, pleased. "Exactly." He looked at Kali
appraisingly. "Are you native Hawaiian?" he asked, with
no hint of embarrassment. "I'm assuming from your tattoos that you are."

"Yes," said Kali, equally at ease. "My grandmother
was an historian here in Maui. The tattoos are to make
sure I never forget my lineage."

Kinard nodded in approval. Kali knew she needn't explain that the tattoos had been received the traditional
way, with a bone needle tapped with a rock, to make sure
the needle pierced the skin deeply enough, while she bit
down on a piece of wood.

"Too much is being lost," he said. "Thank goodness
people have come to their senses, and the language is

being reintroduced to schoolchildren. I used to despair that the culture would simply disappear." He paused. "May I ask who your grandmother was?"

"Pualani Pali," Kali said.

Kinard looked up, his eyebrows raised. "My goodness. I knew her, you know." He walked over to a bookshelf on the opposite wall, extracted a hardcover book, its cover showing that it had been frequently used. He walked back over and handed it to Kali,who placed the club back into its empty slot in the display case.

"*Lore and Legend of the Hawaiian Archipelago*, by Pualani Pali, Ph.D.," she read. She looked up at Kinard and smiled.

"Look just inside the cover," he said, and Kali opened the book. Inside, there was an inscription, written in her grandmother's familiar, graceful script: *To my dear friend and colleague, whom Hawaii has embraced as one of her own.*

Kali touched the writing gently, then handed the book back to Kinard.

"We met at the university during one of her many lectures there. She was a brilliant woman," Kinard said, his voice clearly reflecting respect.

"She was, indeed," said Kali, suddenly overcome with a feeling of acute loss. She turned back to the case and bent over slightly as she looked closely at the other pieces, trying to regain her composure.

"These all seem to be koa wood," she noted.

"They are. As I'm sure you know, it's very long lasting and resilient. And quite hard. The teeth vary. Several of the clubs have teeth from more than one type of shark. One has boar's teeth."

"I don't suppose you've sold any of your pieces or had anything stolen from you over the past few years?"

Kinard looked surprised. "No, indeed. I've been gathering these pieces since my days at the university. I invest only in the authentic weapons, of course, and they're surprisingly hard to come by. Plenty of cheap replicas floating around, but I'm not interested in those, not even the more well-made ones. Occasionally, I get a request from someone who'd like to see them."

"How often does that happen?"

"Rarely. I think the last time was about a year ago. A young man making weapons was interested in seeing how they were constructed by early indigenous peoples."

Again, she felt the chill.

"Do you remember who that was?"

He frowned. "I'm afraid I don't remember. He wasn't Hawaiian—I do remember that—but if you ask me to describe him, I won't be able to. I seem to remember that he had an accent, but I'm afraid I really don't remember much about the visit other than the knife discussion."

She glanced again at the contents of the glass case, trying not to show she was bothered by what she'd just heard. Silently, she berated herself for allowing herself to be suspicious that it might be Elvar. The very idea was ridiculous in the extreme, and she pushed the thought away.

"How did you find the pieces you've invested in?" she asked.

"Several pieces were advertised, but the others belonged to families that were dispersing the belongings of someone who had recently passed on." He peered at Kali, knowing that she understood the implication.

Kali nodded. "Of course. As I'm sure you're aware, there are still many traditional Hawaiians who believe that keeping the belongings of a family member around after the person has died can bind the spirit to a place," she said. "Giving away personal items allows the spirit to move on unencumbered."

"Yes," agreed Kinard. "Though, from a practical standpoint, valuable items are often sold, rather than given away. When I've been fortunate to hear of something of this nature becoming available for purchase, naturally, I follow up to see if there might be an item worth adding to my small collection."

Kali looked at one of the clubs, which was shaped like a broad paddle. "That's a nice piece."

"Again, the teeth are from a tiger shark," said Kinard. "What many people don't realize is that the clubs weren't necessarily used to hit or strike an opponent with force, but were often used with a slicing motion. The teeth would rip the skin and cause considerable damage. If the teeth were long enough, and the club was handled by an expert, the damage might extend to broken bones or pierced organs."

Kali moved toward the door. Kinard closed and locked the case, then replaced the key in his desk drawer.

"If someone broke in here," Kali said, "that case doesn't offer much of a challenge. Especially not with a glass top and the key a few feet away in a drawer. Do you have anything else, perhaps more valuable, stored elsewhere?"

Kinard smiled. "Everything I have is right here in this case," he said. "I'm afraid I hold no illusions about security. In my nearly eighty years as a resident of this planet, I've learned that if someone is determined to rob you of something, they are unlikely to be dissuaded by the small gestures made by locks and keys. I choose to go about my final days in as trusting a manner as possible. Shame on those who would take advantage of that."

Shame on them indeed, thought Kali.

"Though you seem certain that no one has had access to your collection, I'm afraid it will be necessary to borrow the pieces for a short time, Professor. I'll help you wrap them up. We should need them only for a few days at most."

"Oh?" He looked at the glass case and back to her, one eyebrow raised.

"Yes. I apologize for the inconvenience, but it's to do with an investigation."

"I understand," he said. He seemed concerned, and Kali sought to reassure him.

"No harm will come to them. You have my personal guarantee."

She wrapped and labeled each item separately, supervised closely by the professor. Kali said good-bye to Kinard after accepting his invitation to come back for dinner in the near future so that they might talk more about Hawaii and her grandmother's work.

She climbed back into the Jeep, where Hilo sat waiting, his head resting on the dashboard, his tail thumping the back of the seat. In the rearview mirror, she could see Kinard standing in his doorway, watching as she pulled away. She gave a brief wave, but he didn't respond.

She radioed the station and was put through to Hara.

"I'm heading over to the Josephs house now."

CHAPTER 30

The sunlight was brilliant, and the afternoon was plea-santly warm. Kali eased back out onto the main road, heading north. She knew this road well but was fully aware of its ability to deteriorate rapidly in bad weather. The earthen cliffs bordering one side could disintegrate into dangerous mudslides when the heavy rains came, and she'd been caught on the wrong side of timing on more than one occasion.

She pulled off onto a small secondary road that was poorly marked by a bent sign, and drove slowly until she found the driveway leading to the home of Franklin Josephs. The house at the end of the driveway was an ill-kempt single-story with a rusted pickup truck parked half in and half out of the garage. The lawn was overgrown, and the trim around the windows and doors had peeled to the point that the paint color was indistinguishable.

Hara was already there. Kali climbed out of the Jeep and joined him beside the police cruiser.

"You can be the tough guy today," she told him. "I'll be the friendly local who's interested in his collection."

There was no reply to their knock on the screen door. From just inside, Kali could hear the sound of a television, tuned to a home renovation show. She knocked again and heard a squeaking sound, as though someone was repositioning themselves on a chair.

"Anyone home?" she called.

There was still no reply.

"Maui police," announced Hara, his voice authoritative. "Come to the door, or we'll let ourselves in."

This time, there was a response.

"What the hell do you want?" It was a woman's voice, sounding extremely displeased. "If you're here for Frankie, I don't know where he is. I haven't seen him for a couple of weeks."

The woman to whom the voice belonged came into view. She was in her late fifties, as far as Kali could tell, and was wearing a nightdress of thin, faded cotton. Her feet were bare, and she looked as though the idea of washing her hair had long ceased to be of any personal interest. Kali did a quick mental calculation, remembering that Josephs had been described as being in his midthirties.

"Are you Franklin Josephs's mother?"

"Well, I'm not his sweetheart," said the woman, looking suspiciously at Kali.

"We're here about his weapons collection," said Hara. "We have a warrant to search the premises."

"What?" she said, frowning at the document Hara extended toward her. "Guns? There aren't any guns in this house. I won't have it."

"Not guns," Kali said. "Historic Hawaiian weapons. We've been told he has a collection, and we need to speak to him about that. It's our understanding that he's—" Kali cut herself off. "We understand that he's considered to be a bit of an expert in the area, and we need some help in a murder investigation."

"Well, he's not here. I already said." The woman's voice was calmer, as though she had been mollified by the idea of her son being useful. "I don't know where he is, or when he's coming back, and I don't care, either."

"Did he move out?" Kali asked.

She shrugged. "His stuff's still here. He just took off with that trampy girlfriend of his. Didn't say when he'd be back. Didn't leave any money for groceries, either."

"Exactly when did you last see him?" Kali asked.

"Told you. A couple of weeks."

"And you have no idea where he's staying?" Hara asked, his tone suggesting he didn't believe her.

"I don't," she snapped. "I've called everywhere. I'm out of beer, I'm out of bread, and I don't have anyone to take me to the bank or the store. He's always been a lousy son."

Kali and Hara exchanged looks.

"Right. Very sorry about your difficulties, but we'll take a look at his collection now," said Kali.

"Suit yourself," she said, pushing the screen door open. Kali and Hara walked inside. Hara looked around with barely concealed disgust. Franklin Josephs's mother was a slob.

"Is this his house or yours?" Kali asked.

"His. He was letting me stay, on account of my no-good asshole of a husband getting hit by a car and not leaving me any insurance."

Kali wondered briefly if he had been hit by the car or had jumped out in front of it on purpose.

"And does Franklin have a room of his own?"

"Room? He has a bleeding suite of rooms, all his." She looked toward the back of the house. "Me? I have the sofa."

Followed by Hara, Kali walked through the living room, past the television set, and into the hallway that ran to the rear of the house. She opened the first door and found herself in a large bedroom. Not tidy, but definitely an improvement on the front of the house. She looked briefly in the closet and the small chest of drawers, but they were filled with clothing.

The next room proved more interesting. For starters, it was locked. Mrs. Josephs shook her head when asked about a key, and Kali didn't argue. If Mrs. Josephs had one, she reasoned, she'd have already been inside to snoop around herself. She looked at Hara.

"Why don't you stay here and keep Mrs. Josephs company? I'll be right back."

She walked outside and located the window to the locked room. Near the garage, she found an old five-gallon plastic paint bucket and carried it to the spot beneath the window, then climbed up to peer inside. There was no curtain, and she could see easily, despite the security grating that had been fitted over the window. The room was sparsely furnished, but there was a small desk, and two large trunks against one wall. The rest of the room was taken up by a large metal filing cabinet and a sagging easy chair.

Kali walked back to the Jeep and opened the toolbox

she kept in the back. She removed a small pry bar and returned to the front door. Mrs. Josephs was standing there, looking out with some alarm at Hilo, who had climbed out of the Jeep and was sitting in the shade it cast on the driveway.

"Is that some kind of horse?" Mrs. Josephs asked as Kali walked past her and opened the door.

"Yup," she said. "Teeth like a bear, though."

The woman stepped back, then followed Kali inside, openly suspicious.

"We're going to open the door to your son's room, as well as the filing cabinet and the trunks inside."

Mrs. Josephs scowled but didn't protest. "Go ahead, honey. Knock yourself out. Wouldn't mind seeing for myself what's in there."

They had the door open in less than a minute. Hara stood, half guarding the entrance and half watching. The trunks were also locked. Kali made short work of the locks, snapping them with the pry bar.

In the first, there were several ceremonial headdresses and an embroidered robe. There was something about them that struck Kali as mass produced rather than handmade, and she set them back inside the trunk, exactly as she'd found them.

The second trunk held the weapons. There were only three, but these were clearly old. Besides a short dagger, there were two war clubs, each wrapped loosely in soft cloth. Kali looked through the desk, but there was nothing she could find that pertained to the weapons collection belonging to Josephs. She noted that the space was wired for high-speed Internet service, but there was no computer in the room. Josephs had to have a laptop, which he'd probably taken with him.

In the filing cabinet, she and Hara found things of more interest. There were neatly sorted files that detailed a fairly successful eBay business trading in Hawaiian artifacts. There were orders and receipts for each transaction, along with detailed descriptions of the items that had been bought or sold, many with pictures attached. There was also information about whom he'd purchased each item from and whom he'd sold it to, including their contact information. It looked as though Franklin Josephs was a fairly professional businessman, even if he hadn't lucked out in the parental genetic pool.

There were too many files to go through on short notice, so Kali instructed Hara to bundle them all up while she collected the war clubs. When they finished, they made their way back to the front of the house. Mrs. Josephs had taken up position on the couch and was staring without any apparent enthusiasm or comprehension as a television presenter mindlessly destroyed a beautiful natural stone wall with white paint.

"We're taking your son's historic weapons and some files," she said. "Officer Hara will give you an itemized receipt. They'll be returned later."

"Take whatever you want," Mrs. Josephs said, not looking up.

"I need you to sign this, then. It says you understand I'm removing these weapons and documents for official purposes, and that you agree the list is accurate."

"Fine," she said, then scrawled her name on the form Kali extended to her. Still without looking up, she asked, more quietly, "Did my son do something awful?"

"Not that we know of," Kali answered, wondering if the woman really even cared, and interested that she should ask. "We'll be sure to let you know if we find out otherwise."

"Yeah, you do that," Mrs. Josephs mumbled. "And bring that stuff back. Maybe I can sell it."

They let themselves out, and Kali whistled to Hilo to get back into the Jeep. As she began to pull out, her cell phone rang. It was Walter.

"Mango," he said.

"Banana," answered Kali, wondering if Walter had suddenly made up a secret code.

"No, damn it," said Walter, sounding slightly more exasperated than usual. "The wood. It's mango. Whatever Kekipi was hit with, it was made of mango wood."

"Got it," said Kali. That, at least, might narrow things down a bit. "I'll fill you in on the collectors when I get back to Hana."

"Looking for a dinner invite?"

Dinner. The invitation to seafood stew with Elvar and Birta. Well, that would have to wait until another time.

"Guess I am," she said.

"I'll warn the missus. See if you can get here by six. The girls have some kind of event to get to later, so we're going to eat early. We can talk after they leave."

Kali drove south along the highway, taking her time on the dirt section of the road as she drew closer to Hana. She was hungry, and whatever Mrs. Alaka'i had prepared for the evening would likely be delicious. Nor would Mrs. Alaka'i care if Hilo made himself comfortable on the wide stone terrace. And, if the past was anything to go by, she'd leave with plenty of leftovers to stash in her sad, almost empty fridge.

CHAPTER 31

The light had just begun to creep across the floor through the uncurtained window, but it was bereft of warmth. Kali rolled over and pressed her face into the back of the sofa, engulfed by a feeling of profound loneliness. She admitted to herself, finally, that the reason she slept here instead of in her own bed was that the empty space beside her was too much to face—more weight at the beginning of the day than she had the strength to carry.

Her mind searched for something normal, something familiar and pleasant that had nothing to do with murder or theft. She thought back to dinner at Walter's. His wife, Nina, had prepared tender pulled pork with sweet potatoes. And there was coconut cake for dessert. Walter's three daughters—Beth, Lara, and Suki, who called her

Auntie Kali—had surrounded her with their laughter and happy noise.

When dinner was over and Nina was busy readying the girls to go out, Walter and Kali had retreated to the lanai. Walter had built a fire in the stone pit, and they had pulled their chairs close to the warmth. Once the sun went down, even Hawaii had her moments of chill, and the two had relaxed for a few minutes, enjoying the warmth, before they'd turned their thoughts to murder.

"The professor said he estimates that over eighty-five percent of the authentic weapons he's looked at over the years have been made from koa wood," Kali had said. "He's seen a few carved from monkeypod and mango, but not many. Koa, being hard, plentiful, and long lasting, was—and still is—the wood of choice. In the past, it was also a class thing. Being especially beautiful and coveted, it was considered a premier wood and a worthy choice for a warrior."

"Snobbery among the war crowd?"

"Something like that. The point is, if the club that was used to kill Kekipi was made of mango, that eliminates a lot of choices."

"Sure. All we have to do is find the one guy with the right mango club."

"The lab is running tests on all the weapons we've collected so far, just in case. And these might help," said Kali, pulling the envelope with its stack of receipts and orders belonging to Franklin Josephs out of her worn canvas messenger bag. "The second collector, Josephs, has been running a fairly profitable buy-and-sell business for about the past ten years, lately mostly Internet based. He's sold three mango clubs in that time. All of them are trimmed with shark's teeth, all of them are at least a hundred years old, and only one of them was sold to a buyer here in the islands. Maui, specifically. The other sales were to mainland collectors."

Walter leaned forward. "So," he said, "assuming that a mainland collector would hardly plan a vacation that involved packing a large tooth-rimmed killing weapon, we should pay a visit to the Maui purchaser."

"Worth a shot."

"Who is it? Do we have a current address?"

"We do." Kali paused, enjoying herself. "The collector is one Polunu Hausuka of Hamoa Beach, just down the road."

Walter made a choking sound. "No kidding? Funny how he keeps popping up, isn't it?"

"I was thinking the same thing. At least we now know what he's been spending some of his hard-earned money on."

"Yeah, it's very nice that he's contributing to the local economy, rather than buying stuff off-island."

"At least he's buying. That, alone, is surprising."

They got up and walked back into the house, still fragrant with the smells from dinner. Walter, looking thoughtful, walked her to her car and told her to go home and get some sleep, that he'd pull another search warrant for their field trip to visit Polunu.

She slept poorly again, unable to remember her dreams. She got up and made herself a cup of strong black tea, then cleaned up the small kitchen. It was nearly ten o'clock by the time she heard Walter's cruiser pull up. She went out to meet him on the front porch and noticed that he had his 9mm Smith & Wesson holstered. He looked at her, an eyebrow raised in question.

"I'm guessing you'll be ready with some obscure

prayer to keep us safe, instead of something potentially useful, like your gun."

She shook her head. There had already been enough gunfire in her life, but she wasn't stupid. "I'm armed. And I'm bringing Hilo."

"No you're not. Hara's already developing a procedural ulcer about civilian dogs in official police equipment, and I'm pretty sure finding hair all over the seat from you bringing your pet monster along would send him over the edge."

"Would you rather take the Jeep? If Polunu's there, the police car will probably spook him."

"Your transmission is shot."

"Just when I go into reverse."

Walter snorted. "Suppose," he said, "that you have to make a quick getaway. Or, heaven forbid, join a pursuit. That thing is likely to fall apart underneath you."

Kali was offended. "It hasn't yet."

They'd reached the police car, and Walter opened the door. "It only takes once, you know."

"I don't have any trouble getting around. You're just heavy handed. Or spoiled from driving this sissy automatic."

"Yeah, that's it," Walter said. "You're navigating, by the way. The GPS is on the blink again. What's our turn-off to Polunu's place?"

"Next right. He lives on the road that heads downhill toward Kipahulu Valley."

"I know the turn."

"Do we know if he lives alone?"

Walter shook his head. "No missus or roommate listed in anything we have on him."

Kali stared out the window. Even petty crooks like

Polunu Hausuka had friends. Mike had thought that the meth dealers had been alone. She hadn't stopped him from leading the raid. The meth dealers had had plenty of friends, and they'd all been expecting the cops.

They parked a short distance from Polunu's house. There was no garage, and the overgrown driveway was empty. There was a light on somewhere in the house, however.

"We've got a white delivery van, nineteen ninety-one Chevy model, registered to him as active, but I don't see a vehicle anywhere in sight," said Walter.

They walked toward the front door.

"Wait," she said, squatting near a set of clearly visible tire tracks. "Look familiar?"

Walter joined her. He looked closely at the mismatched tracks and gave a low whistle.

"Mind if I give a cautious 'Eureka'?" he asked. "These look like they could be a match for the tracks in the clearing. See the big patch mark on this one, about two inches from the edge?"

"I see it. We'll get photos while we're here."

They approached the house carefully.

"Light's coming from the kitchen," she said, keeping her voice low. "No sound of a television or radio."

Walter turned to Kali. "Okay, let's knock on the door and say hello."

They climbed the front steps. Kali stood beside the door, just out of sight, while Walter knocked, his gun drawn. There was no answer. He tried the handle and glanced at Kali. The door was unlocked.

He called out loudly enough for anyone inside to hear. "Polunu Hausuka, you home? Maui police. We've got a pizza for you."

There was no answer. Flies buzzed against the door's outer screen. Kali and Walter waited, listening for the sound of any movement from within.

"Shall we?" Walter asked, and Kali nodded in agreement. Kali eased the door open and stepped aside, allowing Walter to enter first. She followed quickly. It took them less than a minute to move through the small house.

"There's no one here," Walter said.

Kali walked through the dim living room, past a cheap-looking sofa, then stepped through a doorway back into the kitchen. The light they'd seen from outside came from a bare bulb hanging over the small wooden kitchen table. On the table, a full cup of coffee sat, cold. The milk had congealed on the surface.

She nodded toward the coffee cup. "That's been here for a while," she said.

"Yeah. Looks like he's out for the day."

Kali said nothing but returned to the living room area and switched on the overhead lights. On the wall over the sofa was a watercolor painting of a hula dancer, framed against an impossibly full moon. The television, a large and very new model, occupied one wall, positioned next to a stereo with an elaborate speaker system. It all looked expensive.

"Little bigger than a candy bar. I'm guessing he didn't walk out of a store with those underneath his arm. Means he's got some spending money," noted Walter. "And look at that," he added, pointing to the opposite wall.

A long spear was displayed, mounted carefully on sturdy hooks.

"Okay." She looked critically from the spear to the sagging sofa. "And he's also making significant financial investments in historic objects instead of furniture. That doesn't explain why he would take a valuable war club to the beach and then hit a teenager over the head with it. What's the connection?"

Walter turned to Kali in mock amazement. "You've actually met Polunu Hausuka, yes? And seen the video that's circulating? Not exactly a brain trust."

"Okay, but why would he be carrying something of historic value around with him?"

Walter looked at the spear, admiring the carving, clearly impressed. "Maybe he was taking it somewhere to show off," he offered. "Or to resell for some fast cash."

"Or," said Kali, thinking about the information they'd pulled on Polunu, "he was using it in the luau show."

"That's a possibility, I suppose," said Walter. "But unlikely."

They made a cursory search of the house. In one of the house's two small bedrooms, they found a carved ceremonial drum.

"Not exactly a weapon," observed Kali, "but it definitely looks valuable."

The closet revealed that Polunu also had a lot of new clothing, including an expensive-looking leather jacket. Walter pulled out the jacket, eyeing it with great curiosity.

"Now, where on earth does he wear that? He'd roast to death in it in Hawaii," he said.

"Where did he even get it?" asked Kali.

Kali walked into the other of the house's bedrooms, a tight space that appeared to be used mainly for storage. She lifted a cardboard box off the floor and carried it out to the kitchen table. She pulled open the flaps and found that the box, though rather large, contained only a small throwing ax, made of koa wood. There was also a shipping receipt. She took it out and examined it carefully. "This is interesting."

Walter peered into the box. Kali held up the slip of paper.

"This receipt is from Josephs," she said. "It's dated over two weeks ago, which jibes with the records we found in his files. The receipt is for this throwing ax, and for a war club made of mango and trimmed with shark's teeth."

Walter and Kali exchanged looks.

"If it's here, it's hidden," said Walter. "But it doesn't make any sense that he'd hide one artifact away and leave the other one sitting here in this box. He's unlikely to have gotten rid of anything of historic value, even if it was used to kill Kekipi."

"We haven't checked the yard or the garage."

"You do that. I'll make one last cupboard and closet search inside. Looks like it's time we brought him in for questioning."

Kali let herself out the back door and into the overgrown yard. The garage was empty except for a lawn mower and a few tools. The exterior wood siding had large gaps in it, and no interior shelves or other places to leave anything, especially something of value. The floor was dirt, much of it sprouted with weeds and tufts of grass, which benefited from the sunlight flowing through the spaces between the wallboards.

She walked to the rear of the garage and looked out of the building's single window. A good-sized aluminum storage shed had been erected behind the garage, completely out of sight from the driveway or the house, half concealed by tall shrubs. She could see that the door was secured with a heavy chain and a padlock. There were no windows visible.

"Walter!"

She heard his footsteps hurrying across the wooden porch on the back of the house. As he joined her, she nodded toward the shed.

"This shed looks brand new, and that's interesting," she said.

"There's a padlock on the door."

"Do we have just cause for a little forced entry?"

Walter pretended to consider the question carefully. "Depends, I suppose, on who you're asking. If you're asking me, I'd say it's time to locate a pair of heavy-duty bolt cutters. There could be a murder weapon inside that shed. Maybe a body to go along with it, if you're seriously questioning a superior officer about his decision-making skills."

Kali looked disapprovingly at her uncle.

"Don't give me any stink face," he told her.

It took them nearly twenty minutes, working in turns, to cut through the heavy chain with the tools they'd taken from the trunk of the cruiser. The door swung open, and Walter stepped inside the shed, shining his flashlight around. There wasn't much to see other than a stack of tarpaulins in a corner and a few gallons of half-used paint. Otherwise, the space was completely empty.

"Well, this is disappointing," said Walter, the disgust evident in his tone. "Why in the hell was it even locked?"

"You want to do a psychological analysis of the way thieves think?" asked Kali.

"Probably just habit," said Walter, "the way you flip off a light when you leave the room, or automatically lock your door behind you."

"I don't think so. The floor looks like something's been repeatedly dragged across it, and the number of tarps could have been used to cover up something large and potentially valuable he wanted to keep hidden. The size of that chain definitely suggests he had something here that he didn't want anyone to take."

"Like?"

"Canoe, propped up on its end? Something historic?"

Walter shut off his light. "Well, whatever it was, it's not here now."

"Yeah," said Kali. "And neither is Polunu Hausuka."

They closed the shed door and put the tools back into the car, then carried the spear, the throwing ax, and the ceremonial drum to the car. Walter filled out a notice alerting Polunu to the whereabouts of his belongings and whom to call for their return.

Later that night, while lying on the sofa, with Hilo nearby, snoring happily, Kali wondered about Polunu and his motivations. His collection suggested that he had some pride in his Hawaiian heritage, as well as an appreciation for beauty. Why, she wondered, was he squandering his time on Earth as a thief?

She fell into a deep sleep. This time, there were no gods or goddesses appearing in her dream space, delivering obscure messages. There was no restless tossing and turning. Just a deep and welcome darkness.

CHAPTER 32

At five thirty the next morning, Walter's cell phone rang. He fumbled on the night table next to his bed and located the source of disruption. His wife rolled over, still asleep.

"Alaka'i here."

"Hi, handsome."

Recognizing the voice, he grunted, immediately annoyed. "What do you want, Makena?"

"Money," came the slightly slurred voice on the other end of the line. "Money, money, money. And lots of kisses."

He disconnected, dropped the phone onto the table, and pulled the light cover up around his neck.

The phone rang again. Walter looked at it with aversion, then grabbed it, slipped out of bed, and walked into the hall and into the kitchen. He continued to let it ring, expecting Makena to give up. She always did. After five rings, the call switched over to his voice mail. But seconds later, the phone began ringing again. He hit the AC-CEPT CALL button, but before he could begin the lecture that was on the tip of his tongue, Makena spoke.

"Money for information, asshole. I saw something, and believe me, you want to know what it was."

"What, no sense of civic duty, Makena? Right and wrong? Balancing out the darkness with a little light?" He knew it was useless to appeal to this side of her, if it even existed. "What did you see?"

"I'll tell you for five hundred dollars."

He laughed. "Even if I trusted you, which I don't, I wouldn't give you five hundred dollars. I don't even *have* five hundred dollars."

Makena swore. "That's okay. You're always such a jerk. I'll just go to the other guy, Mr. Fancy Boat. Bet he'll pay."

Makena hung up, and Walter felt suddenly uneasy. Was Makena playing at blackmail? Maybe she *had* seen something. He shrugged, dismissing the feeling. Chances were if she had actually witnessed a crime involving a boat, it was nothing more impressive than someone dumping trash overboard, or a local official with his pants down, taking a cruise with someone else's wife.

He went out to the front porch and looked at the sky. It was a clear morning, and he needed to locate Polunu. He decided to start by checking his address again to see if he'd come home. And if he had no luck there, he'd drive over to the resort and see if anyone on the luau staff had any idea where he might be. *Drunk in a ditch, most likely*, thought Walter. Or laying low, in the hope the resort manager hadn't yet caught wind of the YouTube video of the incident with the woman tourist.

After a cup of strong Kona coffee and two bowls of cereal—the second one doused with coffee creamer—Walter got dressed and headed out.

Several miles away, Kali was also beginning the day. Like Walter, she had been jarred awake by a call from Makena, which she'd ignored.

She could hear the *ding*, *ding*, *ding* of a hammer striking an anvil and put down her coffee cup. Elvar was up and working. It would probably be a good idea to stop by and offer her apologies for ignoring his dinner invitation to share in Birta's freshly made soup. Her thoughts turned involuntarily to his weapons commission.

The grass along the pathway was still damp with dew. She could see the glow from the already hot forge, as well as Elvar's back as he slipped a piece of iron into the forge's belly.

"Good morning," she called, hoping she wouldn't startle him.

"Hi there," he said, smiling over his shoulder.

"Sorry I didn't call to say I wasn't going to make it over for dinner," Kali said. "I hope your sister's not furious with me."

Elvar laughed. "No, no, everything's fine. No one got out the fine china or anything. Just a casual invitation." He fumbled a bit as he answered. "Of course, Birta probably wanted to know if you've located the missing solar panels yet and locked the thief safely away."

Kali smiled wryly. "Working on it. No luck so far finding out who's behind it or where the panels are going."

She looked curiously at the blob of molten metal protruding from the forge. As usual at this stage, she couldn't really tell what he was making.

"Something new?" she asked.

"Yes, a commission from a boar hunter. I'm working on a spear tip. He wants a Hawaiian hunting scene worked into the long handle. It's a little more challenging than the usual weapon shape I make. I really need a bigger forge."

She took a deep breath. "Have you ever had a commission for a war club with shark's teeth?"

He turned, looked at her with curiosity.

"Sure," he said. "Why do you ask?"

She made an effort to keep her voice even when she said, "Just curious. I know a lot of authentic weapons have to be made from specific kinds of wood."

"The older, the better," he said. He smiled, but it seemed forced.

"Where do you find old wood?" she asked.

"It's around if you look for it."

She was about to ask him for details when her cell phone rang again. She nodded to Elvar and walked back along the path, out of earshot. It was Walter on the other end, and he didn't sound especially happy.

"You're up bright and early," she said.

"Banner day, Kali. Makena's been a pain in the ass all morning, and Polunu Hausuka just showed up."

Kali heaved a sigh of relief. Talking to Polunu was a priority. "He have anything to say about a missing war club?"

"He hasn't said a thing," said Walter. "Nor is he likely to, considering we just fished his body out of the seaweed down on the beach at Hana Bay. Looks like he's been dead at least a couple of days."

Kali caught her breath. "That's not too far from where Kekipi's body was. Does it look like an accident?"

"Not unless he tied a rope around his own ankle before he jumped into the water."

"Great," said Kali. "Anything else?"

"Not yet. CSI officer from the main station is there. Hara's talking to everyone who was around the area. He's still recovering from taking the call this morning from some tourists, and being the first one of us to see the body. I recognized our favorite pickpocket as soon as I saw what's left of him. We've got a team combing the immediate area, and both the police chief and the mayor have already called to ask me why in the hell people keep finding bodies on our stretch of beach."

"And?"

Walter sighed. "I told them it's our new tourism campaign. *Come to Hana and never leave.* No one thought it was very funny."

"Maybe because it's not." She frowned. "And what did you say about Makena?"

"She's been calling me all morning, trying to sell some info about something she saw on the beach . . ." Walter's voice trailed off.

"She called me, too," said Kali, "but I didn't bother to answer it."

"Hell. You don't think she actually saw something, do you? She said she was going to take her offer to someone with a fancy boat."

Kali felt a prickle of uneasiness. Was it possible that Makena had seen something that involved Polunu? Most likely not, but it would be a good idea to find her and ask, even if it took a bribe to get an answer out of her.

"It seems unlikely, but I'll see if I can find her," she said.

Trouble was, there was never any easy way to find Makena, especially if she didn't want to be found.

"I'll check in as soon as I have something to tell you," Kali said. "I'll call her back. Meanwhile, let's issue an official alert—tell everyone to keep an eye out for her. No telling where on the island she might be."

Walter hung up, and Kali felt the worry settle in and take hold like a deep, unwelcome frost. Makena was nothing but trouble, but Kali didn't want her next encounter with her to involve identifying her lifeless, needle-scored body.

CHAPTER 33

It was perfectly true that Makena was a whore and a drug addict, but she wasn't entirely without ambition. And she certainly possessed her share of street smarts. She had clearly seen one man dump a second man into the water out of a small boat. And it had certainly appeared that the first man's feet were tied together.

She made her way along the beach trails in Waianapanapa State Park, just north of Hana. She walked slowly along the interior park paths, waiting until she saw a young couple leave their cabin and head for the beach. She broke one of the cabin windows and climbed inside, then took a hot shower and helped herself to a pair of clean shorts and a blue T-shirt advertising some obscure concert. They hung on her small frame, far too large, but they were free of the stench of months of sleeping outside, unwashed.

She made herself half a peanut butter sandwich out of supplies she found in a cooler in the kitchen, leaving smears of peanut butter on the cooler's lid, and the loaf of bread open on the floor. By the time she had helped herself to a man's watch, which had been left on the shelf above the bathroom sink, and had borrowed one of the two toothbrushes that were drying in a water glass, she'd come up with a plan of sorts.

Collecting any money for what she'd seen would involve finding out who owned the fancy boat. The name, *Beryl*, had been written clearly in blue script on the stern, which should be useful. Her plan was to head for the marina at Hana Bay, across from the hotel complex. Someone there should be familiar with a powerboat as large as the *Beryl*.

After walking to the main road, she hitched a ride from a sympathetic woman in a gray Toyota and got out near the hotel. She made her way down to the marina and found the small office that dealt with slip rentals, fuel pumps, and general maintenance issues.

The manager was at the desk. He looked up as she came in, a preoccupied expression on his face. It changed to one of caution when he saw Makena.

"What is it, honey?" the manager asked, his voice far from friendly.

Makena scowled, nervously twisting a strand of hair in her fingers. "I'm trying to find a boat called the *Beryl*." Even as she spoke, her eyes scanned the racks of food near the cash register, then assessed the manager's proximity. "You know where it is or who owns it?"

The manager frowned at her disheveled state. "Someone owe you a twenty?" he asked, his voice unkind.

"Piss off," she said. "I left something on the boat, and I need to get it back."

His face was blank. "Nope. Never heard of the *Beryl* and don't know who she belongs to," he said. "Could be docked anywhere. This is an island. It's nothing but coastline and coves. Now scram. And don't let me see you around here again."

She tried again, her voice cajoling. "You don't understand. I left my mother's necklace on the boat while it was in the cove by the state park. It's valuable. I have to get it back, or you know how it is. My parents will throw a fit."

He laughed. "Oh, sure. A valuable necklace. Family heirloom with rubies, was it?" He leaned across the desk. His voice was sharp when he said, "Listen, kid, I don't know what you're up to, but if you've stolen something, lost some drugs, or have gotten yourself pregnant, I don't give a crap. Get out of here now, or I'll call the cops."

Makena turned and flounced out the door, then slammed it behind her. She walked to the edge of the marina and sat down on the wooden planks, then leaned her back against a piling, fuming. She had no backup plan. She got up and found a spot closer to the office that offered some shade, and made herself comfortable. She was used to having nowhere to go.

Inside the office, the manager did a quick search on his computer for boats registered in Hana. The *Beryl* was listed, and it didn't take long to come up with a phone number. Giving the owner a heads-up that some crack kid was looking for him could be a smart move. There might even be a reward for passing along the information.

He dialed the number and let the phone ring. There

was no answer, but on the fourth ring, an answering machine picked up.

"Aloha . . ." He hesitated. "This is Hana Marina. There was a young woman here earlier, trying to track down the owner of the *Beryl*. Says she left a valuable necklace on board while your boat was moored at the state park. It didn't sound legit somehow, so I told her we weren't familiar with the boat, but it seemed to me that you might like to know someone's looking for you." He hesitated again. "Okay. Well, anyway, hope you're having a nice afternoon." And with that, he hung up.

CHAPTER 34

Police chief Leo Pait tapped his long, thin fingers on the surface of his desk. On the other side, Walter sat stiffly on a metal folding chair. Pait's office was being redecorated, and most of the furnishings had been covered up with paint cloths.

"Walter, what we have here is a public relations disaster," said Pait, leaning back and pushing the fingers of one hand through his thinning strands of hair. "Three bodies—one a grandmother, one a schoolboy, and the other an infamous local criminal with a sinker attached to him. The tourists are getting spooked. A couple of Hana bed-and-breakfasts and both the small hotels have advised their guests to stay off the beaches at night."

"The grandmother killing happened in Kihei. And Polunu Hausuka was a pickpocket, at best," said Walter defensively.

"What? Oh, the thief. Regardless. Violent loss of human life, et cetera. Doesn't look good on the local news. And that actor with the podcast is getting everyone all stirred up. What we want is reporters covering cultural festivals, restaurant openings, film stars staying at the resorts."

"Chief, I—"

"Don't give me excuses, Walter. I've known you too long. Are you and your cadre of law enforcement misfits going rogue on me over there on the other side of the island?"

Walter sighed, regarding Pait with a degree of apprehension. The man was intimidating. Pale skinned, extremely tall, and equally thin, he reminded Walter of a ghostly basketball player.

"Hardly, Chief. We've been devoting every spare resource to trying to find out what happened to the boy. And we've got this solar-panel investigation in full swing. As you know, we just had a major breakthrough in determining what the murder weapon was in the case of the boy."

"Likely was. You haven't produced an actual weapon."

"Granted, but we've got some good leads."

"Like the one that washed up on the beach this morning and gave a bunch of tourists the heebie-jeebies?"

Walter was silent for a moment. "A setback, sir. That's all."

"Tell me again what the connection is between the grandmother, the boy, and the second body?"

"I didn't—"

"Damn right, you didn't. And that's my point. You don't even know if there is one."

A desk sergeant stuck his head around the office door. "Painters are here, Chief."

"Send them in," said Pait. "Get out of here, Walter. Find out what the hell's going on over there on your beaches, and fast. Clear?"

"Yes, sir." Walter got up and left Pait's office. He walked slowly through the building, then out into the glaring sunshine of the parking lot. The medical examiner's office was a few blocks away, and he drove there next, fully expecting another lecture.

He was shown through the front of the building to the stairs leading to the lower level and the autopsy room. He made his way down the stairs, not looking forward to what was likely to be on display. Stitches was there. She looked up and saw him enter the autopsy room's viewing area, which was separated from her work space by a wall of glass. She nodded to the young doctor assisting her and walked through the connecting door, removing her gloves and mask.

"I assume you're here for Polunu Hausuka, not Grace Sawyer, but you don't want to go in there," she said in greeting. "Stinks to high heaven. He was in the water awhile, and the fish had a go at a lot of his soft tissue. Only one eye left."

Walter felt his stomach lurch. "Thanks for the image," he said.

"But you can look from here," she said, standing at the glass and gesturing for Walter to join her. In the next room, Polunu's disfigured body was laid out under a set of glaring lights. Stitches pushed a button on the wall next to the edge of the glass, activating an intercom.

"Lift up his right leg," she directed the other doctor. He did as she asked. Walter could clearly see a section of rope hanging from the blackened ankle. "His ankles were tied together and probably weighted, though we don't know what with. The rope was tied clumsily, so it came loose, probably through the motion of the current. Most likely, he was dropped off a ways from the shore, but not very far. Otherwise we probably wouldn't have seen him for much longer—or at all, if something bigger found him and was hungry enough."

"So, carried from the beach out into deeper water?"

"My guess would be he was dropped off a boat at some point fairly close to the shore, then dragged along underwater by the current until he got lodged on some submerged lava. The skin on the body—particularly the legs—is scratched and broken, but those injuries occurred after death and are consistent with repeatedly hitting sharp rocks."

"How long was he in the water?"

"Three days at most. Given the rate of the current, that would suggest he might have been put into the water somewhere in the vicinity of Haleakalā National Park, up near Kipahulu."

"And he drowned?"

"Yes, but the interesting thing is that his wrists weren't bound. Whoever tied his ankles probably did so just to make the body sink, not to keep him subdued. We're testing right now to see if there are any correspondingly significant amounts of narcotics or alcohol in his system."

"If there are, then he probably knew the person who put the weight around his ankles."

"Probably. As I'm sure you're aware, statistically, most murders are committed by someone known to the victim."

Walter was silent. In Polunu's case, there was most likely a long list of people he'd made enemies with over the years. Walter had a sudden urge to go home and take a nap.

"Anything else?" he asked, preparing to leave.

"He wasn't circumcised."

Walter looked at Stitches and shook his head. She was a mystery. And as far as he was concerned, she could stay that way.

CHAPTER 35

Located at latitude 20.30° North and longitude 156.00° West, the Alenuihaha Channel between Maui and the village of Hawi on the northern tip of the Big Island was over thirty miles of deep, treacherous water. In places, the depth of the water dropped to more than six thousand feet, and the coastal mountains that bordered the channel on both sides helped to create a wind tunnel with a legendary appetite, one that had claimed more than one boat and more than one life.

The builder was happy to disregard what others might consider risky, and willingly made the channel crossing whenever enough solar panels had been accumulated by his Maui contact to make the trip worthwhile. He was unlikely to let rumors or legends about a stretch of sea deter him from increasing his already considerable profit margins.

He'd learned two important lessons early on in the construction business: first, that anything perceived as environmentally friendly, or "green," was a huge psychological sales tool that appealed to a certain home-buying demographic; and second, the less he spent on building materials, the more he could shuffle into his own bank account. The money he was saving on solar arrays alone was going to finance amply a large private compound on the relatively undeveloped island of Kaua'i. He'd already drawn up the plans, and after he settled in, he'd spend his free time traveling around the world.

A slender woman poked her head up through the hatch of the cruiser's galley.

"Hungry, Dad? I'm thinking of making a salad. Would you like one?"

"Sounds great, honey. Extra bacon bits for me."

She rolled her eyes. "Okay, but under duress. You know they aren't good for you."

"Nice to know someone cares."

She shook her head. "It's my job to keep you healthy. I'm going to give you grandkids someday. And at some point I plan to leave them with you for a few months so I can go to Paris and relax."

He laughed as she disappeared belowdecks. He motored along the coast, captaining the sleek craft from the deep upholstered seating area of the cockpit. At the marina, he pulled the boat up carefully next to the fueling station and tied the boat to the cleats on the dock, then removed the nozzle from the diesel tank. He inserted his credit card in the pay station, and an error flashed across the screen: out of order. He swore, looking up toward the office area. The marina was very quiet, and most of the boats bobbed peacefully in their slips. A few people were visible, going leisurely about their business. He put his card back into his wallet and walked the length of the dock, then climbed the narrow stairs that led to the office area.

When he walked through the door, the manager was stocking shelves with bags of snack chips. The manager made no sign that he'd noticed a customer walking in.

"Any chance you could help me out over here?" the builder called out, his voice conveying annoyance. He took his credit card out and tapped the edge of the card impatiently against the counter.

The manager abandoned the snack chips and walked over, positioned himself behind the counter at the cash register. The builder handed his credit card across the counter. The manager looked up when he saw the name on the card and did a double take. His face registered surprise.

"Oh, hi there. You got the phone message, then?" the manager said.

The builder looked at him blankly. "What phone message?"

The man looked confused. "Day before yesterday? About the girl who was here looking for you?"

When the builder made no response, the manager continued. "She was here trying to track you down. Says she left a necklace on your boat when it was moored over by the state park."

The builder's brow creased. The *Beryl* had been moored in one particular spot for the transfers on at least a half-dozen occasions by now.

He smiled at the manager, keeping his voice even when he said, "Oh, I see. I've been off-island for a few days, so I'm afraid I didn't get the message if it was left on my office number. Did she leave a name or a place to reach her? I had quite a party on the boat a few weeks back, so I'm afraid I'm not really sure who might have lost a piece of jewelry."

"No, she didn't actually leave her name or any phone number," the manager answered, realizing suddenly that he should have at least asked. "But," he said, nodding toward a set of large windows overlooking the parking lot, "you're in luck. She's been hanging out here since she first showed up a few days ago. I saw her this morning over by the picnic tables."

"Well, that's certainly lucky," the man said smoothly. "What does she look like?"

"Shoulder-length dark hair, looks Hawaiian Asian. Very thin," he said. "And she was wearing shorts and a T-shirt."

"Great. Thanks. The diesel-pump pay station's not working, by the way."

"Sorry about that," said the manager, running the credit card through his register. He printed a receipt and handed it to the man, who was looking out the window toward the picnic area. "But hey, if you hadn't come inside, you'd have missed the girl."

The man took the card and the receipt and slipped them into his wallet.

"I must have been born under a lucky star," he said before he exited through the front door. He turned immediately up the path, his pace slow as he scanned the faces of the few people who were walking about.

He walked to the rim of the parking lot, then searched the shadowy light beneath the trees along that area, where a stretch of parkland had been fitted with a half-dozen picnic tables and benches. Makena was almost immediately visible, picking through a garbage can near the tables. As he watched, she waved a horde of flies away and pulled the leftovers of someone's sandwich from the trash. Without even examining it closely, she began to eat it.

He walked toward her, calling out in a friendly voice. "Hello there. Are you the girl looking for the *Beryl*?"

She paused and looked over at him, curious. "I might be. Why?"

He pointed back to the marina, where the *Beryl* waited by the fuel pumps. "There she is," he said.

She dropped the sandwich and walked closer to the parking lot. There was the boat just a few hundred feet away. She looked at him closely, trying to determine if he was the same man she'd watched from the hillside. "Do you know whose boat it is?"

"It's my boat," he said easily.

She looked from him to the boat. A young woman could be seen moving around on the deck. Makena turned back to the man. His eyes were cold, despite his smile. He said nothing, waiting for her to make her move.

"I need some money," she said.

His shoulders lowered, relaxing. "Don't we all?"

"Some of us more than others, seems like," she said, her voice calculating. "For instance, I don't have a boat. Not even a dinghy."

His smile became a thin line. "Well, now. That's a shame. But if I understand correctly, you lost a piece of jewelry on my boat, even though I'm pretty sure I've never seen you on board."

Her face twisted into a sneer. "I didn't lose anything.

But I saw something. And I bet what I saw is worth a little bit of your hard-earned cash."

The air crackled with tension. The man spoke slowly, his voice low. "How much cash are we talking about?"

Makena looked from him to the boat, considering. "Two thousand dollars."

"Really?" He raised his eyebrows, as though surprised. "And yet you still haven't told me what it was you saw that should make me want to pay you anything. New at the blackmail game, are you?"

She shifted her feet, looking toward the *Beryl*. She took a deep breath and leaned closer to him. "I saw you push that man into the water," she said, her voice a hiss. "So don't give me any crap. Two thousand dollars, and I'll keep your dirty little secret forever."

His eyes narrowed. "He slipped," he said, a dark smile on the edges of his lips. "Happens all the time. Could even happen to you."

"Don't threaten me," she said. "I have good friends on the police force."

"Is that so? Listen, sweetie, just because the cops know you by name doesn't mean they're your friends."

She drew back, alarmed by his tone.

"Anyway, I certainly don't need that kind of trouble," he said, his voice friendly again. "I'll give you the money, but you have to promise me that's the last I'll ever see of you."

"Sure," she said, not meaning it any more than he did.

"You do realize that I don't have two grand in my pocket, don't you?" He glanced back toward the marina office. "And even if I did, it would be a bad idea for anyone to see me giving you a big wad of money. Might get the wrong idea about our relationship."

"I'm not dumb," she said. "I didn't think you'd have it on you."

He nodded toward the *Beryl*. "As it happens, I do keep a little extra cash stashed on the boat," he told her. "I'm not sure if there's that much, but it's probably close."

"Well, let's go and see," she said.

"My daughter's on board. I don't want her to get caught up in this."

"Afraid I'll ruin your reputation?"

"Just do what I tell you, and you can take your money and get lost."

He walked between the picnic tables and along the edge of the parking lot, then took the stairs that led down to the floating docks and the fueling station. She came behind, but not too far away.

He climbed onto the deck of the *Beryl*, then turned to her.

"Would you like to come on board?" he asked. "Or you can stay right here on the dock, if it makes you feel more comfortable. It will take me a few minutes to get the safe open."

Makena looked around. Only a few other people were visible, sitting on boats in slips farther away. It was broad daylight, and a scream would likely attract plenty of attention. She hesitated, then stepped toward the deck.

"Yeah, sure," she said. "Just hurry up."

The builder reached out, extending his hand, and helped her on board. She backed up against the deck rail.

"Places to be?" he asked, making no attempt to hide his sarcasm.

"Got to spend that money, don't I?"

He eyed her carefully. "You look like you're about to run off with the silverware." He gestured toward a seating area. "Sit down. Put your feet up. You'll understand if I don't invite you inside and take a chance of you seeing where my safe is."

She shrugged. "I'm fine where I am. Thanks."

"Please yourself."

As he turned, the young woman came up from the galley into the sunlight. Makena could see him shake his head at her, as if to discourage her from saying anything. Then he took her arm and said something quickly. The woman smiled at Makena, her head tilted slightly to one side, as though she were making an assessment of some kind, then followed the man down a short stair belowdecks.

They were gone only a few minutes. When they returned to the deck, Makena was still standing exactly where he'd left her. He made a pretense of looking around cautiously, then flipping through the stack of twenty-dollar bills in his hand to get her attention. She stepped forward, her eagerness replacing any remnant of common sense. As she reached for the money, he slipped a heavy black Glock out of his waistband and shoved it deep into her gaunt side.

"Right now, you have a choice to make, and you'd better make it really fast," he said, his voice a fierce whisper. "Be a good girl, and we'll just go for a little cruise down the coast. Be a bad girl, and I'll knock your teeth down your throat and swear you tried to rob me. You can take your chances that anyone believes a crack whore over a respectable businessman."

Makena looked at his face and knew he was serious. "Maybe I should just get off the boat now, and you can keep your money."

He shook his head. "A little bit too late for that, isn't

it?" He nodded toward the cockpit. "Climb up there in front of me. Now."

She did as he told her, making her way carefully up the ladderlike steps.

"Now sit down and be very quiet while I pull out of the marina."

She sat down on the thickly upholstered bench.

"I'm not going to dump you in the water, if that's what you're worried about," he said. "Too many people out and about. We're going to pull out of here and head for deeper water till the sun goes down, and then I'm taking you to my daughter's house."

Her face reflected a dawning sense of terror. Her eyes welled with tears. "I'm not going to tell anyone anything," she said, her voice a whimper. "I swear it."

"No, I don't think you will," he agreed.

Watching Makena from the corner of one eye, he cranked the engine. The boat shuddered slightly. He climbed down the stairs and cast of the lines, never taking his eyes off of her. He climbed back up into the cockpit and eased the boat out past the harbor markers and into the deeper water beyond the bay. He set the autopilot at a slow cruising speed and turned back to Makena.

"Okay. Below deck, princess," he said, pointing the gun at her. She got up and retraced her way down the steps from the cockpit. He led the way down another set of steps and opened the door to the lounge. Roughly, he pushed her inside. Below deck, the surroundings were impressive—all gleaming wood and brass, with a deep, thick carpet. The other woman was there, next to the door, waiting.

"I need you to stay quiet for a while," he said to Makena, handing the Glock to the other woman. "My daughter will keep you company."

The woman's face was blank. "You Hawaiians. It's really impossible to clean you up, isn't it? Well, no one can say I haven't tried," she said.

Just as Makena was about to reply, the woman raised her arm and hit her across the side of her head with the gun. She crumpled and fell to the carpet, unconscious. Followed by his daughter, the man picked up Makena with one hand by the front of her shirt and dragged her into one of the forward staterooms, where he left her face-down on the floor. He looked down at her, as if considering. His daughter grinned.

"I don't think ninety pounds of unhealthy flesh is much of a threat, Dad. I'm certainly not staying in here with her. She smells like a leaking septic tank. Leave her on the bed and we'll lock the door."

The man lifted Makena and dropped her onto the bed.

"We're going to have to burn everything to get rid of the stench—sheets, cover, pillows, carpet," he agreed, locking the door behind them.

"Now what?" the woman asked as they made their way back up to the deck. She handed the gun to him. "Wait until dark and head back out across the channel, where she can accidently fall overboard? Or can I play with her first?"

The man looked away, ignoring her remark. "I'm afraid this has turned into something of a mess. We should be sitting by the pool right now, enjoying dinner. I'm a rich man, and you're a rich woman." He reached out and squeezed her shoulder. "Sorry about all of this, pumpkin. Life is supposed to be easy for people like us."

CHAPTER 36

Kali parked the Jeep outside of George's Island Market. She'd left Hilo at home for the day while the search for Makena continued. George was inside, ensconced behind the cash register with the day's tabloid, his calm presence providing a false sense of normalcy to the day.

"They found another mermaid in Norway," George said by way of greeting. "In one of those fjords. You'd think the water would be too cold for a mermaid to want to hang around."

"You'd think." She smiled briefly as the image of a mermaid in a Scandinavian sweater flitted through her mind. "I'm looking for Makena Shirai, George. Has she been around?"

George looked up sharply at Kali's tone.

"She was," he said reluctantly. "I think it was about

three days ago. Maybe not that long. She came in and asked to use the phone."

Kali waited.

"I made her leave," said George. "Which, I'm going to guess, is probably not what you want to hear."

"She called me from somewhere about then, and now we can't find her. The number traced to a stolen cell phone. I'm afraid she's in trouble."

Kali could feel George scrutinizing her face, seeming to sense the genuine worry.

"Drugs?"

"Not this time. It appears she's pedaling some information, playing at blackmail."

"You checked the waterfall areas? I heard she's been working a couple of the parking areas fairly recently, helping herself to whatever the tourists leave in their unlocked cars."

"Good grief. You'd think we have enough signs posted everywhere telling people not to leave valuables in their rental cars."

"Tourists," said George, shaking his head. A wry smile played at the corner of his mouth, but he kept his voice somber. "Of course, they have to stop here next, to buy more sunglasses and tanning cream and disposable cameras. It's important to appreciate the way the universe works."

Kali nearly smiled.

"We've been back and forth, up and down the road," she said. "Every possible spot, from Hana Airport to where the road turns to dirt. Couple of sightings, but no sign of where she's been sleeping lately."

"That would be tough to figure, anyway, wouldn't it? I've found her sleeping behind the Dumpster before.

There's a lot of remote land on either side of the road. A lot of places to disappear to if you don't want to be found."

Kali leaned against the counter, suddenly exhausted. George was right, of course. There were plenty of areas of Maui that were still raw and wild and that offered ample hiding places. Outside, the wind had picked up again, and clouds were scuttling across the sky. Hawaii was not bright and shiny today, and she could sense a darkness welling up from its deceptive garden surface. Chances were good they'd find Makena's body in a ditch somewhere, overdosed and discarded.

"No news yet on Kekipi Smith or the other guy that washed up?" George asked. His voice suggested that the possibility of a connection between recent events and the search for Makena had not escaped him.

"Not yet."

"Girl like that," said George slowly, "creates her own trouble. Remember that, Detective. Some people just can't be helped."

"Yeah. I know." Kali straightened up and turned toward the door. "Got to do what I can, though, George. You call me right away if she shows up or if you hear anything about her."

"Will do." He reached behind himself into a small refrigerated cupboard, then tossed a pineapple soda to Kali. "For the road," he said.

Kali nodded her thanks and walked back to the Jeep. She opened the bottle and drank the contents, then rubbed the cool, beaded surface of the empty glass across her forehead.

She headed north on Highway 360 toward Hamoa

Beach and stopped several times along the way to ask if anyone at any of the food stalls that dotted the length of the road had any news to share. Just as she had finished speaking to the proprietors of the shave-ice stand just out of town, Walter's voice crackled over the radio in the Jeep.

"Where are you?" he asked.

"Just talked to George, and he says the last time he saw her was a few days ago, when she came in to make a phone call, but he sent her away. Anything on your end?"

"Hara took a complaint call late yesterday afternoon from someone over at the marina at Hana Bay. The caller said a drug dealer, a female, was working the parking area. The description fits Makena. We just checked, and the same girl was seen getting onto a big swanky boat earlier today. We've got an ID on the boat, a big cruiser, and the Coast Guard is looking for it right now."

"What's the boat, and who owns it?"

"It's registered as the *Beryl*. Technically belongs to a building company on the Big Island."

"Name?"

"Just the company, Sunspot Ltd. But we have a description of the company owner. Male, midfifties, stocky, height five feet, ten inches."

There was silence on the radio. She waited, knowing him well enough to know he needed his moment of drama.

"Sunspot Ltd.," Walter said after a suitable pause, "is actually an umbrella group for not one, but multiple housing developments here and on the Big Island that specialize in solar-powered homes. And one of the developments is Secret Haven."

"Billy Shane."

More crackling. To Kali's ears, it was filled with tension.

"We ran his records twice, because you didn't like him. They were spotless. The only things that came up were personal."

"Right. Something about a daughter?"

"Lived back and forth with him and the mother following an ugly divorce. Kid was in and out of hospital facilities. Psychiatric. Exhibited strong sociopathic tendencies and was expelled from two different schools for acts of cruelty against other life forms."

"You didn't tell me the details," she said.

"Didn't seem related to what we're looking at."

"What kind of things did she do?"

Walter grimaced. "Locked another girl in a storage shed behind a school when she was eight. But first, she cut off all the other kid's hair. Showed zero concern about it."

"And?"

"Set some hamsters on fire in the school science lab when she was ten. They found her standing there, watching them burn. Again, no sign of remorse or even an understanding that what she was doing was wrong."

Kali felt her stomach twist.

"I've got a bad feeling," she said.

"Yeah, agreed. There was also something about the daughter's husband. Local guy from Kaua'i Island, killed in a hit-and-run. The case is still open. There'd been one domestic violence call a few months before, but not what you think. The husband was having an affair, and Shane's daughter apparently beat the crap out of him when she found out. While he was sleeping. Anyway, you need to head over to the marina. Roger Blake with the Guard offered to swing by and pick us up on the launch. He's got the full backstory, and we already have a statement from the marina attendant that a female matching Makena's description followed Shane onto his boat, which had come in briefly to refuel."

"So she probably wasn't lying to us. At least not completely."

"She's been hanging around for a couple of days, trying to get info on the boat, based on some bullshit story about a lost necklace. I'll meet you over there."

Kali swung around on the road, wishing for once that she was in a vehicle with a siren. She made her way down the busy stretch of road packed with tourist traffic and pulled into the marina about fifteen minutes later. Not good time for a drive that was less than three miles from the shave-ice stand.

Walter was already there, waiting on the dock. As she made her way from the parking lot at a jog, Kali could see the Coast Guard cruiser coming in, slowing as it approached the inner harbor but still moving fast enough for its wake to rock the boats at rest in their slips in the marina. Roger Blake waved from the controls and pulled alongside the dock. Walter and Kali boarded, then joined Roger at the controls as he opened the throttle and headed back out of the harbor. His speed indicated he was far less concerned about his exit than he had been about his entrance.

Walter regarded the darkening sky with apprehension. Roger caught his glance.

"Weather moving in," he shouted above the noise of the engine. "Either of you have any constructive ideas about where to look? I've got three boats in the water. There's no sign of him."

"We've got a black-and-white parked in view of his house on the Big Island," Walter shouted back. "No one's there. Best guess is he has Makena in open water." He paused. "Hopefully, still on board," he added for Kali's benefit.

Kali picked up a pair of binoculars and began to scan the water. The few boats she could see were clearly sail-boats, and they were making their way back toward the harbor. The deteriorating weather, she knew, would at least have the effect of thinning the number of craft that would have to be checked out.

She looked up at the sky again. She was suddenly sick of storms, sick of kids on drugs, sick of a society that had become so unbalanced that the bad guys really did stand a chance of winning. The rain began to fall in sheets, ob-scuring the lenses of the binoculars. She wiped them against her sleeve, feeling a sense of depression descend.

They'd been doing sweeps up and down the coast for about half an hour, each pass slightly farther out, when a call came in. The *Beryl* had been spotted.

"We'll do the approach," called Walter. "Tell everyone to stand back, but close enough, in case we need them. He sees too many Coast Guard uniforms, he may do something stupid."

In the distance, they caught sight of a large, gleaming cabin cruiser. Kali pointed, and Roger swung the wheel.

"Slow down," she cautioned. "Don't want to spook him."

Her spirits lifted. Maybe they weren't too late. Maybe there would be plenty of days the bad guys would go home with the prize. *But maybe*, she thought, *not today*.

CHAPTER 37

From the deck of the Coast Guard boat, Kali peered through the binoculars. The *Beryl* was still at a good distance, but the lenses were strong, and she could make out the large *B* at the beginning of a short name on the stern. She passed the binoculars back to Walter, who nodded in agreement.

"You guys care to share your game plan?" Roger asked.

"Approach slowly and use the weather as an excuse," said Kali. "Tell Shane that we've got a major storm warning and want him to move to shore."

Walter looked dubious. "He'll have seen it on his own radar."

"He's not heading for a known port, so it looks like he's unaware," said Kali.

"And he's going to say thank you and follow us in?"

"You have a better idea?" Kali asked. "Please . . . I'm all ears."

Roger turned to them, tense. "Okay, people, you two try not to look like a police search party, and I'll use the loudspeaker to make contact."

"We need to board," said Kali. "If Makena's still with him, she's probably not sunbathing out on the deck, within easy access."

"The closer we get to the harbor, the easier this will be," Walter insisted. "And safer. If she's still on the boat, he's not going to toss her over while we're in the vicinity."

Kali frowned. She wasn't completely sure that Walter was right, but how to get on board without making a bad situation potentially worse was going to be risky from any angle.

"Okay," she said. "We're getting close. Pull up beside him and let's see what he has to say. I'll stay out of sight, in case he remembers me."

Meanwhile, from the deck of the cockpit, Shane tracked the weather. Large raindrops were falling, splashing on the gleaming white surface of the boat. He was about a mile from the shore—close enough to get in quickly, but far enough out that no one could observe anything taking place on board. He cruised slowly, parallel to the coast, making his unhurried way back to Kaupo and his daughter's private dock.

He went below deck, then listened at the stateroom door where he'd left Makena. There was no sound from inside. He made himself comfortable back in the cockpit, where he was sheltered from the weather. His daughter stood at the helm, looking perfectly at ease. The boat rocked in the growing chop of the channel waters, the dimming light and the acrid scent in the air foretelling the imminent arrival of the coming storm. The panel barometer was clearly visible and was rapidly dropping.

The horizon was nearly empty. To the east, toward the Big Island, the only other craft in sight was the distant shape of a container ship. To the west and the Maui coast, there was another boat, smaller than the *Beryl*, cruising slowly at a distance.

Ten minutes later, the other boat appeared to be in the same position as before. His daughter pointed to the distant shape of the smaller boat.

"They've been running parallel to us for a while."

He squinted into the distance and the dimming light. "Probably some idiot trying to make one last catch before the storm causes an exodus of fish. The locals drive me nuts with their stupid legends."

Her face was expressionless. "It's so easy to scare them."

He reached out and rested his hand on her shoulder. The gesture was protective, forgiving. She made no response.

Not far away now, the smaller boat turned, making its way through the mounting waves. It was growing closer. Soon, it became clear that it wasn't a fishing boat, but a Coast Guard vessel, heading directly for the *Beryl*. Shane swore and banged his fist against the control panel.

"Every damn thing's gone wrong ever since that kid showed up at the loading site and the video with that moron Polunu got out on the news." His voice carried over the wind and the engine. "It was just a matter of time till he brought his bad luck to us. And now here it is."

From below deck, the sound of Makena calling out could be heard.

Shane swore again. "Keep us on course. I'll go deal with the noise."

He made his way to the stateroom, then pulled the gun out of his waistband. After unlocking the door, he opened it just enough to see inside.

"You need to shut up right now," he said, his voice menacing.

"I swear, I won't tell anyone what I saw," Makena said. Dried blood had matted the hair above her ear, and she stood unsteadily. One hand was pressed against her head; the other held tightly to the edge of a fixed set of drawers.

He pushed the door open farther and went inside, gun drawn. She backed away, watching him with slightly unfocused eyes.

"Here's what's going to happen," he said, keeping his voice even. "You're going to come up on deck with me and play house for a few minutes. There's a Coast Guard boat on its way, and you're going to smile and look happy and make sure everyone knows you're on this little cruise because you want to be. Friend of the family, right?"

She said nothing.

"Do you understand what I'm saying, sweetie? One wrong word out of you, and I'll blow a hole through your belly. Takes a long time to die from a belly wound, they say. Supposed to hurt like hell."

She swallowed, nodding her assent.

"Good. Now come up with me and stand on the rail. Smile at my daughter and wave to the people on the other boat like you're having the time of your life. Got it?"

Makena nodded again and walked slowly out of the stateroom. Shane followed her closely, the gun in her side. When they came up on deck together, Shane pulled her to the rail. He slipped the gun into the back of his waistband, within easy reach.

The wind had begun to whip across the surface of the water, and the rain was growing intense. There was a flash of lightning, followed by a loud crack of thunder. The Coast Guard boat slowed to a crawl, just a few yards from the *Beryl*. Roger stood at the bow, holding a megaphone.

"Ahoy, *Beryl*," Roger called. "Severe storm rapidly approaching. Typhoon conditions are expected. For your own safety, we need you to follow us into port immediately."

Shane pulled Makena close to his side.

"Is that really necessary?" he shouted. "Got a little party boat thing going on here."

The sharp edge of the gun dug into Makena's upper ribs.

Roger pointed to his ears and shook his head. He spoke into the megaphone. "Afraid I can't hear you! Too much wind. Just follow us, please, and we'll make sure you reach the marina safely."

He put down the megaphone and returned to the cockpit, swinging the bow of the boat back toward shore. He turned and looked up at Shane, then made a "Follow me" gesture with his arm.

Shane waved in response and turned toward the cockpit stairs, pushing Makena in front of him.

"You keep smiling, honey," he said. "Or else."

She began to climb the steps, moving cautiously. They

reached the cockpit, and she started to sit down. Shane pulled her up, close to the wheel and next to his daughter, and forced her to stand beside them.

"I get it, I get it," she said, whining.

He nodded to his daughter, and as she turned the *Beryl* in line with the Coast Guard vessel, the bow rose from a trough and hit the crest of a wave, causing them all to nearly lose their balance. Shane grabbed at the wheel with both hands as his daughter lurched to one side.

As he steadied himself, Makena's hand darted forward and pulled the gun from his waistband. He swung around and grabbed at her, but she was already on the stairs. She jumped shakily to the deck below, turned, and pointed the gun at his chest.

Makena wiped at the rain collecting on her face. "I might not be able to hit your head, asshole, but I'm going to bet I can at least hit something. Maybe I'll make a great big hole in your bitch of a daughter."

"You stupid slut!" he screamed. "What are you doing? I wasn't going to shoot you."

"Sure," she said. She adjusted her aim. She pointed the gun at his stomach and pulled the trigger three times. The first bullet missed. The second hit his shoulder. The third bullet made contact with his abdomen, and Makena watched expressionlessly as he fell to the deck below and a pool of blood spread out beneath him.

CHAPTER 38

The sound reverberated through the thick, wet air. On board the Coast Guard cruiser, Kali and Walter jumped.

"Gunfire!" Kali shouted. "Pull around! Pull around!"

On the deck of the *Beryl*, Billy Shane lay writhing on his back, blood spewing from his belly. They could see Makena standing above him, looking down, and a second woman sliding across the wet deck before disappearing into the interior of the boat.

The cruiser pulled alongside the *Beryl* and rode parallel. Kali picked up the megaphone.

"Makena! Who has the gun?"

Makena waved it lazily in the air.

"Where's Billy Shane?" Kali shouted.

Makena pointed behind her, toward the deck.

"Turn the boat! Turn the boat! You have to turn the boat or cut the engine!" Kali screamed to Makena, the sound amplified by the megaphone, rising above the noise of the boat striking the waves, as well as the thunder, now very close.

Lightning slashed through the darkening sky, and from the deck of the Coast Guard cruiser, Makena could be seen silhouetted against the white surface of the *Beryl*. She was shaking her head, mouthing words.

"She doesn't know how!" Walter yelled.

Kali looked across the water. Rain sprayed in sheets across her face. The coast was approaching.

"I have to get over there!" she shouted.

"What?" Walter yelled. "How the hell you going to manage that?"

Kali looked at Roger. She screamed against the wind, "Can you get close enough to get a grappling hook over the rail?"

Roger looked uncertain, his eyes calculating the space between the boats. They were moving fast, and the water was tossing the smaller boat around.

"Can try! You think you can pull yourself up?"

Kali had no idea. But she couldn't think of any other options. In another ten minutes, it would be too late to do anything except watch the *Beryl* explode as she impacted with the rocky shore, and Makena becoming an inevitable part of the debris.

"It's not worth your life, Kali!" Walter took her arm, his voice pleading.

"Can't make that call. Give me your cuffs!"

Walter passed her his handcuffs, and she shoved them into the waistband at the back of her jeans. She didn't say what she was thinking in her heart, that perhaps everyone would be better off if Makena was no longer on the edge of their lives. That maybe this was the universe cleaning up one small mess and preventing some future disaster that none of them could see. Then she thought of Mike, of his face covered with the spatter of his own blood as he lay dying in front of her. Maybe Walter was right—maybe some people simply couldn't be saved from themselves.

Roger held the wheel as Walter moved to the boat's storage area, where he removed a webbed line fitted with a thick grappling hook on the end. Together, Walter and Kali quickly tied a series of huge knots along the length. Walter reached back into the storage locker, fished around, and produced a pair of thick gloves, then handed them to Kali.

"Put these on," he said. "There's not a lot of room for error here. Stand back while I swing. Roger! Radio ahead. Make sure the shoreline in our path is cleared out, in case we wind up with an out-of-control cabin cruiser making impact on the beach rocks."

Walter braced his feet. He turned to her and grabbed her arm.

"Don't tell me not to, Walter," she said before he could speak, "It's my fault Mike died. I can't be responsible for this, too. She's his daughter. This is for him, not Makena."

Walter shook his head. "It wasn't your fault."

"I knew those kids had an arsenal in there. I wasn't there to help; I wasn't there to stop or protect him. When I got there, they were shooting."

"What the hell are you talking about? Mike knew those dealers had guns. He knew all along. It's why he took the call without you—to keep you safe!"

She felt dizzy. Walter let go of her arm and swung. The hook missed the rail, struck the side, and bounced back, narrowly missing the windscreen of the Coast Guard boat. He swung again, and this time the hook found its mark. He held the length of the line taut, his feet splayed, pressed against the deck. She stood in front of him and grasped the line as far out as she could, then wrapped her hands securely around one of the knots, trying to stay upright.

"Ready," she yelled, and as Walter let go, Roger swung the smaller boat away to create an arc, leaving Kali momentarily suspended.

For the briefest moment, she felt a tremendous calm. Mike had been protecting *her*. There was no wind, no movement. There was no sound but the beating of her own heart, an acceptance that good or bad, there was no way to change what had already taken place. She was in a place of light, some of her grief sliding away, leaving her afloat, leaving her ready for whatever happened next.

Then her feet hit the water, and she crashed against the sea. The drag was excruciating, and her arms were nearly pulled from their sockets. The line swung against the side of the *Beryl*, and she sank below the surface. Then she rose. She gasped, spitting out the briny water, trying to catch her breath.

Every muscle in her body crying out in pain, Kali pulled herself forward to the next knot and tried to find a knot lower down to leverage her feet. The line flapped wildly, and she hit the side of the boat hard with her shoulder, knocking the breath from her lungs.

She was being pummeled by the speed of the boat against the brutal surface of the sea. As she hit the boat a second time, she found the next knot and reached up, then closed her hand around the deck rail. She held on, trying to get her breath. Then, gathering all that was left of her strength, she pulled herself up, feeling the pain rip through her shoulder, swung one leg over the rail, and fell with a crash to the wet deck. She lay on her back for a moment, filling her lungs with air.

As she struggled into an upright position, Kali saw Makena standing against the rail, watching, her face strangely calm, almost disconnected. The gun was still in her hand, pointing downward, her grip slack.

From where he was sprawled nearby, Shane made a small movement with his feet. He groaned, calling out. "Van . . ."

From the stairs leading below, Shane's daughter appeared. Her face was covered with a full mask, white and blank, punctuated with tiny holes, which allowed her to see and breathe. In her hand, she wielded a war club rimmed with shark's teeth. She stood framed against the hatch.

Makena spoke, her voice clear above the engine and the wind. "Your lousy father's going to die," she said.

Shane's daughter took a small step forward, and Makena raised the gun, pointed it in her direction.

"Put the gun down, Makena," said Kali. "Just put it down. I need your help . . ."

Already, the sound of the warning sirens could be heard from the shore, and a flash of red and yellow lights swirled on the beach. From the corner of her eye, Kali saw the woman spring toward Makena, swinging the club at the hand holding the gun.

Kali lunged at the same moment, and careened across the wet surface. She tackled the woman, pinned her to the deck, and wrestled the club from her hand. It skittered on the polished teak, then disappeared behind a built-in cooler. Kali ripped at the mask, pulled it away. She looked with shock at the woman's face, at her blond hair, and recognized her immediately from Uru's warehouse.

The woman twisted, kicking and screaming. "You stupid, filthy natives! We'll show you! We'll own this whole island, and you can all—"

Kali shoved her knee into the woman's chest and pressed hard. She leaned down, her face inches from the other woman. "You killed the boy, didn't you?"

The woman hissed. "So what if I did? He was going to ruin things for me."

"And the old lady? What was she going to do to you?"

The woman laughed, then bit at Kali, nearly making contact with her wrist. Kali fought against the pain coursing through her shoulder and arm and elbowed her with all her strength, making full contact with her jaw. She dug the handcuffs from her waistband, pulled the woman's hands together, and fastened them. The woman continued to kick as she rolled on the deck, shouting obscenities. Makena backed away.

"Stay here!" Kali shouted to Makena. She took the gun from Makena's unresisting grasp.

They were careening toward the beach, the line of rocks close enough to show the cracks in the lava. Kali heaved herself up the stairs to the cockpit and grasped the wheel, then pulled it to the right at hard as she could. As the boat shuddered and swerved, Kali heard the rip of fiberglass as the hull was breached by the rocks just below the water's surface.

The Coast Guard cruiser slowed, closing in on them, and Kali cut the engine of the *Beryl*. Walter was already clambering over the side, his face flooded with relief.

Makena had slumped against a bulkhead. Kali reached the bottom of the cockpit ladder and knelt beside her.

"Are you all right?" she gasped, searching Makena's face. She tried to wrap her arms around her, but Makena pushed her away.

"I told him," Makena said, her voice eerily calm. "No one ever believes anything I say."

Kali looked at her, not understanding. "What was it you said to him, Makena?"

"I told him I had friends on the police force. He should have listened."

CHAPTER 39

By the time they had all reached the harbor, Billy Shane had completed his journey to the next world, and his daughter had been taken away. Makena, concussed and sporting a huge lump on the side of her head, was transported to Kula Hospital, near Wailea. Kali accompanied her to have her shoulder, which had become dislocated, attended to. Walter came along to take statements.

"I hope you know exactly how I feel about the whole 'swinging from a rope at sea in a storm' scenario," he told Kali as they waited for the doctor on duty to examine her shoulder. "You didn't learn to do that at the police academy."

"No, you're right." She smiled at him. "It's all the yoga. I keep telling you to come to class with me."

He ignored her and turned to where Makena was being

escorted into another examination room, accompanied by a policewoman.

"She'll never say thank you, you know," he said.

"I don't need her to say anything."

"In fact, she'll—"

Kali raised her palm to Walter, interrupting him. "Walter, shut up. Seriously. Just stop talking for a little while, will you?"

He grunted. "Okay, but just until your shoulder feels better."

"Thanks." She shifted on her seat, moving carefully to keep her arm still. "I'll be surprised if Uru had anything to do with this. The cat he was trying to save . . . I'm guessing that was Vanessa, deliberately messing with Uru for her own sick brand of amusement. And the grandmother was supposed to be away, not at home during the theft."

"Agreed. Hara had Uru picked up for questioning, just to see what light he can shed on the details. Looks like Shane's daughter may have taken the job to glean as much information on the solar panel sales industry as she could. It also looks like she was intercepting requests for information or orders, sending them on to her father, who was offering far lower rates."

"There are too many huge houses in his development to be supplying them with just the number of panels that have gone missing."

"True, but that was only part of the business model. The books on the big developments give every appearance of being legit, as they include actual large-scale purchases from manufacturers. I think he was just getting started on something smaller, which would have brought huge profits in the long run."

A nurse stuck her head around the door of the examining room to ask if they'd like some coffee sent in. She smiled at Kali.

"Yes, that would be great," Walter said. He turned to Kali. "You never finished telling me about the volcano guy. How's that going?"

Kali looked uncomfortable. "No idea. Guess he should know pretty soon if he's getting a transfer out here or not."

"Oh, how nice. Then you can pretend he's not here at all, kind of like you do with the hunky Icelandic guy next door, right?"

Kali took a deep breath. She didn't want to think too hard about the suspicions she'd begun to have about Elvar, or about the ridiculous idea that he'd somehow been involved in Kekipi's death. Just one more thing, she told herself, to add to the collection of weights around her neck.

"Yup. Just like that. You seem to know everything, Walter. I'm so lucky to have you on my side."

"Damned right you are," said Walter.

He got up from his seat and surveyed Kali with no small degree of amusement. She was dressed in a set of blue scrubs, donated by the hospital staff so that she didn't have to make the drive home in her own wet clothing.

"Let's get that coffee to go and get out of here," Walter continued. "You can come to dinner at my house. The girls will love this story. And I want them to see you wearing that outfit. You look great in that shade of blue."

Dinner at Walter's was good, with coconut pudding for dessert. Walter's wife and daughters fussed over Kali, making sure her own clothes were washed and dried while she ate. Despite his threats, Walter made no mention of the day's events beyond saying that Kali had fallen into the water while boarding a boat. He seemed content that she was safe and warm and dry, and sitting beside him among his family.

As Kali was preparing to leave, a plastic container of leftovers carefully balanced in one hand, her cell phone rang. It was the hospital calling to say that Makena Shirai had disappeared from her room, and that a number of needles and an assortment of painkillers were missing from a medical supply cart.

"Don't beat yourself up," said Walter when she told him. "You've done what you can, and I'll say it again. She's not worth it. Mike would never have wanted you to be saddled with that kind of burden."

Kali didn't answer. Where, she wondered, did the responsibilities of love begin . . . and did they ever truly end?

CHAPTER 40

Kali stood at the edge of the west-facing cliff, looking down at the sea below as it crashed against a mass of partially submerged lava boulders. The wind carried the sea spray up over the rim of the narrow spot where she stood, as if it were a fountain. Each time the spray of water droplets ascended from the waves below, the sunlight, reflecting from behind, created a small rainbow. This was a sacred place, known to the Hawaiians as Leina a ka ʻuhane, one of the secret locations in the islands that was believed to be a leaping place used by spirits when they were ready to jump into the eternal realm.

Next to Kali stood Lys; Kekipi Smith's mother, Anna; and his younger brothers and sisters. A few feet behind them, waiting quietly, were Walter and Sam Hekekia. Kali's arms were raised above her head, and a strand of large brown kukui nuts was around her neck. She was chanting, and her rhythmic voice rose and fell with the sound of the waves, the ocean offering a backdrop to the words of her prayer song that wished Kekipi safety in the afterlife.

In her hands, Anna held her son's surfing leash by its narrow collar, which had once fitted around his ankle. Lys stood beside her, holding the other end. As the sounds of Kali's song began to fade, Anna and Lys lifted the leash and pressed it to their cheeks. Then Anna took it and walked to the very edge of the cliff. With a single movement of her arm, she cast the leash over the edge and into the sea. Below, the current caught it and carried it out into deeper water so that the receding tide could bear it far away.

This was her offering, her *ho'okupu*. No longer would Kekipi's spirit be tethered to this world. Now, his *'au-makua*, the loving ancestor god who guarded him and his family, would come forward to meet him. Attended by this spirit, he would board a canoe and slip away across the wide sea on his journey to heaven.

Anna turned to Kali and Walter. She hugged each of them in turn, her back straight, her eyes clear.

"Thank you," she said. "I can feel that my son's spirit is on its way home at last. Someday, he'll come back for me, when it is my turn to leave, and he'll help me into that canoe. And then there will be no more good-byes." She gazed out over the ocean. "There he goes, for now," she said, raising her hand and waving.

Walter stepped forward and took Anna's arm, then gently guided her toward the path leading away from the cliff.

Kali stood quietly, her head bowed. She had sung these prayers before, and would sing them again. *Bal-*

ance, she thought. Briefly restored for now, for this day at least. But balance was a temporary, tenuous thing, and not, she believed, a state that could be sustained for any length of time in the earthly world.

She walked across the green, living grass, letting the fragrance of the wildflowers fill her lungs. She reached the Jeep and climbed in, then sat quietly for a moment before she started the engine. She watched as Lys walked away along the cliff path, and as Anna and her children got into Walter's car and pulled away. Kali knew that Walter would make sure that they reached home safely, and that Anna's friends would come to spend the day with her, that they would speak of Kekipi and of all his accomplishments, of all the things they'd most loved about him.

The engine turned over, rumbling, and Kali eased slowly out onto the road, heading for home. Hilo was waiting for her, and she would stop at the market to see what fresh fish was available today. She thought maybe she'd pull out her grill, the one Mike had once fussed over so proudly, and ask Elvar and Birta if they'd like to come over and share a meal with her. She needed to make amends for her disloyalty to someone who had never shown her anything but friendship, even if she had never given voice to her suspicions. And, she admitted to herself, she didn't really feel much like being alone today. The way she figured it, there'd be plenty of time for that tomorrow.

If you enjoyed THE FIRE THIEF, be sure not to miss
Kali's next investigation in

THE BONE FIELD

**A series of strange cold-case ritual murders leads Maui
detective Kali Māhoe on a trail of legendary vengeful
spirits and more human monsters in paradise.**

Kali Māhoe, Hawaiian cultural expert and detective with
the Maui Police Department, has been called to a bizarre
crime scene. In the recesses of a deep trench on Lana'i Island, a derelict refrigerator has been unearthed. Entombed
inside are the skeletal remains of someone buried decades
ago. Identification is a challenge. The body is headless, the
skull replaced with a chilling adornment: a large, ornately
carved wooden pineapple.

The old field soon yields more long-buried secrets, and
Kali is led along an increasingly winding path that brings to
light an unlikely suspect, an illegal cock-fighting organiza-
tion, and a strange symbol connected to a long-disbanded
religious cult. Her task is to dispel the dark shadows linger
ing over the Palawai Basin plains, and to solve a puzzle that
no one wants exposed by the bright, hot tropical light.

To discover the answer, Kali will be drawn deeper in the
mysteries of the island's ancient legends—stories that tell of
an enraged rooster god and man-eating monsters. For Kali, a
detective of sound logic and reason, it's not easy to consider
the unknown for explanations for what appears to be a series
of illogical links in a twisting chain of deadly events. Or
safe. Because the dormant pineapple fields of Lana'i have
yet to give up their darkest and most terrifying secrets.

On sale June 2021 wherever books are sold.

CHAPTER 1

The midmorning sun hammered down on the old pineapple field's rutted surface, imparting a relentless, blazing glare. The ocean breeze had failed, on a colossal scale, to deliver a cooler version of tropical air over the lip of the coastal cliffs and down into the Palawai Basin plains of Lāna'i Island's central region. It was hot, and it was early, and it was going to get hotter.

Detective Kali Māhoe peered once again into the recesses of the freshly dug trench at her feet. She'd been in, out, and around the hole for most of the morning, and her sleeveless green T-shirt, tied in a messy knot just below her breasts, was soaked with sweat. Streaks of dirt partially obscured a tattoo encircling her upper left arm, depicting a stylized, slightly geometric interpretation of a thrusting spear.

At the bottom of the hole in front of her was an old refrigerator, its door flung open and partially resting on the mound of red-tinged dirt that had been created during its excavation. There was a small backhoe parked close by, on loan from the island's community cemetery. It was close enough that she could feel the additional heat radiating from the surface of its recently used engine.

The area around the open ground had been enclosed by crime scene tape, while a makeshift tarp on poles covered the hole, tenting it from the unlikely possibility of wind interference on this unusually still morning, and fending off the sun's glare for the benefit of the police photographer. In place of the abundant natural island light, bright, artificial lights had been set up around the perimeter, angled to illuminate the depths of the hole.

The tarp had proven completely ineffective at providing any semblance of shade. In the trench, Maui medical examiner Mona Stitchard—commonly known as "Stitches," but only behind her back—was kneeling beside the refrigerator, taking measurements and making notes in a small book. Her hooded, sterile white plastic jumpsuit clung to her arms and the sides of her face, held in place against her skin by a layer of perspiration. Kali could see that her narrow eyeglasses were sliding down her nose.

Kali studied the peculiar contents of the open refrigerator, then took a long swig of water from a bottle hooked onto her belt, leaning her head back as a few drops trickled down off the edge of her chin.

Police Captain Walter Alaka'i walked up and stood beside her. He regarded the refrigerator with curiosity, his frown giving way to a row of creases in his wide brow. "Well, I gotta say this is definitely a new one. Any brilliant initial thoughts you're not sharing?"

Kali shook her head, considering the question. "Sorry.

Nothing yet, beyond the obvious, slightly bizarre component."

She looked away, across the field, and then back down into the hole. What she didn't say was that she was keenly aware of a residual sadness and loss still clinging to this space, filling the molecules of earth around her feet, newly disturbed after untold years.

Stitches glanced up at Kali and Walter.

"Well, I suppose we all like a challenge." She waved her arm at a fly buzzing by her face. "And this should certainly be interesting."

The three of them regarded the derelict refrigerator. It was an older General Electric model, with a single, large main compartment and a smaller freezer door on the top. The shelves from the main compartment were missing.

"My mother had a refrigerator like this one," said Walter, pointing at it with the opened bottle of water he was holding. "And a matching stove. She was crazy proud of them. Horrible shade of yellow, if you ask me."

"Technically, the color is harvest gold," said Stitches. "Hugely popular from the 1960s all the way through the '70s."

Walter frowned at her.

"You think it's been here that long?"

"Hard to say," she answered, shrugging. "Though it doesn't seem likely someone would bury a new one."

She stood up, passing her medical bag to Kali with one hand and stretching out the other toward Walter, which he grabbed and pulled. Emerging from the depths of the trench with impressive composure, she tugged the plastic hood away from her face and hair, now plastered wet against her head. She peeled off her jumpsuit with relief, and stood beside them, taking off her glasses to clean them. Walter passed her the bottle of water he'd been holding for her. She replaced her glasses and took the bottle, drinking from it gratefully.

There were a number of people milling about the area surrounding the trench, each involved in either further securing the scene or attending to some detail: Tomas Alva, Lāna'i's only full-time cop, officially part of the Maui County Police Department; a police photographer busily loading equipment into the back of his car; the crime scene team from the main station in Wailuku on Maui; Burial Council officials who were required to attend the scene of any uncovered grave that might have a cultural tie; and a terrified-looking young couple who were clearly tourists, huddled by a rocky outcropping at the edge of the field. They were dressed in matching brightly patterned Hawaiian shirts, and on the ground beside them were two metal detectors, their long, narrow handles clearly visible.

Looking over at the couple, Kali sighed. "I guess I should go and talk to them one more time before the woman passes out or starts wailing again," she said.

The offer sounded half-hearted, even to her own ears. Stitches glanced at her. Walter regarded her with a raised eyebrow.

Kali glared at them. "Seriously? Surely both of you can see she's one wrong word away from another bout of hysteria," she said in a defensive tone. "And yes—before anyone points it out, I'm fully aware I'm not at my best with overexcited twenty-somethings."

Both Stitches and Walter turned toward the young couple, considering.

"Probably put a big dent in her day, right?" said Walter, his smile lopsided. "They're just kids on vacation.

Not every day you go looking for buried treasure and turn up something like this."

Kali exhaled. "Okay, okay. Point made."

Walter's grin widened. "One of these days, you'll realize I'm always right."

Kali snorted. "Playing the uncle card?"

He reached out and patted her lightly on the shoulder. "I can safely say that not only are you my *only* niece, you're absolutely, without doubt, my favorite one."

He turned to Stitches, who had begun to wad her used jumpsuit into a ball.

"You all through here?"

She nodded. "For now. I'll know more, of course, once we've moved everything back to the morgue and I can do a proper examination." She surveyed the long-abandoned appliance in the hole. "Meanwhile, good luck with the search. Hopefully you can find something that will be useful in ascertaining an identification."

"Well, we've searched as much as we can with the fridge still there," said Walter. "Maybe there's something still hidden beneath it. We'll see, I guess." He wiped a few drops of sweat from his brow with the back of his hand. "I'm going to head back to Maui after we get the body and fridge loaded up on the launch."

Stitches had already walked off, making her way toward a waiting car that would take her to the harbor for the roughly nine-mile boat crossing back to Maui across the 'Au'au Channel. Walter strode toward the backhoe, gesturing to the driver. The engine turned over. Parked beside it, a truck fitted with a flatbed also roared to life. The drivers of both vehicles made their way slowly toward the open hole, guided by Walter.

Kali peered once more into the depths of the trench.

Lying inside the no-longer-gleaming harvest-gold refrigerator, dressed in a pair of rotting overalls, was a skeleton, its bony hands folded neatly across the chest. It was
lying on its side, both legs bent at the knees, feet pressed
together. She had the impression it had been placed there
with great care—even reverence, perhaps. She looked
more closely. Her initial feeling suggested to her that
whoever had performed this strange burial had possibly
cared about the dead person in some way.

   She supposed it looked like a small man, but it was
difficult to tell. Resting on the corpse's narrow shoulders,
in lieu of a skull, was a large, ornately carved wooden
pineapple, a macabre adornment that gave no sense at all
of who the long-dead figure might have been—or how
he'd come to be resting here, in a dormant field of fruit,
bereft, headless, and utterly alone.

CHAPTER 2

It was well after noon by the time Kali had compiled her notes with details about the burial setting and finished her final interview with Brad and Jan, the tourist couple. As she'd predicted, the woman had broken down into a fit of wild crying midway through her account of the morning's events.

Brad had been more pragmatic, even a little excited.

"We thought maybe we could find some old coins, you know? Something to take home as a souvenir that didn't come from a gift shop."

Kali refrained from pointing out that removing a historic artifact from the islands wasn't likely to be looked upon kindly by the authorities. She watched his face, fascinated by the difference between his reaction to the discovery of a body, and that of his girlfriend.

"When the metal detector starting going off, we dug

around the spot and kept hitting metal. Jan thought it might be a treasure chest, but I figured it was probably some old piece of harvesting equipment that got covered up." He patted the girl on her leg, as if consoling her for the loss of an imaginary fortune.

Kali frowned. "And when you realized it was an old refrigerator, why did you keep digging?"

He grinned. "Well, why would someone bury a refrigerator? I mean, maybe something important had been stashed inside of it. You know, valuable—not just a pile of old bones."

He fumbled as he saw the expression on Kali's face. "I mean . . ."

"You mean that the body of some long-dead human being, perhaps a local person, is of no possible concern, or any value." She watched as he squirmed. "Correct?"

"Well, no, of course not. It's just that . . ." He looked from Kali to Jan, and back to Kali. "Jan called 911 right away, you know? I mean, a body, right?"

"Yes, a body. Exactly right."

Jan made a fresh sobbing noise. "I didn't want to open it," she said, making an effort to keep her voice from breaking. "In the movies, opening the box buried in the remote field never turns out to be a good thing. I knew there was something bad in there. I just knew it."

"The skeleton belonged to an actual person, you know," said Kali. "A living human being who probably had a family and friends."

"And at least one enemy," Brad joked.

Kali swallowed her irritation at his shallow response, doing her best to temper her character assessment with some degree of kindness. She turned to the woman, ignoring Brad.

"You could look at it this way: Thanks to you, maybe someone will finally find some peace and closure knowing that their loved one has been found."

The woman grasped at the thought gratefully.

"Well, glad to have helped, of course. I mean, anything we can do . . ."

"You're absolutely sure you didn't find anything else?"

Exchanging glances, Brad and Jan shook their heads. They looked directly at her with no apparent subterfuge.

"No," said Jan. "Nothing at all."

Kali waited, but they just sat there, disheveled and sweaty. The woman's shoulders sagged. Kali noticed a small tear in her shirt, as well as soil stains on her beige sneakers. "I'd appreciate a call if anything occurs to you."

Again the couple looked at one another, before Jan spoke.

"So, it's okay if we go back to Maui tonight? We have a flight home to California the day after tomorrow. Should we cancel it? Will you need to hold us for more questioning or anything like that?"

Kali suppressed a smile. There were, she thought, simply too many police shows on television these days.

"I don't think that will be necessary, but we'd appreciate it if you could keep all of this to yourselves until we've been in touch," she said, keeping her voice even. She could tell they were more than ready for cold showers and the hotel bar, where they'd most likely retell their story over and over, no matter how many times she might ask them not to. "Just make sure Officer Alva has all of your contact information before you leave." She lent them a more serious gaze. "Just in case."

* * *

The refrigerator, still holding the body, was carefully lifted from the ground and loaded onto the flatbed truck. To give them space to work, a command center for the police and crime scene crew had been set up near the parking area. The surrounding area was searched diligently, the soil sifted for any small item that might shed some light on the moment when the refrigerator had been covered and abandoned. As the day lent itself toward dusk, more lights were set up around the now-empty hole. Armed with a bucket, sieve, and small shovel, Kali helped turn over the loose earth meticulously.

She could see the undulating landscape of the pineapple field rolling off into the distance, shrouded by the growing shadows. Tomas Alva stood just outside the line of light, waiting patiently. Like Kali, he was covered in dirt.

"We're going to shut this down for the night," he said wearily. "Probably take forever, but we've got a team using ground-penetrating radar coming in the morning, and a crew to start digging up the rest of the field if necessary . . . in case the head's nearby."

It won't be, Kali told herself. The pineapple suggested that the burial had had some sort of ritual significance, and it was unlikely that a head had been relegated to a separate box and conveniently planted somewhere in the vicinity. She kept her thoughts to herself. It wouldn't hurt the SOC crew to spend a few days with backhoes and shovels. The last thing she wanted to do was keep anyone from feeling useful.

She felt Tomas's eyes on her. They'd known one another for years, and she suspected that he'd likely read the gist of her thoughts. He said nothing, only grinned tiredly.

"I'll give you a ride into town when you're ready," he said.

She brushed herself off, succeeding only in making her hands dirtier than they already were.

"I'm going to make a mess of your car seat," she said, somewhat apologetically.

"Can't get any dirtier than my seat will be," he said. "Come on. Let's get you settled, and I'll go and see if there's any supper left for me at home."

They walked to the car and climbed inside. For a moment, Tomas sat with his head back against his headrest. He reached forward slowly, turning the key that had been left in the ignition. As the car's engine rumbled softly, he backed out of the makeshift parking spot and pulled onto the narrow track leading to the two-lane main road.

They rode in silence for minute. Then Tomas turned to Kali. "Can you think of any reason someone would replace a head with a wooden *hala kahiki*?"

She considered his question. "Well . . . it's an obvious way to conceal the victim's identity, at least in the short term," she offered. "But I think it's more likely there was something significant about the choice. Why not a real *hala kahiki*? It's not as though there's a pineapple shortage here. Market shelves are full of them."

"That's what I was thinking. Seems like someone went through considerable effort to find a wooden one."

Not if the person's death had been planned in advance, and the carved pineapple had been conveniently at hand, she thought. That scenario suggested a premeditation that might somehow tie to the image of this particular fruit. "I don't love these cold cases," she said instead. "It's bad enough when we know who the victim is to begin with, but when we have to figure out who it is before we can hunt for a reason, I start losing sleep."

"Maybe," Tomas responded, his voice thoughtful, "it was a natural death, or an accidental one, and the pineapple was an afterthought."

She looked at him sideways. "Natural death by decapitation?"

Tomas shrugged. "Yeah, it does sound a little crazy, doesn't it? What about an accident, maybe with some of the equipment, and someone wanted to hide it?"

It was Kali's turn to shrug. "I'm sure stranger things have happened. But in all likelihood this wasn't just an accident."

They drove the rest of the short distance in silence. Darkness had almost completely fallen as Tomas pulled the car up in front of the entrance of the Hotel Lānaʻi in Lānaʻi City.

She unclipped her seat belt and opened the car door, already anticipating the magic of a long shower and late dinner.

"Mahalo for the ride," she said, climbing out. "I'm heading back to Maui early, but I'll be in touch before I leave."

"*Pomaikaʻi*," called Tomas, using the Hawaiian word for "good luck." He gave a wave as he pulled back out into the street, taillights fading as the road curved away into the night.

Kali turned, gazing at the small plantation-style building that housed the hotel. It was painted a soft yellow and surrounded by blooming foliage. She climbed the front steps, stopping halfway with her hand on the rail, scanning the tranquil setting in appreciation. The designation of "city" was stretching things more than a little bit, she thought. The tiny town was hardly more than a pretty square bordered by a few shops and restaurants, with beautiful residential neighborhoods spreading out beyond.

Never the tourist magnet that continuously drew hordes of visitors to Maui and O'ahu, the island of Lāna'i had become identified with the sweet, prickly crops of fruit growing in orderly rows across its face. The small hotel had once served as private lodging, and was modest in comparison to the two enormous resorts located in other parts of the island.

While the nickname Pineapple Island had eventually become popular, promoted in newspapers, magazines, movies, and television, Kali knew that the island's dark history had little to offer in the way of sweetness. Lāna'i, so green and peaceful, was steeped in dark myth and violent legends that whispered of man-eating spirits that stalked the living.

"I wonder how many of the tourists who make their way across the channel know about the Lāna'i monsters?" murmured Kali, half to herself.

"Probably none of them," answered a male voice.

Kali started, surprised that anyone had heard her. A very old man was standing on the porch above her, partly in the shadows near the rail, looking out toward the dangling moon, which was surrounded by faint, glittering stars. She halted her ascent up the stairs just before the stranger.

"Do you think it would make a difference to them if they did know?" she asked.

The old man shrugged. "I doubt it," he said. "Just fodder for T-shirt slogans, I would think. No one believes in anything anymore unless they can see or taste it."

She mused over his words, and the abundant truth in them. "Or unless it touches their own life directly," she added.

"Exactly so," he said. He bowed slightly in her direction, then turned back to the rail, resuming his observance of the moon's widening glow. "You must excuse me. I have an agreement with Hina, you see, that I will, whenever possible, greet her as she arrives to light the night."

Kali was surprised to hear him speak the name of Hina. *The Hawaiian goddess of the moon.*

"That's quite an honorable agreement," she said, her voice carrying a genuine respect. "I'm sure, Grandfather, that she looks forward to seeing you each evening."

The man smiled broadly, evidently finding her use of the title *grandfather* friendly. They stood together in companionable silence for several minutes, looking at the sky as the cool night breeze whispered across their faces. As she turned toward the door, she noticed the deep lines around his eyes; there was old grief written there, but laugh lines as well, deep crevices that came from a lifetime of many smiles. For a fleeting moment she wondered what her own face revealed, and if others might someday look at her and see nothing but regret, or the disillusionment that regularly arose from constantly dealing with the results of the cruelty and selfishness of her fellow humans.

"*Aloha ahiahi,*" she said softly to the man, nodding her head. As he returned the gesture, she opened the door quietly and passed into the hotel foyer, imagining the imminent comfort of climbing beneath the fresh, cool sheets of her temporary bed, where she might dream, all the while bathed in Hina's silvery light.